SEEDS OF GLORY AND RUIN

A MAGE'S INFLUENCE SERIES

Seeds of Glory and Ruin

Vines of Promise and Deceit

Thorns of Hope and Betrayal

Forests of Grandeur and Malice

And set in the same world:

A MAGE'S APPRENTICE SERIES

Winds of Courage

Storms of Allegiance

Tempests of Truth

SEEDS OF GLORY AND RUIN

A MAGE'S INFLUENCE BOOK 1

MELANIE CELLIER

LUMINANT PUBLICATIONS

For my intelligent and talented niece, Chelsea,
who shares my love of reading

HIDDEN CITY
NOMAD LANDS
Kingdom of CALISTA
VIRIDIAN RIVER
CALINARA
CELADON RIVER
LAKE ATERRA
CADENCE'S HOUSE
HUNTING LODGE
NOMAD LANDS
CELADON RIVER
Kingdom of TARTORA
TARONA
VIRIDIAN RIVER
N
W
E
S

CHAPTER

ONE

I heard the distant sound of hoof beats long before I saw anything unusual. Springing up, I spun toward the noise, but the surrounding trees blocked my view.

I spared a second's glance at the basket by my feet. The berries inside were the last of the season and represented several hours of work. I had been dreaming about the pies they would make all day.

With a shake of my head, I left them where they sat. The basket was an awkward shape, and its load had grown heavy. It would only slow me down.

Weaving between the trees, I ran. My breath soon rasped in and out, but I didn't slow. Five riders were on a course that would lead to my sister. I didn't stop to question my certainty— I just knew they promised disruption to the monotony of my isolated life.

The possibility of danger didn't give me a moment's hesitation.

At first, as I raced across the uneven ground, I told myself it was concern for Airlie that lent my feet wings. But the image of my formidable older sister danced across my mind's eye, calling a lie on the noble sentiment. I revised my internal justifications.

Airlie might not need any protection I could provide, but she would certainly be worried on my behalf—she always was. If there were other people in this remote area, she would want us to stick together.

But I could feel the less flattering truth behind even that excuse. Curiosity drove me on above everything else, its fires stoked by the thrilling possibility of disruption to my boring life. What was danger compared to that?

The wind shifted, bringing with it the biting smell of smoke. My pace faltered, concern leaching through my excitement. We rarely ventured away from our isolated house in its protected valley, but we did make supply runs to the nearest villages. And hadn't I heard talk of some new band of brigands on our last such brush with humanity?

Airlie had been quick to turn us away from the conversation, but I had caught the worried looks and hushed voices. At the time, it had seemed like the usual anxieties of those who needed something to complain about. Airlie and I had been living for two years without our father—a soft target for thieves—and we had never seen anyone near our house.

But why else would there be smoke on the wind? It was far too much for a simple campfire.

My feet slowed of their own volition, proving I did have some care for danger, after all. Apparently some natural caution remained. The hoof beats had stopped, replaced by voices, the lower tones of a man punctuated by the familiar sound of my sister. I slipped through the remaining trees, creeping up the gentle slope toward the place where they stood.

I had directed my approach to avoid the majority of the smoke, but it still stung my eyes, the occasional breeze forcing me to suppress a cough. If the newcomers had torched the long abandoned and derelict shack we had been using as a base for the last two nights, they must surely be brigands. Who else would possess such a destructive nature?

My heart had barely slowed despite the halt in my exertion, but my sister's even tones gave no hint of fear. I eased myself behind the last tree, the ground ahead of me bare of anything more than waist high bushes.

For the first time, I had a clear view of the source of the smoke.

As I had suspected, it was the shack that was burning. The structure had already collapsed, the flames smoldering rather than leaping high as they might have done with a juicier target. Smoke still billowed out, however, providing an impressive backdrop to Airlie.

She stood tall and confident, having claimed the high ground directly in front of the fire. A few steps below her, a man in a purple cloak faced her, four mounted men behind him.

I frowned at his companions. Three of them were dressed in the blue and gold livery of royal guards. I had seen royal guards only once before, during a visit to a distant village, but their garb was too distinctive to mistake. Not brigands, then. And hardly likely to have set a crumbling shack on fire.

Had they been drawn here by the smoke? Perhaps they had driven the brigands away?

If so, Airlie didn't appear grateful. Rather she looked like a monarch, barring entry to her domain—no matter how devastated that domain might be.

I sighed. It wasn't only my lack of height that denied me such an authoritative presence. Despite our shared features— long brown hair, startling blue eyes, a heart shaped face, and a willowy frame—Airlie and I had never been alike. More like opposites, in fact.

The two of you possess the seeds of glory and ruin. The voice of our father sounded as clearly in my head as if I had heard him issue his favorite pronouncement yesterday instead of two years earlier. My stomach soured at the memory. It had always seemed the path of wisdom not to inquire which of us was which. Given the warmth of pride in his eyes whenever they rested on Airlie, I didn't think I would like his answer.

More words I couldn't catch were exchanged between the men and my sister, and then the one in the cloak pointed at the burning shack. A waterfall of rain appeared from the clear blue sky, directly above the fire. It fell in a solid sheet, causing the flames to sizzle and sputter, even more smoke pouring forth. A moment later, the water cut off as abruptly as it had begun.

I bit my lip. An elements mage. And a strong one to produce so much water without a cloud in the sky. That explained the attendant and three guards.

"Cadence! Please join us." Airlie's raised voice reached me, her eyes somehow finding me despite the distance and covering foliage. How did she always do that?

I didn't dwell on the irritation, however, spurred on by the return of my earlier excitement. If Airlie was beckoning me into the open, that was confirmation the men weren't a threat, despite the burning building.

I jogged across the short distance, avoiding the column of smoke as best I could, as well as the small huddle of men and horses. Within moments, I reached my sister's side.

From this position, I could see the newcomers more clearly. The four mounted men kept half their attention on their horses as they stomped and snorted, nostrils wide at the smell of smoke. Only the fifth man looked entirely unconcerned about the situation. Despite the height disadvantage from his position on the ground, he maintained an air of confidence and command that put even Airlie to shame. Even without his earlier display, I would have had no doubt who the leader of the small band must be.

The cloaked man looked back at me, the slight lift of his brow suggesting surprise.

"It is really just you and your sister? These are remote and lawless parts for two youngsters on their own." His eyes shifted to the burning building behind us.

I snorted softly, drawing his gaze back to me. I braced myself for anger—or at least irritation—but his gaze held only a trace of amusement.

Interesting.

Given our usual isolation, I spent our supply runs watching the people who inhabited the villages as closely as possible. And while I might not be an expert, it hadn't taken much experience to learn that men who carried themselves with such assurance rarely appreciated being laughed at by sixteen-year-old girls.

I hadn't been able to help my response to his words, though. He had spoken as if he were a gray beard instead of a young man only a handful of years older than Airlie.

I examined him more closely, but the answer didn't lie in the messy waves of his dark brown hair or the angled lines of his honey-colored face. His authority was no more a physical attribute for him than it was for Airlie—it came from within him, and it clearly carried weight with the four older men who followed him. The one closest to us was eyeing me with all the distaste his leader lacked, apparently more defensive of his dignity than the man himself.

"Don't mind Sutton," the leader said without turning to look at the man behind him. "His face falls that way naturally."

The disapproving lines on Sutton's face deepened, but he still didn't speak.

"I'm Evermund," the leader continued with a friendly nod.

"This is Cadence," Airlie replied before I could introduce myself. "My younger sister."

I suppressed a surge of irritation. I wasn't a child, unable to give my own name, but this was hardly the time for a squabble between siblings.

A resounding crash behind us made me flinch. Fresh billows

of ash and smoke erupted as the sagging remnants of the shack collapsed. Airlie, on the other hand, held herself steady, the barest tremor rocking her slim figure.

As I fought against a flush of embarrassment, I thought I detected a hint of admiration in Evermund's eyes as they dwelt on Airlie. No surprise there. Young men in the villages we visited usually did look at Airlie that way.

No one directed such approval in my direction, but at least Sutton was no longer glaring at me, instead busy keeping his horse from bolting for the trees. I gave the animal a sympathetic look. I would have preferred some distance from the smoldering ruins myself, but Airlie and Evermund were apparently trapped in a competition to see who could show themselves less affected by our proximity to a burning building.

Or perhaps Evermund truly was unbothered by it. A powerful elements mage had no reason to fear fire.

"You are both remarkably self-possessed young women to take the loss of your home and all your possessions with such calm." Evermund's words sent my gaze whipping from him back to my sister.

Although she refrained from meeting my eyes—keeping her attention on Evermund instead—I could feel a strong emotion radiating off her in waves. If it wasn't for our audience, she would no doubt have been glaring at me, warning me not to react to the incorrect assumption. I immediately moderated my response, wiping the surprise from my face.

A curious gleam had already leaped into Evermund's eyes, however, and I read the annoyance on Airlie's face. Not that a stranger would be able to detect her hidden emotion. Just as the arm she placed around my shoulders no doubt looked maternal to an outside eye.

"We would indeed be distraught to have lost all our possessions," she said. "But we were just returning from an extended gathering trip and thankfully have our packs with us. Naturally our most important belongings are carried with us always."

She gestured at two large packs half concealed behind her on the ground. I hid my frown, making sure to give them only the briefest glance despite the fact my pack had been inside the shack when I left to go berry picking. I didn't understand what was going on, but I trusted my sister.

"It wasn't much of a home anyway." I gave the smoldering timbers a glare. "I'm not sorry to see it gone." Even the fire could only do so much to conceal the decrepit nature of the building.

Some of the invisible tension leaked from Airlie's body, her arm around me relaxing slightly at this evidence that I intended to play along with whatever game she was playing.

"I'm glad you weren't around to encounter whoever lit that," Evermund said. "But the fate of your home—an unsatisfactory one by your own claim—must stand as evidence to the unsuitability of this location. Surely you have family elsewhere who would take you in?"

I shook my head. "Our parents have been dead for years. We only have each other."

"So your sister informed me." His focus was still on Airlie, a faint crease between his brows as if he couldn't quite work her out.

She drew herself up to her full height. "I will be nineteen this coming winter. I am the proper person to have guardianship of my sister."

"Nearly nineteen?" The crease smoothed out of Evermund's eyes. "That explains it, then, I suppose. But why don't I recognize you from the Mages' Guild? You must have a strong ability. Few in your position would risk living in such an isolated location so soon after completing their apprenticeship."

I opened my mouth to inform him we hadn't just arrived in this remote area—we had been alone here since our father's death. But I thought better of it, snapping my mouth shut again. Our father had been obsessed with secrecy, always insisting we rotate our trading visits between as many villages as possible to ensure we never made real connections with anyone. He would have been horrified to hear me reveal any information at all to a stranger, let alone that we actually lived in this border region—an area shunned by most sensible Tartorans.

"What is your affinity?" Evermund asked Airlie, his concern replaced with curiosity. When she didn't reply, he asked again, with a touch of impatience. "What type of power do you wield?"

She still gave him no answer, meeting his look with a hint of defiance.

"I don't owe you anything," she said, and I caught her eyes flicking sideways to Sutton for the briefest second.

I hid another frown. What was Airlie playing at now? She and my father had always insisted we do everything possible to avoid notice. Why provoke these strangers? There was more to her response than a reluctance to admit she wasn't a mage.

Evermund said nothing, but Sutton's horse responded to a heel in his side, taking several reluctant steps in our direction.

"Don't you know who you're addressing? This is the Royal Mage, an elements master and direct emissary of the king." He transferred his attention to his companion. "Really Evermund, we have tarried here long enough. The fire shows no danger of spreading, and no one has been injured. There is no reason to prolong the delay. Test the girl, if you must, and have done with the questioning. It is well within your rights."

Evermund regarded him for a moment before giving the briefest of shrugs and turning back to us. But in that short moment, he missed the tightening of Airlie's muscles and the sudden squeeze she gave my arm. Whatever she had been attempting to orchestrate in this encounter, it had been leading to this. For some reason my sister wanted this master mage to test her.

"Very well, Sutton." Evermund gave us a measured look. "As a master mage I am permitted to test anyone I encounter. And since we have detoured from royal business, I must ascertain whether or not you are two defenseless and homeless minors in need of royal sanctuary."

I kept my mouth buttoned closed. There was no chance we were going to meekly accompany them to the closest town to be dumped on some unsuspecting matron, but I knew better than to overset whatever plan Airlie had underway.

Evermund looked almost apologetic as he continued. "There are some masters who don't live at the Guild, so it's possible you've completed your two years' apprenticeship without us crossing paths. And if you are indeed a qualified mage, then I can allow you to go your own way with a clean conscience. But I must be sure."

Airlie said nothing, and Evermund sighed. Prompted by instinct, I slipped out from under her arm. I had no idea what a Royal Mage was, but if Evermund was a master mage, able to control the elements, I didn't want to be caught by whatever storm Airlie had just provoked.

Far from trying to keep me at her side, Airlie gave me a subtle push to encourage me away. If Evermund noticed, he didn't comment, and neither did he make any gesture or utter any grandiose words.

But something emerged from him anyway, racing through the air between him and Airlie to encase her in an invisible bubble. I couldn't see anything, but I could feel it, the tiny hairs on my arms standing on end.

A radiant smile—almost a triumphant grin—transformed my sister's face in the second before the air around us shook and an unnatural thunder rent the air, setting my head ringing.

CHAPTER

TWO

I stumbled and fell, landing painfully on my rear and only just catching myself with both hands before I fell all the way back and struck my head. But at least I didn't have a mount to deal with.

The horses, driven past forbearance, whinnied loudly, three of them rearing up to strike at the air with their front hooves. Two of the guards and Sutton fought to control the animals, while the remaining guard disappeared into the trees on a mount that had decided to bolt instead.

Evermund, with his feet on solid ground, fared better. Although he staggered briefly, he didn't lose grip on his horse's reins and soon had the animal back under control.

Only Airlie was completely unmoved, as if the bubble surrounding her had protected her from the unnatural movement of the air. But even as I thought it, I realized the bubble had gone. I could feel no trace of it now.

Evermund ignored his four companions, his eyes wide and lips tight as he stared at Airlie. She had lost some of her self-assurance, meeting his gaze with a look of penitence. It was as if —having achieved her aim—she now had the grace to acknowledge her role in whatever piece of subterfuge she had just engineered.

I scrambled back to my feet, about to demand some answers, but Sutton beat me to it. Sliding down from his still quivering horse, he abandoned the reins, his whole body shaking with anger.

Striding forward, he loomed over Airlie.

"You foolish child! What have you done? Do you think to entrap the Royal Mage? You will soon discover—"

"Sutton!" Evermund's commanding tone whipped across the space between them, pulling the older man up short. "That is enough."

Sutton turned back to him, an appalled expression on his face. "You cannot allow this nobody to get away with such an appalling trick. You are—"

"Bound by the same laws as everyone else, regardless of my position." Evermund had regained his previous calm. "As for a trick, you are forgetting Hayes." He turned a questioning eye on one of the mounted guards.

"Is our new elements mage truly eighteen?"

"Aye, Master Evermund. I would have told you if there was any untruth."

I gaped at both of them. The guard was a mage who could tell truth from lies? What sort of power allowed that?

I scrambled to remember my own words from earlier. My comments about the shack hadn't been a lie, even if they had been misleading. When our father died and Airlie was forced to take over the hunting, she had insisted I couldn't be left behind on my own. We had discovered the derelict shack on our first trip, and she had laughingly dubbed it our hunting lodge—a home away from home for the time we spent foraging and hunting. But it smelled foul and creaked ominously in the slightest wind, and I had always hated it. I had spoken the truth when I said I wasn't sorry to see it gone.

But the revelation about the guard's ability wasn't the only shocking part of Evermund's words. He had called Airlie a new elements mage, and all five of the men were now regarding her with varying levels of shock. But my sister wasn't a mage of any kind—not even our father had been.

"Airlie, what's going on?" I asked, noting with concern that she looked nervous, although she was hiding it well.

Evermund frowned thoughtfully at my question, looking between me and Airlie. "You must know how unusual it is for someone of your age not to have been activated." He hesitated, the furrow in his brow deepening. "Or perhaps…" He looked between us. "Have you had any training—formal or informal—on the ways of power? Of seeds and activation and influence?"

Airlie stiffened but didn't speak. Was she ashamed to admit to ignorance? I felt no such compunction. I didn't bear the blame for the hole in our education.

"None," I said. "Our father undertook our education before his death, and he always refused to speak of such matters, no matter how many times I asked."

Airlie's hand slipped into mine and squeezed approvingly. I shook my head slightly. I must have misunderstood her reluctance to respond.

"That explains it then," Evermund said. "And whatever our personal feelings on the matter, the law is clear. As the mage who activated your power, I am now personally responsible for your training. We will return to the Guild immediately."

He glanced at the collapsed walls and blackened ashes of our lodge and then at the sun which had already begun its descent toward the horizon. "I believe we can manage another hour or two of travel before we need to make camp."

"Back to the Guild?" Sutton stared at him. "But what of our mission? I concede our hands are tied on the matter of the apprenticeship, but the girl can tag along easily enough. Given how you were trapped into the activation, she cannot expect you to drop everything and see to her—"

Once again Evermund cut him off. "How many seeds have you seen activated in your years, Sutton? Have you ever witnessed anything like what just happened?"

Sutton shifted uncomfortably. "I was there when Master Drake activated you, Evermund, and still remember how the air shook. Everyone agreed that nothing like it had been felt since his own activation."

"I, too, remember the occasion." Somehow Evermund managed to keep the impatience out of his voice, which suggested he had the forbearance of a saint. "And I spent the next four years striving to live up to such a promising beginning. I do not, however, remember thunder nearly splitting all our eardrums."

Sutton gaped foolishly at Evermund, whatever disbelief he was feeling apparently outweighing his natural inclination toward self-importance.

"What exactly are you saying, Evermund? Are you suggesting..."

"I'm saying that we will return to the Guild immediately. Our mission can wait or be assigned to another. This is too important."

"The villagers whose homes and lands have been burned and pillaged might not agree," Hayes said quietly behind them both. "Nor the ones carried off by the raiders—if the rumors of such are true."

Sutton glared at the guard—apparently he was the only one allowed to question the Royal Mage—but Evermund showed no sign of offense.

"If they understood the broader picture, they might. Airlie must undergo formal testing immediately. If we have discovered something new, it might prove crucial in protecting the outlying Tartoran villages and ending this raider threat once and for all."

Airlie stepped forward, half shielding me with her body. "I take it you wish me to accompany you to the capital? I'm not going anywhere without my sister."

Sutton turned a dull shade of red, bristling with anger. "An apprentice doesn't question the orders of a master, let alone her influencing master."

"Excuse him," Evermund said with a friendly smile, "he's rather old-fashioned. I assure you I am as fallible as anyone and will not crumble at the least sign of opposition."

Sutton sputtered, but Evermund ignored him, his tone turning apologetic. "But in one respect he is right. When I activated your seed of power, I bound us together, little though I intended to do so. You are now officially my apprentice and must remain so for the next two years. As such, the law does require you to accompany me back to the capital. It is my home, you see, and I can hardly train you if you remain out here in the borderlands."

"I am more than willing to take up residence in the capital," Airlie said with a stubborn tilt of her chin that I knew all too well. "But I will not go without my sister." An edge of entreaty entered her voice. "She is only sixteen and has no one but me. Surely you see that I cannot abandon her out here alone."

Evermund ran a hand over his chin, surveying me with a calculating air. I tried to look as small and helpless as possible. I was going to the capital if I had to trail behind them the whole way there. I knew enough of tracking to manage it, but I would much prefer to travel as one of their party—especially since it appeared the talk of brigands in the area had been true. I shivered, and apparently my fear tipped the matter in my favor.

"Very well," he said. "You said your birthday is in the winter, and you will be nineteen. Since you will be of age in a matter of months, we can stretch the matter and claim your sister as your dependent. As such, she is entitled to your care and protection even above any responsibility you owe to me."

Airlie's tension melted away, and she gave him a true smile. He blinked once, a strange expression traveling across his face before it was quickly suppressed. I gave a small sigh. No one had ever been forced to hide their reaction to my blinding beauty.

I shook my head. I had no reason to complain about my sister's many talents. Apparently they were great enough that she had won us both a position in the capital—the very place to which we had spent the last two months planning to move.

"Is it really true?" I murmured. "After all our plans—and your insistence that we not go until we were fully ready and provisioned—are we just leaving everything and walking away?"

"Not everything," Airlie said. "We have our packs."

I shot her an unimpressed look, but something in her words gave me pause. No one had ever disturbed us in our snug, well-built cabin a full day's travel away. We had never seen any evidence that anyone had even come upon it, tucked out of sight in a remote valley. And yet every time we left, Airlie insisted we take our most treasured possessions with us, despite the slower pace our heavy packs required. How many times had I grumbled that we were not snails to need to carry our home upon our backs?

Had Airlie always been prepared for such an eventuality as this? It seemed impossible when she had spent two years insisting that we not leave our home to join one of the neighboring villages as I had wished.

Two months ago, when she suddenly announced we needed to start careful preparations for a move to the capital, it had seemed like a complete about face. Now I wasn't so sure. Had Airlie always been open to the possibility that every time we left our home we might never return? Had she been planning our eventual departure—one way or another?

I watched her out of the corner of my eye as she slung her pack on her back and brought mine over toward me. Whatever excess of emotion had overtaken her in the immediate aftermath of her activation—whatever activation even was—she was now back to her usual air of calm confidence.

Although a certain buzz of excitement underlaid her manner. Was it possible my staid, responsible sister—always preaching caution and the need for concealment—wanted to go to the capital as much as I did? If that was true, why had she drawn out our plans for the move to such an extent? I had been sure she was lingering at home, unwilling to actually leave. Some days I had doubted it would ever really happen.

I accepted my pack, noticing for the first time that something was missing from its usual place strapped to the top of hers.

"Wait! Where's—"

"Shush!" she hissed at me, and I instantly fell silent.

But despite her efforts at subtlety, Evermund hadn't failed to note the exchange, watching us with an unreadable expression. He didn't comment, however, merely directing the guards to take our packs and secure them on the back of Hayes' and Sutton's horses. As soon as that was accomplished, he directed the remaining two guards to take us up in front of them. Apparently he was the only one to remain unencumbered by our unexpected presence.

Not that he held himself aloof from either of us. He was the one to lift first Airlie and then me up to the guards waiting to receive us. I tried to remain unflappable during the proceeding, desperate not to show my inexperience. We had learned to ride on Father's old mare, but she had passed away two years before he did, so it was a long time since I had been in such close proximity to a horse.

And I had never been in such close proximity to a strange man.

I held my breath as his arms encircled me, knowing he needed to position himself that way in order to hold the reins. When his movements and attitude remained detached and impersonal, I soon relaxed. The furor in my mind left little room for me to obsess over my physical situation.

The day had started as so many before it had done, and now suddenly my whole world was upended. How many times had I pleaded with first Father and then Airlie that we should leave our isolated home and travel to a nearby town? After Father's early responses, I hadn't dared suggest the capital, but a small village hadn't seemed so ridiculous a proposition. He had always remained adamant, however—claiming we were safer in our home. And Airlie had held the same line for two years— only she claimed we had to respect our father's wishes.

I had been over the moon when she first announced our intended relocation to Tarona. I had always dreamed of seeing Tartora's capital. But when the weeks passed by and we spent our time gathering a ridiculous pile of supplies we would never be able to carry, the excitement had ebbed, swallowed by the belief we would never actually leave. But now, apparently, the unexpected arrival of Evermund and his group had propelled her to action. I just wished I knew why.

Not that I intended to repine. Whatever the cause, for the first time, we were leaving our home behind with no intention of returning.

Should I feel sad? Or melancholy, perhaps, to be leaving behind our parents' graves? I couldn't muster the emotion. Father had loved us—I didn't doubt that—but he hadn't been one to encourage sentimentality.

The memory of Airlie's desperate declaration that she wouldn't go without me sparked a bloom of warmth in my belly. For all my frustrations with my sister, I loved her with a fierceness my father had never managed to evoke. From my earliest memories we had turned to each other for the affection that he seemed to find so hard to display. She was not just the only family I had, she was also the only home that mattered. There was nothing to tie me to what we left behind.

The mage's words about destroyed villages made me scan our surroundings with heightened awareness. Given my late arrival on the scene, and the subsequent pace of events, I still had no idea how our temporary protection had ended up burning. Were we in imminent danger of crossing paths with brigands?

A scuffed section of ground caught my eye, a familiar object clearly visible, although it had been abandoned half under a bush. I nearly called out for us to stop but a moment later thought better of it. Craning my head around, I tried to keep the spot in sight as it disappeared behind us.

A muttered complaint from the guard behind me—a man whose name I had yet to catch—made me straighten again. As soon as I looked forward, I encountered Airlie's glare.

I returned it without hesitation. I didn't need her warning. I hadn't said anything, had I? I might not have my sister's trick of commanding a room, but I had always kept up in our studies, despite the age difference between us. I didn't need further reminders not to go blabbing our business to these unknown mages.

And what right did she have to glare at me, anyway? I wasn't the one behaving strangely and keeping secrets. I was the same old Cadence I had always been—the one with such terrible aim that our father had never bothered to craft me a bow of my own. The one who had to gather berries while Airlie hunted.

Maybe it was petty of me, but I had always suspected my ineptitude fueled my sister's great pride in her archery skill—and in the adult sized bow Father had gifted her at the age of

18

fourteen. She loved that weapon, so why had it been abandoned beneath a bush? And why had she shushed me when I noticed it was missing?

Positioned downwind, she would have seen the smoke long before I did. But she would hardly have abandoned her weapon in such a situation—quite the opposite. Panicked on my behalf, she would have clung to it all the more tightly.

I mentally reviewed the scene I had just glimpsed from the back of the horse. Already we were well past the abandoned bow, joining a little used road that led away from our distant home and toward the nearest town. But I could still picture the scuffed ground easily enough. And now that I was paying attention, I realized that the bow and quiver of arrows hadn't been the only abandoned items. I pushed my mind, questioning my memory, but the image was clear. The small leather pouch my sister always kept attached to the quiver had been there—but lying several feet away, its contents scattered across the ground. Almost as if it had been used...

I jerked back hard enough to hit the man behind me, provoking another protest. I murmured an apology, having been so caught up in my memory I had forgotten his presence. But even now, my racing thoughts barely slowed enough to acknowledge him. That pouch had been our father's final gift to Airlie, one she wore with determination and pride. It was one of the tools she always swore would keep us safe.

Thoughts of brigands melted away as I considered the evidence before me. Airlie had been at the shack when the men arrived, although she should have still been out hunting. I had assumed the smoke brought her, just as it brought them. But now I knew Airlie had opened the pouch where she kept the items needed to transform her arrows into flaming projectiles. And then she had abandoned the evidence among the trees.

There was only one conclusion. I stared at my sister's back. Why had Airlie burned our makeshift home? Had she heard

Evermund and his men before I did? Had she lured them to us on purpose? If so, it wasn't the work of a single impulsive moment.

My earlier musings took on new weight. Despite her words to me about staying in our home, Airlie truly had been living in a constant state of readiness for us to leave—readiness to take some action I still didn't understand.

Everything I thought I knew about our life shifted, tilting and sliding beyond recognition. Our father had always been a secretive man, but I had thought Airlie and I open with each other. Now, for the first time, I wondered what other secrets my sister might be hiding.

THREE

My churning thoughts kept me so occupied that it was some time before I noticed how quickly the road was speeding past beneath the horses' hooves.

"Should we be going so fast?" I asked the guard behind me. "I must be a heavy extra weight for the horse."

It was the first attempt at conversation between us, but he responded readily enough.

"None of the horses will be able to keep it up for long, but the light won't last much longer, either. Master Evermund wants to cover as much distance as possible before we camp. We won't travel at this pace all day tomorrow."

"I should think not, poor boy." I pressed my hand against the warm coat of the gelding.

Now that I was paying attention, I noted we had left the trees behind us and were no longer sloping downhill. Instead, the road shot straight ahead, cutting a level path between endless fields. The ground had already been stripped bare of its usual harvest of grain, and the resulting barren view was rather bleak. We had never come this way so late in the season before.

Ahead of us, a small stand of trees broke up the horizon, and

I fixed my gaze on it. Evermund must mean us to camp there for the night.

But when we reached the shelter of the overhanging branches, the mage at our head didn't slow, although the sun had nearly hit the horizon.

"I thought you said we were to stop." I shifted, trying to gain a more comfortable seat without slipping off the horse's back altogether.

"Not among the trees." The guard's focus on the road ahead didn't falter. "Master Evermund will want somewhere with a clear view of our surroundings. So no one can approach unseen."

I nibbled on my lower lip, trying to get a glimpse of Airlie on the horse in front of me. They believed brigands were in the area and had burned the shack not long before their arrival. Should we tell them the truth? From their previous words, they considered Airlie irrevocably bound to Evermund, so they couldn't abandon us now, whatever we said.

But even knowing the truth of what Airlie had done, the niggling anxiety over brigands lingered. Hayes had spoken of a whole village razed to the ground, so they had more reason for their unease than our burned shack. I sighed. I wouldn't say anything now, but as soon as possible I was finding an excuse to seize a moment alone with my sister.

"There!" Evermund's raised voice broke through my irritation.

His extended arm directed my attention to a wooden shelter in one of the fields, a short way ahead of us. A rough structure, it had only a roof and three walls, leaving one side open to the elements. No doubt it had been used to store the harvest while the reaping was ongoing. But whatever produce had sheltered here had long since gone to market, leaving it empty.

"Perfect." The guard behind me straightened. "It will shelter us from easy sight while giving a clear view of the surrounding countryside."

I couldn't take offense at the lecturing note in this voice—I had already betrayed my ignorance on such matters.

Before long, we were huddled beneath the meager roof. Thankfully these fields must be plentiful because there was room enough for seven people and five horses. Enough hay even littered the ground for one of the guards to scrape together an extra snack for the horses.

The five of them worked in easy tandem, pulling out food and unrolling bedrolls as if they had done it many times before. No doubt they had.

Airlie and I rarely spent a night on the road—that was why we had our hunting lodge. But we still had bedrolls to lay out and some reasonably fresh bread to contribute to the general supplies.

It didn't take us long to dig the food out of our packs and lay it beside the small fire being carefully nurtured by Hayes. As soon as that task was done, I tugged Airlie out of the shelter. I was expecting her to protest, but she came willingly enough. She must consider me a danger—liable to explode with the effort of restraining my tongue around so many questions. Silence had never been one of my stronger attributes.

As soon as we were far enough clear, alone in the middle of the stripped field, I turned on her and put my hands on my hips.

"Did you burn down the hunting lodge?"

She shrugged. "When I spotted them from the trees, I had to think fast."

"You burned our house down just to get their attention? Granted it worked, but what if you'd burned half the forest down with it? A bit much, don't you think?"

She shook her head. "Evermund is an elements master, he would never have let it get to that point. Besides, I couldn't let them get a proper look at that shack. They would never have believed it was our main home if they had."

"Airlie! Where do I even start with that answer? Are you telling me you knew who Evermund was? How? And why did you need them to think we lived there? What is going on, Air?"

She hesitated as if considering not answering. I turned my strongest glare on her, and she sighed, giving way.

"I don't know him personally, or anything."

I sighed, impatient with her half answers. "Obviously not! When would you have had the opportunity for that? Even in the border villages, Father always avoided anybody official. So how did you know who Evermund was?"

"I recognized from his cloak that he was the Royal Mage. That's all I knew. Other than the royal family, only the Royal Mage—a position awarded to a trusted master of great strength—is permitted to wear that shade of purple. And the current Royal Mage is known to be an elements mage, so…"

My mouth hung open. "Known by who?"

She shrugged again. "Everyone."

"Not by me! Who taught you that? Father would never answer my questions about the Mages' Guild or the Triumvirate." I answered my own question. "But it must have been him who told you. There's no one else. All those times he sent me off to do chores. I can't believe you didn't tell me any of this!"

"There was good reason for my silence. I was trying to protect you, Cadence." She was using her responsible older sister voice.

"I don't need you to protect me, Airlie! We're supposed to be partners, remember? That's what we vowed after Father died. That we would always look out for each other. You're not my parent, and I'm not a child."

Guilt clouded her expression. "I needed you to be able to answer honestly. It really is for your own good, Cadie. When we get to the capital, you'll see. It will be much easier for you this way."

My eyes grew even wider. "You mean you knew they would have some sort of truth mage with them? Is that why Father always required us to tell the absolute truth? He was forever droning on about the importance of choosing our words carefully. Are you telling me he was preparing us for truth mages?"

Airlie nodded slowly, clearly reluctant to give away even that much.

Betrayal colored my thoughts, the angry feeling swirling out to prickle in my limbs, making it hard to stay still. "We used to complain about what a hypocrite Father was, requiring nothing but truth from us while he held so many secrets and mysteries. You used to be just as frustrated as me!"

She shifted her weight to the other foot. "I didn't know back then. He only told me toward the end."

I took a deep breath, trying not to let my anger get in the way of answers. I still had so many questions; it was hard to order them. "Was it Father who told you to conceal our true home? What's that about, Airlie?"

She huffed in irritation. "He didn't need to tell me that. And you shouldn't need me to explain either. I know you daydreamed through geography, but even you know where the border is." She gave me a significant look.

"Who cares about geography?" I asked impatiently. "What do borders matter when the Kingdom of Tartora shares this continent with no one but the nomad tribes? The nomads don't care about borders, and the fallen kingdom is empty now. There's no one left there to take umbrage if their land is encroached."

"Cadence!" Airlie lowered her voice. "You know it matters very much. It matters because our home is on the wrong side of the border! And you know how Tartorans feel about Calistans and their desolate homeland."

I frowned. "What does it matter if we lived across the border? I know Father was excessively secretive about it, but that was because we only ever had contact with superstitious border villages with a dislike for Calistan refugees. Surely? The villagers may believe the empty Calistan lands are cursed and unsafe to traverse, but we know that's nonsense. And Evermund doesn't strike me as the superstitious type. I'm sure he's just as aware as we are that Calista is safe enough—even if the long-ago invaders poisoned the soil so no food will grow."

"It's more than superstition." She glanced around, as if to check we were still alone. "And it's not just the soil. The lands of Calista are forbidden ground for a reason. The fallen kingdom has protections still, left by its long dead rulers."

I raised skeptical eyebrows. "I know Father told us tales about the protections on their empty capital, but they can't be over the whole kingdom. I've never noticed any of these so-called protections."

She met me look for look, raising a single eyebrow of her own. The seconds stretched out as she waited for me to put two and two together.

When I continued to look confused, she finally spoke. "The protections are against outsiders, not Calistans."

"Calistans?" My brain was starting to strain under the weight of the day's revelations. "Just because we live over the border doesn't make us Calistans."

"We don't just live over the border," Airlie hissed. "Where do you think the house came from?"

"I thought Mother and Father found it after they were married. Don't you remember Mother talking about it?"

Mother had died when I was young, but I remembered her stories about growing up in the Tartoran capital. And she often spoke of her love for our sturdy dwelling and how she had felt when she first sought sanctuary there.

"Mother may have been born in Tartora, but Father was

born in that house," Airlie said quietly. "Didn't you ever wonder why he didn't tell similar stories? In fact, I always had the impression he didn't approve of her talking so much about her past. And I've wondered if he resented the experiences he never got to have."

"Are you saying that Father lived his whole life in that one valley?" I stared at her, trying to process what that meant. "He was always so confident and sure, as if he understood the world. But if he was born there, where did his parents come from?" I gave her a suspicious look. "He always refused to answer my questions about our grandparents. Did he tell you? Apparently he told you all sorts of things he didn't bother to tell me." I tried to keep the petulance from my voice, despite my hurt.

"You know many Calistans survived the invasion, and many sought refuge in Tartora—where they were hardly welcomed. Can you blame Father's parents for choosing to remain in their home, given it was isolated enough to avoid notice? Especially since they were close enough to the border for regular provisioning trips."

I could feel the blood draining from my face. "But...that means...we really are Calistan."

Every slur and sneer I had ever heard directed toward a Calistan repeated through my mind. They were the butt of every joke and the scapegoat of every minor conflict, despite the fact that after nearly a century, most of them had managed to blend into the regular populace.

Airlie nodded. "See? It's easier not knowing. Father was only trying to protect you by never spelling it out."

"And what about you?" I glared at her. "You could have told me after he was gone!"

Her eyes slipped away from mine, and fresh anger shot through me. I propped my hands on my hips, leaning forward.

"You thought I would slip up and give us away in one of the villages, didn't you? Thanks for nothing, Airlie!"

For a moment she hesitated, as if about to acknowledge fault, and then she straightened.

"You can't afford to be childish about this, Cadence! Now that you know the truth, you'll need to forget it just as fast. We won't be welcome in the Tartoran capital if it's known—even the precious laws of apprenticeship might not bind us. Nearly a century might have passed, but Calistans are still reviled here."

I rubbed at my temples, my irritation disappearing into fear as my shoulders slumped. "How have you carried this secret all this time?"

She wrapped her arms around me, something in her bearing strangely light, despite the tension between us—as if the weight settling on my shoulders had come from her own. The thought gave me pause, and I embraced her back.

What sort of burden had this knowledge been for her? My anger shifted toward our absent father. Had he extracted a promise of secrecy from her on his deathbed? He had certainly been furious and resentful in those final days of his illness—fighting with every breath against the fate that was coming for him.

After a long silent moment, I drew back. "I'm still confused, you know. Don't think I haven't noticed there's a lot you still haven't explained. Like why you wanted to draw Evermund's attention. Or what in the kingdoms was going on back there with all that weirdness."

A bubbling laugh erupted from her. "Was there some part of the day that hasn't been odd?"

Despite myself, I grinned back. "Well, there were all those hours I wasted gathering berries."

She sighed wistfully. "I was looking forward to those berries."

"Me too. But don't think you can distract me. I was talking

about the strangeness in the air—from Evermund and then from you. And the thunder, and everything."

She pinned me with an intense look. "You felt something from Evermund? Before my..." She made a general gesture with her hands as if even she didn't know how to label what had happened to her.

I frowned. "What of it? Is this another thing Father explained only to you? When he used to mention seeds, I always thought it was metaphorical, but Evermund mentioned them too."

Airlie's lips twisted at my reference to our father's favorite mysterious pronouncement. She had never liked it any better than me.

"And the thunder," I pressed on despite a noise behind me. I was working up momentum now. "What was that about? Why does it mean we all have to hurry for the capital?"

"I..." Airlie paused as if unsure how to begin answering.

Before I could demand she at least try, a polite throat clearing made me whirl around. Evermund gave me a smile that wasn't as natural as the friendly ones he had been dispensing back at the shack. Alertness braced his whole bearing now, and his gaze kept darting away to sweep the horizon.

"It's growing dark." His calm voice gave no hint of the concern in his bearing. "It would be best if you rejoined us in the shelter."

I glanced around. In the intensity of the conversation, I hadn't noticed the light disappearing.

"I'm sorry, Master Evermund," Airlie said. "The unexpected events of the day somewhat overset my sister."

"I'm fine," I snapped, immediately regretting the petulance in my tone. I cleared my throat and tried again. "It's certainly been a surprising day, but I'm perfectly willing to return. I've no desire to bring brigands down on us."

Evermund's smile brightened slightly, a hint of amusement creeping in that I tried not to resent.

"I'll be more than happy to explain matters further once we all have some food in our bellies. It's the least I can do for my new apprentice and her sister."

He grimaced suddenly, running a hand through his hair. "It really is an awkward situation. But there's nothing to be done but make the best of it. And if the signs at your activation were any indication, what we have to gain will far outweigh any minor irritants from having you under my influence." He shook his head. "Of all people!"

"Your influence?" I couldn't help the small chuckle that escaped. "You make it sound like you're a bad one. I wouldn't have pictured a royal mage as a rebel."

"Not *a* royal mage," Sutton snapped from behind us, stepping up to Evermund's side. "*The* Royal Mage. And of course he's not a rebel. What are you suggesting?"

"Peace, Sutton." Evermund sounded weary. "There was context you're missing. No one is accusing anyone of treason."

I stiffened, my conscience tender from the revelations my sister had just imparted. But I didn't need her warning hand on my arm to force myself to relax. I would have to adjust to the reality of our position sooner rather than later. Otherwise I would find myself responsible for turning my longed for adventure into a nightmare.

Evermund glanced at me, but there was no accusation in his gaze. "I will explain influence along with everything else. It will all make sense, I promise. But first, let us eat."

"Yes, that's why I came out here. None of us should be out here, exposed like this," Sutton said in a sharp tone, looking relieved to regain the high ground.

None of us bothered to reply, instead staying close together as we hurried back toward the wooden structure. Now that the last of the light was fading, I had no inclination to linger, keeping close on the heels of the others. And the smell coming from the small fire only increased our pace. Clearly one of the guards was skilled at cooking to be able to produce such an aroma from travel rations.

It turned out Hayes was our cook, and both Airlie and I heaped so much praise on his head that his cheeks turned pink. We both ate more than our fair share, savoring the food. I hadn't had anything as good in two years. For all his less admirable features, our father had been an excellent cook, and both Airlie and I sorely missed his cooking.

Six of us sat in a rough circle, while one of the guards took a bowl out to eat on watch. Mostly we ate in silence, but when the tiny fire had burned down—the merry flames replaced with glowing cinders—Evermund cleared his throat.

"I promised answers, and I'm a man of my word."

I straightened, glad no one could see my eagerness in the dim glow of the dying fire. From Airlie's mysterious comments, I suspected I was the only truly ignorant one in the circle.

But Evermund didn't continue, the silence growing weighted. When he finally spoke, I could hear the grimace in his voice.

"I must confess, I was never much good with small children, so I've never before had the task of explaining the basics. Sutton, I think you'd better take over. You'll do a better job of it than me."

I flushed at this reminder of the depth of my ignorance. No doubt Sutton would resent the task.

But when he spoke, his voice, while pompous, gave no hint of irritation. Perhaps he truly did enjoy teaching.

"You must know something of power and how it is wielded, but given the gaps in your education, it will be simplest if I assume you know nothing."

I rolled my eyes in the darkness. Sutton might prove adept at teaching, but clearly tact wasn't among his attributes.

"Of course I know that everyone has power of some sort," I said, unable to resist defending my lack of knowledge. "And that there are different types. I've seen it in the villages we visited. But Father always brushed my questions about it aside and said that it was a matter for adulthood."

I didn't add that he had claimed his power kept us safe and that was all I needed to know, leading me sometimes to secretly wonder if he had no power at all and that was why he refused to talk about it. I had certainly never seen him use it as the ordinary villagers did, and the business of mages was something distant—a matter for the far away capital.

"Of course," I continued, still defensive, "I learned about the Mages' Guild and the Triumvirate and their significance in the kingdom. It's just the details of how their power worked that I—"

Sutton cleared his throat, irritation now evident.

"Those different *types* are called affinities. But, as I said, it will be best for me to start with the basics rather than attempting to weed out what details you may or may not already know."

It was clear from his tone of voice that he considered it likely that anything I thought I knew was wrong. And given the events of the day, even in my own mind, I couldn't defend my father against the implied accusation. He had apparently denied me education that even the youngest Tartorans received.

"Sorry," I mumbled.

Sutton cleared his throat a second time, somehow imbuing the sound with approval this time, and began again.

"Everyone is born with a seed of power inside them. But this natural ability lies dormant until it is activated by someone else's power."

So your power had to be activated. I ran the implications of that information through my mind. That must have been what happened at the hunting lodge. Somehow Airlie had tricked Evermund into activating her power.

I didn't waste any time wondering if it had been intentional on her part. Evermund might choose to give her the benefit of the doubt, but I had spent a lifetime in close companionship with my sister, and I knew her well enough to read the signs. While I didn't yet understand why, I knew with certainty she had orchestrated that scene for some unknown purpose.

Uneasiness shifted inside me. I had never dreamed Father meant something so concrete when he spoke of the seeds inside us. Seeds of glory and ruin. My eyes strained to see Airlie, her face obscured by the darkness although she sat beside me. Clearly from the reactions of these men, Airlie's seed was spectacular. But what of mine?

Had our father known what lurked dormant inside me? And what had he meant by ruin?

"So Airlie's power is now activated," I mused aloud, forgetting I wasn't supposed to be interrupting. "Does that mean someone is going to activate mine? Airlie, perhaps?"

Her warm hand slid into mine and squeezed, the familiar gesture more comforting than I wanted to admit. Whatever lurked inside me, my sister, at least, would never abandon me. I didn't know what game she was playing, but I knew whatever she did was to protect me.

Evermund jumped in, an unexpected note of excitement in his voice.

"How old are you, Cadence?"

"I'm sixteen. I'll be seventeen in the spring."

"Oh." His clothes rustled as he settled back into position. He didn't attempt to explain his obvious disappointment.

Sutton resumed his lecture without deigning to note Evermund's interruption. "Activation is dependent upon age. If you will grant me the indulgence of continuing with the plant metaphor, you can think of your seed as lying dormant on rocky ground. Only at the age of seventeen does the soil become fertile enough for the seed to grow."

"Just like that, on your seventeenth birthday?" I asked.

A suppressed chuckle came from Hayes. "Your power is as much a part of you as your arms and legs. And biology doesn't work to such exact timeframes. It isn't a door that's opened on your birthday."

"No, indeed." Sutton resumed control of the conversation. "It is merely a general timeframe. In some cases, power can be activated as much as two months before the seventeenth birthday. Other times it lags several weeks behind. That is of little consequence."

But it wasn't of little consequence. Not to me. He had barely begun his explanation, but already so much was becoming clear to me that had been obscured before.

No wonder they had assumed Airlie's power would already be activated—and had even considered the possibility she might have completed a two year apprenticeship. If her power had been activated early, it was possible—just.

Of course I knew that you came of age at nineteen—everyone knew that. But now I understood why—as well as why formal apprenticeships didn't begin until seventeen. Father always said it was simply the way things had always been done, which was a less than satisfactory answer. Now I realized it was because it allowed all of the apprentice's abilities to be trained.

But that was only the smaller of the revelations that rocked me off balance. My father's final days paraded through my mind. His anger and frustration that had been so obvious, and —less obvious, lurking behind it—a fear that grew stronger as his strength failed. I had been surprised to see my confident, capable father in such terror of the end.

Now I understood the truth. It hadn't been fear for himself that gripped him, but fear for us. Airlie had been only months from her seventeenth birthday. No wonder he had held on with every ounce of strength despite the physical ravages of his illness. The image of Airlie's golden-brown curls bent low over his sickbed, spooning broth into his mouth, filled my memory. How desperately they must have tried every day to activate her power, hoping that extra day had made the difference. But he had not been able to hold on long enough.

Whatever I had suspected in the past, clearly power of some significance did lurk in our family. So perhaps our father truly had been using his to keep us safe in some unseen way. No doubt he had intended to hand the mantle on to Airlie. And if Airlie had been activated, she could have activated me when my time came. But instead we were left alone and powerless in the remote wilderness of a fallen kingdom—one haunted by a curse and reviled by all. No wonder my sister had been desperate enough to launch this scheme despite the many unknowns. I could only wonder we'd survived so well for two whole years.

Consumed by my thoughts, I had only been half-listening to a short conversation between Evermund and Airlie about her exact birthday. But when Sutton resumed speaking, I forced myself to pay attention again.

"The power we each wield comes from inside us, and there are limits to how it can be used. Not only are there limits of strength, but also of usage. We are each born with an affinity for certain aspects of the world around us, and our power can be used to shape only those aspects."

"Think of it as a natural understanding," Evermund's warm voice interjected. "I was born with an instinctive understanding of the elements that Hayes, for instance, lacks. And so the power in me reaches out to the elements and shapes them. It's as easy for me as reaching out with my arm and picking up my pack."

Sutton snorted. "Easy thanks to years of rigorous training."

The faint outline of Evermund's shoulders shrugged. "I can

only pick something up with my hand because I spent consider-able time and effort strengthening my arm muscles and devel-oping the coordination required. Or so my mother assures me. I was too young to remember it."

Sutton grumbled under his breath but let the point stand. "There are three affinities: the elements—air, fire, and water; healing—which deals with all manner of breathing creatures; and—"

"Wait, what about earth?" I interrupted. "Isn't that an element?"

Beside me Airlie sighed softly, and I bit my tongue. I had never been an ideal student, as she often reminded me.

Evermund chuckled. "I remember asking my father the same thing. We already knew I had an elements affinity, and I was personally affronted that it didn't include the ability to manipulate the earth. I think I pictured myself striking great chasms in the ground to swallow my enemies or some such foolish nonsense."

"If I had been allowed to continue," Sutton said stiffly, "you would have heard that the ability to manipulate the ground belongs to those with an affinity for plants."

"Oh. That makes sense." I winced, annoyed at myself for letting my impatience get away with me.

"Yes," he said coldly. "It does. Now, as I was saying, there are three affinities, and a simple test will determine which seed you possess."

"A test like the one Evermund used on Airlie?" I couldn't help a frisson of anxiety.

"No," Sutton sounded disapproving. "The test I speak of would be administered by one with a healing affinity. They are the ones with a connection to the human body, and it is a simple matter for them to sense the traces of your seed inside you. What Evermund did was a test permitted to master mages to probe the power of another mage."

"Of course, such a connection with a seed will activate it—if the person in question is over seventeen and not yet activated," Evermund said ruefully. "Which isn't usually a problem, since such tests are reserved for mages, not children."

I turned to Airlie, expecting to hear her defend herself. She had never liked being called a child—even when she'd been one.

But instead, the false security of our small, dark circle was broken by the sound of running feet. The guard on watch dropped to one knee beside Evermund.

"They're coming!" He spoke in a rough whisper. "They will be on us in minutes."

FOUR

For half a breath we were all suspended in stillness, shock rendering us frozen. But a quiet exclamation from Evermund broke through our paralysis. We scrambled to our feet.

Airlie lunged for her pack, securing it to her back without bothering to attach the bedroll. I scrambled to copy her, even as Evermund hissed for us to leave them.

We both ignored him. These packs were all we had left of our old lives, and neither of us intended to abandon our only remaining memories of home and our parents. The other five, however, had no such compunction. They reached only for their weapons, muttering to each other quietly as they armed themselves.

Airlie spared me a single glance, checking my pack was secured, before grabbing the arm of the closest guard.

"A bow! Do you have a spare bow? I can help."

"She's an excellent shot," I said, backing her up.

The guard hesitated, turning toward Evermund.

"Give her a bow," he commanded. "And you, Cadence? Can you shoot as well?"

I winced. "Not well enough to waste the arrows."

"Cadence has terrible aim," Airlie said matter-of-factly. "But she's decent with a knife."

Hayes grunted. "Let's hope it doesn't come to that."

All around me, the others muttered fervent agreements. I swallowed. What manner of attackers threatened us? We had four trained fighters—if I included Airlie—plus a master mage. They must be a large party to threaten us.

"Fight or run?" Sutton asked Evermund in a near whisper. His pompous manner had melted away, replaced with an efficiency and ready obedience that hinted at why Evermund might have chosen him as a travel companion.

Evermund hesitated, and I felt as much as saw him look toward the two of us.

"I'm sure we could hold them off if we had to, but we don't know how many might be coming behind them. Just by being here, we're putting this whole region at risk. We need to get to the capital."

Airlie stepped forward. "Then someone needs to leave now. A few minutes up the road there's a turning on the right. It leads to a farm that has horses in the barns. These people are coming for me, yes?" She didn't wait for confirmation. "If I'm the one they're interested in, then one of the guards might be able to slip away unnoticed if he leaves now. He can meet us on the road with two more mounts. We won't be able to make the necessary speed riding double."

I expected Sutton to protest at the idea of stealing, but it was Evermund who spoke in a carefully neutral tone.

"You suggest we just take what we need?"

Airlie gave an impatient shake of her head.

"There's no time for debate—between us or with the farmer. Speed is our best chance now. You just said that my presence here puts this whole region in danger. We're doing this for the farmer as much as for us." I could almost hear her eye roll. "And the horses can be returned later with enough gold to make up for any inconvenience caused by their temporary loss. I assume as Royal Mage you have gold enough to spare?"

For a moment I thought Evermund would react to such blatant antagonism, but he merely nodded. When his eyes flicked to one of the guards, the man seized the reins of the only saddled horse and disappeared into the night.

I shook my head, impressed. It took a confident leader not to feel the need to respond to being challenged in such a way.

Not even Sutton spoke up in the Royal Mage's defense. All of them were utterly focused on saddling the remaining horses and discussing defensive positions.

"I guess I passed," Airlie whispered to me.

I bit my lip. "It did feel like a test, didn't it?" I hesitated. "Are these brigands really after you, Airlie? It all seems so impossible!"

Airlie's face suggested she found the whole thing as surreal as I did, but she didn't have a chance to reply. Hayes held out a bow half as tall as her, and she grabbed at it eagerly.

Stringing it with quick, competent movements, she swung it into position to test the tension in the cord. With a satisfied nod, she accepted the quiver one of the guards handed her, slinging it over her shoulder where it jostled with her pack for space.

"But why you?" I persisted, desperate to understand what was happening to us.

"Seeds of glory and ruin, Cadence," she whispered, before taking the few short strides to Evermund's side.

I gaped after her, wishing I could see her face clearly. But there was no more time for reflection. Hayes appeared from nowhere, puffing slightly.

"There are twenty of them. This must be the band we've been tracking. They're coming fast, but they aren't mounted."

"Twenty?" But even as I repeated the number in shock, I felt utter certainty of it. They were out there, closing in on us.

These must be the brigands who had burned a whole town. And, for reasons unknown—at least by me—they had come for Airlie.

For nineteen years she had lived without attracting the least attention. Whatever this gamble she had embarked upon, it was a dangerous one.

"If there are no horses, then we still have a chance to get away clean." Evermund snapped out the words, his men starting to move before he'd finished speaking. "We ride now."

Someone's hands grabbed me in the darkness, tossing me onto the back of one of the horses. It was an undignified affair, with me scrambling to find a stable position. Unlike last time, I rode behind, leaving my companion's arms free to steer the horse. It was less comfortable, but I didn't complain.

When our mount stepped out of the shelter, meager moonlight illuminated some of our surroundings. We led the way, Hayes following seconds later. Behind him, Airlie held herself stiff and straight, her bow at the ready. I didn't bother drawing the dagger inside my boot. It wouldn't do me any good on horseback.

Evermund and Sutton emerged a moment later, my mount surging forward to keep ahead of them. The moon sailed out from behind a large bank of clouds, and the light grew noticeably stronger.

A yell rang out from across the field behind us, accompanied by the sound of running feet. Evermund shouted, and all four horses leaped forward as if simultaneously kicked by their riders.

I clung tightly to the guard in front of me, but I couldn't resist peering back at our pursuers. I could make out little beyond their dark forms, although several held weapons of different types. At least they were still beyond arrow range.

Air rushed past us from the direction of the brigands, making my eyes water. Hayes gave a warning shout, although it was hardly a strong enough gale to knock someone from horseback.

A moment later an eerie whistle made me smash my face against the back of the guard in front of me as an arrow flew past, almost close enough to nick my ear. The horse gave a terrified whinny and increased his pace.

Where had the arrow come from? A moment later, understanding dawned. The sudden wind hadn't been natural, but neither had it been intended to knock us down. Instead they had used it to bring us within range of their bows. A clever trick to utilize a weaker ability. I just hoped it meant they didn't have any strong mages in their number.

More arrows whistled past, all of us hunkering down over the horses' necks as much as we were able. Not even Airlie attempted to return fire, despite being unencumbered by reins. With the wind against us, our own arrows would have no hope of reaching our assailants.

Evermund dropped back a little, his horse appearing in my side vision. He still appeared focused on the road in front, but he thrust an arm backward, away from us. He said nothing, his serious face drawn and strained. But a louder rushing instantly sounded, a counter wind springing up to circle us.

The air around me writhed and bucked as the two winds fought for dominance. At least no more arrows were making it through.

"Steady," Hayes said from Evermund's other side. "A tornado won't help us any."

"Unless it blows the brigands away," I muttered and felt the rumble of a chuckle from the guard in front of me.

"Now there's an image," he murmured back. "If only luck could be counted on in such a fashion."

I sighed a wistful agreement. It was a foolish thought, but it was better than the flat out panic that feathered at the edge of my consciousness.

"We're gaining distance on them easily at this pace," Sutton called, not adding what we must all be thinking.

How long could the horses hold up? They hadn't had nearly enough rest since their last exertion carrying us all to the shelter.

"There, ahead!" Airlie pointed down the road.

I craned to see around the guard in front of me. A group similar in size to our own waited to one side of the road.

Were they friend or foe? Something about them looked odd.

A moment later, I realized what. Although there were five horses, they were accompanied by a single person.

As a group we slowed, bringing the horses to a walk. The wind that circled around us held its place, still protecting us despite the changing pace. I shivered at the unnatural feel of it, but the waiting guard paid no heed to the strange behavior of the air.

"We were in luck!" he called as soon as we were close enough to hear. "The farm was closer to an estate, and the owner and his sons were in the stables when I arrived. They were alarmed to hear brigands are in the area and are more than happy to help the crown lead them away—in fact it took me some effort to dissuade them from accompanying me. They've sent every one of their riding horses and swear they can make good speed."

"Excellent." Evermund's crisp words easily cut through the sound of his wind. "Sutton and my mounts are the freshest. I want the rest of you to mount up on one of the new horses and secure your current horses behind. Quickly now!"

I slithered down without waiting for assistance, staggering when my feet hit the ground. I managed to keep my feet, however, dashing for the smallest of the new horses. There was no time to dwell on my rising anxiety—but I wished it hadn't been so long since I last rode.

In the chaos of moving men and beasts, no one asked if I

needed help. So it was just as well a convenient fence post stood ready. Scrambling atop it, I launched myself across the saddle, hiking my skirts up to allow me to settle into place.

The horse, a pretty chestnut mare, tossed her head and nickered loudly. I patted her neck, adjusting my grip on the reins. My anxiety was already melting away as the familiar sensations returned to me.

The wind around us settled, the noise of its gusting giving way to the sound of pounding feet. My flinch carried through to the mare, setting her prancing. Our pause had allowed time for our pursuers to catch up.

"Arrows!" Airlie cried, and we all ducked.

With a muttered exclamation, Evermund sent another wind swirling around us. This time, however, it refused to settle into a proper shape, twisting and pulling away before slamming back against us.

Evermund growled, throwing his hand out toward the empty air, as if to lend weight to whatever silent command he was giving. Sutton, beside him, looked pale, peering behind us as if he could visibly discern which of the brigands was giving trouble to a master mage.

"Let's go!" Evermund called. "Ride!"

I dug my heels into my mare's flank, loosening my hold on the reins and urging her forward with my words. She proved more than amenable, shooting forward so quickly, she nearly left me behind.

I shouted and clutched at her mane, managing to regain my balance before I lost my seat. Already the angry cries behind us were growing fainter, and whatever chaos was happening with the wind, it was at least preventing any projectiles from reaching us.

The tightness in my muscles unwound slightly. Now that we were all mounted on separate and relatively fresh animals, we would soon leave the brigands behind. It would likely be an uncomfortable journey to the capital, given our need to hurry, but I was used to enduring small discomforts on our hunting and gathering trips.

The brigands would surely abandon the chase at some point. It was one thing to harry us in this border region, but another altogether to push in toward the more heavily populated areas of the kingdom. Tarona, the capital and home of the king's guard, was never harried by brigands.

We flew down the road, all my attention concentrated on keeping our course steady given our headlong gallop. Soon we would need to slow our pace or even these fresh horses would tire beyond swift recovery.

As soon as the horses in front of me eased their pace slightly, I pulled gently at the reins, signaling the mare to drop to a slower gait. She responded beautifully, and I crooned praises at her, trying to ignore a new unease that centered on the path ahead.

A harsh, guttural scream ripped apart the quiet night. Flailing horse flesh surrounded me. Some impediment had appeared, blocking our way, and the two horses in front reared up in protest, their hooves flashing as they tried to avoid a collision.

I tugged my reins right as those of us behind swerved, scattering to either side of the road. In the confusion of movement and moonlight I couldn't spot my sister.

"Airlie!" I screamed, trying to rise higher in the saddle to gain a view of her.

My mare veered wildly, however, forcing me to sink back into my seat and grab for her mane. A hulking figure loomed out of the darkness, the new horse considerably taller than my own mount.

The surprise wrenched a scream from me, and my mare took off. I fought with her, but she had the bit between her teeth, and I was reduced to a mere passenger.

Pounding hooves beside me indicated another horse had pulled in alongside us. Relief flooded me when I recognized Hayes. Before I could call for his help, however, other hooves sounded, these ones in pursuit.

I risked a brief glance backward and spotted four unfamiliar riders pursuing us at full pelt. They wore dark clothing that looked rough and unkempt beside the crisp blue of the royal livery worn by my companions—an effect that was only exacerbated by the palest skinned among them who had smeared his face with mud to hide from the moonlight.

The services of a bath would have turned any one of them into someone indistinguishable from the villagers I had grown up visiting—if not for the bared teeth and angry eyes. Their strange familiarity only heightened my fear. On the rare occasions I had pictured brigands, it had always been with a vague assurance of otherness.

My stomach dropped away. The longer legs of the pursuing horses were eating the small measure of distance between us. And my mare was already running at the full pace of her fear. She had nothing left to give.

My pulse pounded so loudly against my temples, I feared I might pass out. Hayes, however, kept his cool. And though his taller mount could likely have pulled ahead, he maintained his place beside me.

Our pursuers reached us, fanning out to gallop past. My tiring horse whinnied loudly and tried to find new speed, but she had nothing left. When they circled us completely, easing in ahead of us, she checked. Slowing, she gradually dropped to a walk.

I threw a wild glance backward, hoping to see help, but the rest of our group were out of sight. Had we been the only ones to swerve right?

No wonder we had all escaped the initial pursuers so easily.

The men on foot must have been a feint, meant to drive us out and into the arms of their waiting ambush.

Perhaps Airlie had managed to slip through, though. My own misfortune might even have aided her escape. I could only hope so.

"Halt!" The largest of our pursuers, a tall man with olive skin and tight cropped brown hair, called the command in a loud, rough voice.

I glanced sideways at Hayes, who was looking back at me. He nodded, his face grim, and I reluctantly complied with the command. My poor, trembling horse had finished her heedless flight and was ready to listen to me again. I only hoped they would treat her gently.

Soon all six horses were still. Hayes and I pressed close together, surrounded by a loose ring made up of three men and a woman.

Despite our new proximity, I could see little of the brigands beyond my earlier fleeting impression thanks to the darkness which made it hard to distinguish their individual features. But it was impossible to miss the moonlight glinting off three drawn swords and an arrow tip pointing in our direction.

I swallowed, my entire body trembling with the aftereffects of our frenzied pursuit. I expected an order to dismount, but instead all four of them peered at me, ignoring Hayes and his official uniform.

"Well?" one of them demanded. "Is she the one?"

I suppressed a gasp. They thought I was Airlie. No wonder they had pursued us so hard.

The leader grunted, holding up a hand to silence the others. A strange, almost familiar sensation struck at my chest. But no air shook, and no thunder sounded. Nothing whatsoever happened.

"Well?" the asker repeated.

"She's not the one." The brigand leader watched me with narrowed eyes. "She's too young to be activated."

The one who had asked the question lifted his blade, the sharp edge catching my eye and making it hard to look away. "No witnesses, then?"

My mount shied and whinnied, catching the fear that made me tense on her back. Hayes also tensed beside me, urging his horse a step closer to mine.

"She's her sister."

That made all four of them pause, their attention turning to him for the first time.

"Her younger sister. And she will soon be old enough to have her seed activated."

Three pairs of eyes turned to the leader who measured us both with his gaze. After a long moment in which I could hardly breathe, he sheathed his sword in one swift movement.

"Keep them both. They might prove useful. Let us hope the others haven't failed miserably." His voice suggested he didn't hold out much hope—and that dire consequences would follow.

He turned back to us. "Dismount."

I slowly slid from the mare's back, taking as much time as I dared. Once my feet were on the ground, I leaned heavily against her. It was more than a show of weakness, given how much my legs still shook, but somehow I would have found the strength to run if I thought the attempt would do me any good.

Hayes complied as well, joining me on the ground. Two of our attackers also swung down, moving with swift, efficient movements as they stripped him of his sword and the dagger at his belt, directing both of us to hold out our hands for binding.

"Take shelter in those trees," the leader directed. "I'll be back soon." He spurred his mount away, quickly disappearing into the night.

The three remaining brigands gathered the reins of the

various horses, one of them prodding us into movement. I stumbled across the uneven ground, barely preventing myself from sprawling on my face.

At last we reached the trees, however, and I sank down gratefully at the foot of a broad oak. Hayes dropped down beside me.

"I'm sorry I had to tell them who you are," he whispered.

The trees blocked out enough moonlight to obscure his expression, but his voice sounded worried and apologetic. But not as worried as the situation seemed to demand.

"Better that than dead at their hands," I whispered back.

His attitude gave me hope, however. If his biggest concern was that he'd given away my identity, then he must know something I didn't. It might be a fool's hope, but it seemed better than none.

If Airlie had escaped capture, she would certainly be looking for me. The thought soured in my mind as I realized it was likely the only reason I was still alive. The last thing I wanted was for Airlie to stumble into a trap looking for me—or worse, hand herself over in an attempted exchange for me. The cold look in their leader's eyes made me doubt the likelihood of his honoring any such agreement.

I straightened, new strength filling my limbs. In that case, there was no time to be wasted sitting around. I needed to find a way to escape before my sister came to rescue me.

Hayes came instantly alert at my small movement, making a vague questioning noise in his throat. Slowly I angled myself toward him, careful not to make any moves that might attract the ire of the woman who stood guard over us. She hadn't seemed concerned at our brief conversation—perhaps thanks to the arrow she was aiming at my chest—so I was hoping a small amount of movement would also be overlooked.

Despite the impediment of her presence, it seemed wise to make our move now, while the other two were busy securing the five horses.

I glanced sideways at Hayes. He wasn't an elements mage, I knew that much. I also knew he could sort truth from lies. But could he do anything more useful to our circumstances? If he could, he hadn't attempted it yet.

I slowly shuffled my feet toward him.

"In my right boot," I whispered.

He threw me a look that might have been startled, but it was hard to be sure in the dim light. He didn't question me aloud, however, instead repositioning himself as slowly as I had done. As soon as he maneuvered himself so our watcher couldn't see his left hand, he reached out.

For a moment his fingers fumbled along my boot, and then he found the hilt. With care, he drew it out, clasping it against the far side of his leg, out of sight. Now I just had to distract our captor long enough for him to use it.

"If you're keeping me in the hope my sister will come after me, you're wasting your time," I said loudly. "She would never risk her own hide for me." Speaking the words, even though they weren't true, hurt more than I expected.

I managed to keep the discomfort from my face, but even so, she dismissed me with a snort.

"The General doesn't need you—or anyone—to bring a mere girl to heel. And we know she was only just activated—we heard it two valleys over. I don't care how much natural strength she has. She's untrained and therefore weak."

Her words caught me off guard, and for a moment I forgot the conversation was merely a distraction. "Then what do you want with me?"

She gave me a speculative look. "I can think of only one reason the General would have kept you alive. Do you truly not know?"

"Know what?" I pushed myself onto my knees, leaning toward her. "What do you mean? What did he find when he tested me?"

She shrugged. "You heard everything I did." Her voice turned gruff. "Now sit back down, or I'll put an arrow through the middle of you, and the General can make do with your sister."

I froze. The threat was likely empty—she referred to her leader with too much reverence to actively defy his commands. But I had no desire to test that theory for the sake of a few questions.

At least I had succeeded in capturing her attention. Hopefully Hayes had managed to free his hands in the meantime.

A surge of movement beside me confirmed that hope. Hayes sprang upward with one strong motion, his arm swinging back and then releasing. Whatever missile left his hand moved too quickly for me to see in the dark, but it found its mark on the archer's forehead. She collapsed with only a quiet, gurgling groan.

I whistled softly, thrusting my bound hands toward him.

"Good thing you're a better shot than me!"

He used my dagger to slice the rope with quick, sure movements.

"It wouldn't have worked if you hadn't interrupted her focus," he said. "Or without your dagger to free my hands. So we can call it a group effort."

As soon as I was released, he passed me the dagger. I took it without hesitation. Having seen his aim, it would be a better use of our skills if I had the blade and he picked up another rock.

I didn't make immediate use of my freedom, however, unsure what our next move should be. I hadn't thought past this point.

Before I could ask Hayes for his opinion, a warning shout broke through the trees. One of our other captors had spotted us.

Giving up all thought of strategy, I fled into the small stand of trees, heading back in the direction we had come. I had to believe the others would be somewhere near, kept safe by Evermund.

Hayes's running steps sounded some way behind me, his breathing heavy. Apparently his usual lifestyle didn't involve a lot of sprinting.

I reached the edge of the trees, and the increased moonlight, just as the third brigand leaped out in front of us, his teeth bared in an aggressive grimace. I reacted on instinct as my father had taught me, slashing forward with my short blade.

The tip caught him along one arm, opening a jagged gash, and he gave a shout of pain. Staggering, he clutched at his arm, momentarily distracted. Hayes appeared from behind me, not hesitating to run the man cleanly through.

He fell to the ground, while Hayes turned his eyes on me.

"Sorry for the delay. I stopped to get this." He hefted his blade, and I nodded, my lips pressed together.

Now didn't seem like the time to mention I had never seen someone killed before. I had no connection to the brigand, but the suddenness and violence of his end was shocking—utterly unlike my father's slow, lingering fade into death.

Hayes seemed to read something of my emotion in my eyes, however, because he glanced from me to the trees behind us. His face turned apologetic.

"I'm sorry, but we have to get moving again. The others—"

We both swung around at a shout from the trees behind us, our two blades rising in unison. I tried not to think how meager mine looked beside the full-length sword.

But the shout was cut off, replaced by hoof beats. Hayes and I exchanged a look. Who was being reinforced, us or them?

A small cluster of horses appeared, racing toward us from the road. As they passed the far edge of the trees, another rider emerged from the shadows to join them. Even after such a short acquaintance, I recognized him. Evermund.

Relief turned my legs weak, making me slow to respond to the sound of steps from among the trees.

Hayes called a wordless warning, and I spun toward him as something slammed into my side, hard. I fell backward, driven by the momentum of the blow, hitting my head against the ground.

Everything spun. My vision blacked out for the briefest second before sharp, searing pain brought me rushing back to consciousness. I bit back a scream, even as someone else, far away, screamed my name.

"Cadence! Cadence!"

I tried to gather the energy to rise. Airlie was worried about me.

But I couldn't seem to coordinate my movement. My hand found the sharpest point of pain—my middle—and encountered liquid warmth pooling around a thin hard stick.

The blackness rushed back for a brief second before I fought it away. An arrow. I had been shot.

The thump of a bow echoed somewhere in the distance, and then the horrible sound of an arrow finding its target. There was no scream, however, just a drawn-out silence, and then the crash of a collapsing body. Airlie never missed.

"Cadence!" She cried my name again, her horse now inside the field of my vision. Despite what she had just done, all her focus was on me.

Pulling her mount to an abrupt stop, she jumped down, crashing to the ground without regard for her own safety. But when she tried to surge toward me, Evermund appeared. He caught her around the middle, holding her back with an iron grip.

Somewhere in the back recesses of my brain, where my thoughts hid from the pain, I noted he was much stronger than he looked. His hold didn't waver, despite my sister's angry attempts to fight him off.

"No," he said. "Give her space."

"But—" Whatever protest she was about to give died when he murmured something too quietly for me to hear.

The remaining fight instantly died out of her, and she stood still within the circle of his arms.

Was there no hope for me, then? Was that the news he had so calmly delivered?

Someone else knelt at my side in place of my sister. It was Hayes. He smiled at me, and I scowled back. He could at least have the decency to pretend sorrow at my imminent death.

He remained cheerful, however, as he placed a hand over my wound. The pain began to ease. Perhaps a sign that the end was near.

I scowled again at the flash of his white teeth as he smiled. Now that we were no longer sheltered by the trees, the moon illuminated us once more, allowing me to give him a thorough examination. While younger than Sutton, he was older than Evermund—perhaps fifteen years older than Airlie.

I had never known anyone of his age before—younger than my parents but so much older than me. How many times had I imagined a warm and loving family, full of uncles and cousins such as himself, filling all the gaps our little family lacked?

Despite his unfeeling cheer, there was kindness in his smile as he bent over me, and I let myself pretend he really was my uncle. It brought further easing to the pain.

Wait! The pain was disappearing completely, my strength returning. I tried to sit up, but he gently restrained me, pressing my shoulder back against the ground.

"Give me another moment," he said softly.

I peered awkwardly down at my middle. When had he removed the arrow? I hadn't even felt it. I transferred my gaze to his face.

"Are you healing me?"

His smile expanded to a grin. "Should I have asked your permission? I assumed you wouldn't mind."

"I thought I was dead!"

"I'm pleased to say, not today. Didn't you know the Royal Mage always travels with a healing mage in his party?"

I shrugged. Just another fact to add to the hefty list of things I didn't know.

"Thank you," I said, as he rocked back on his heels, a look of satisfaction on his face. "I don't know how I can ever repay you."

My hands explored the tear in my clothing and the impossibly smooth skin beneath.

"Nonsense. Healings are common enough."

"Are they?"

Such a world was hard to imagine. Father would still be alive in a world like that.

He gave me a quizzical look. "Of course. You can't think the healing mages would simply leave people to die?"

"Can you heal anything, then?"

He pursed his mouth. "Let us rather say...most things. There is nothing I can do if the person is too close to death."

"He's being modest." Sutton appeared at Hayes's shoulder and handed him a wet cloth. "Hayes may only be a proficient for now, but he will likely complete his mastery exams soon. Not all healing mages are so strong. And ordinary people with a healing affinity can soothe only the most minor of ailments."

Hayes gave Sutton an exasperated look as he scrubbed his hands clean. He didn't dispute the words, though, instead turning back to me.

"Your wound was clean, and none of your major organs were damaged. Plus you are young, healthy, and haven't been healed before. Combined, it presented a straightforward healing. I worked no miracles here."

"How do you know I've never been..."

"I can tell." He smiled, offering a hand to help me up. "It was actually quite refreshing. The body develops a certain resistance to healing over time—the reason we all die in the end, no matter the power of the mages that surround us—and the more healings, the stronger that resistance gets."

I hauled myself to my feet with his assistance, grimacing as I did so. My wound was gone, but plenty of bumps and bruises remained.

"I'll bear that in mind and try to stay out of the way of arrows in the future."

"You certainly will—because I'm not letting you out of my sight again!" My sister collided with me, nearly sending me back down to the ground as she wrapped her arms around me.

"Oof! Airlie!"

She didn't respond, so I rolled my eyes over her shoulder and returned the embrace.

Naturally she would forget all about her declaration the second she decided to go haring off toward danger herself. At that point, she would decide that I was on no account to remain near her.

"Where are the others?" I asked instead of mentioning this inevitability. I wasn't in the mood to repeat a conversation we'd already had several times. "The woman referred to him as the General."

"General?" Evermund stepped forward, exchanging a sharp look with Sutton as he did. "What else did you overhear?"

I considered my captor's mysterious comments about this General wanting me for more than just being Airlie's sister.

"Nothing of relevance," I said, half expecting Hayes to contradict me.

He said nothing, however, and I wondered if I was placing too much significance on her cryptic allusions. Perhaps it truly had been nothing. She might have merely been attempting to put me off balance, as I had been attempting to do to her.

Evermund looked disappointed, but he didn't press further.

"It seems the rumors that the General has turned to abduction in order to expand his numbers by force are true," he said. "We need to get moving again. I'm hoping we've seen the last of any pursuit, but I'd rather not put that to the test."

One of the guards came trotting out of the trees, a string of five horses behind him. With the mounts of our three captors, plus the extra horses from the farmer, we now had a total of thirteen. Everyone except me—as the lightest—would have a change of mount now.

Evermund nodded approval at the guard.

"Mount up!" he called, and everyone erupted into movement.

Airlie let me go with reluctance, but I clung on for a moment longer, asking about the other brigands and the missing General.

"Evermund and Sutton fought them off." Her voice had a breathless quality, and her eyes shone in the moonlight. "It was incredible. They both have an elements affinity—like me. I'm going to be able to do that one day, too, Cadie! Neither of us will ever have to be afraid again."

"You mean they're all dead? Like..." I glanced toward the two bodies that lay in view before quickly averting my eyes.

She shook her head. "A couple of them, perhaps, but the General fled with a number of the others. They weren't expecting Evermund, I think. He was too strong for them."

I bit my lip. "No, they weren't expecting him because they were after you, Air! But why?"

She frowned. "Evermund said this General person leads a large band of raiders who have been striking at the border villages for some time. He says the easiest pickings are gone now, and they're growing desperate. They heard my activation, and they understood what it meant about my future strength. It looks as if they're recruiting by force at this point." She shrugged, acknowledging it wasn't much of an explanation.

"But—"

"Mount up!" Evermund called again, a hint of rebuke in his voice, and I realized we were the only ones not in the saddle.

I sighed but ran for the horse Hayes held ready for me. As

much as I wanted answers, I wanted to be away from this horrible place and the remaining members of the General's raiders even more.

"We'll send someone to bury them," Hayes said quietly when he saw me carefully looking anywhere but the bodies. "For now we have to focus on speed."

I nodded once and settled myself in the saddle. There would be time for answers later.

CHAPTER

SIX

We didn't gallop as we had before—the horses couldn't sustain it. But we didn't stop either, except to grab food and swap mounts. Someone had found my pack and secured it to one of the spare horses, and now that I was out of immediate danger, I was immensely grateful it had survived the adventure.

I couldn't speak for the others, but neither Airlie nor I would have managed the marathon ride that followed without the kind intervention of Hayes. Several times he approached us during the short breaks, asking permission to heal our aches, pains, and blisters.

I suspected he did something to keep us awake as well because we rode through the night. Eventually I fell into a sort of daze, my eyes locked on the tail of the horse in front of me as the hours stretched on endlessly.

At some point, a distant part of my brain registered the sound of water, and I realized our road must follow the gentle curve of the Viridian River. We never came close enough to see it, however, and I couldn't muster the appropriate enthusiasm at traveling so far from home for the first time.

By the time the horses' hooves clattered against the cobblestones of a sizable town, not even a healing mage could have kept me awake much longer. After the shock, fear, and injury of the day—followed by the interminable ride—I had reached my limit.

With the sun peeking over the horizon, the town was fast on its way to earning the description of bustling. People walked up and down the spacious roads, and some sellers had already set up stalls along the footpaths.

Everyone we passed turned to stare, their eyes lingering on Evermund's distinctive purple cloak and my torn, blood-stained clothing. I squirmed beneath their eyes, my desperate desire for a bed giving way to an equally desperate desire for a chance to wash.

Evermund led us into the courtyard of a sizable inn, and I dared to hope I might soon achieve both dreams. The innkeeper hurried out, bowing repeatedly and sending orders flying to servants and grooms alike. His wife appeared behind him and listened to only a few words from Evermund before she shrieked the word *brigands* as if it was a question and exclamation all in one.

Hurrying over to Airlie and me, she swept us before her into the inn and down a wide hallway to a large washroom. I almost tripped over my own feet at the billow of steam that rushed out to welcome us when she opened the door. Two women—other guests, presumably—were already there, preparing to enter the available tubs.

The innkeeper's wife swept them aside, however, helping me strip off my ruined clothing and slip into the closest bath. When one of the women protested—there were just three tubs available—the proprietress issued a quiet stream of agitated words. The only one I caught was *brigands*, but whatever she said set the two women clucking with sympathy.

I stopped trying to listen, sighing with contentment as I

sank lower in the blissfully hot water. Airlie made similar noises from the tub beside me.

"Someone at this inn obviously has an elements affinity," she said. "Just think, Cadence. If only Father had lived long enough to activate my power, we could have been bathing like this for the last two years."

"I remember someone at one of the villages we visited with Father boasting that their inn offered hot baths," I said dreamily. "Naturally Father wouldn't consider such a thing worth wasting time and money on, but why have we not been back to that town in the last two years? If I'd known what we were missing out on..."

My energy was too low to muster any true irritation, however, my eyes having already drifted closed. I was devoting the majority of my remaining mental power to staying awake. I didn't want to survive an arrow to the chest only to drown in my own bathwater.

"Where are you from that you're not used to hot baths?" a woman asked from the third tub, her voice half horrified, half curious.

I opened my eyes and glanced over at her. Her straight gray hair was scraped up onto her head in a severe bun, but her eyes held a gleam that I liked. She must have beaten the other woman to the remaining bath while I was luxuriating in the most incredible experience of my life.

I glanced around the room and, sure enough, the remaining woman sat on a long bench attached to one wall, a slightly sour expression on her face.

"Our home is very remote," Airlie said, her words careful. "We are used to living just the two of us."

"How dreadful!" The woman shook her head, tutting sympathetically. "I can't imagine."

Airlie shrugged, making the water in her bathtub ripple. "It wasn't so bad."

"Actually," I said, "now that I've experienced a hot bath, I think perhaps it was that bad."

Airlie laughed and, after a moment, the woman joined us.

"Mages are worth their keep if they produce wonders such as this," I continued.

"Mages?" The woman chuckled again. "You won't catch a mage wasting time heating water at an inn."

I frowned across at Airlie. "I thought you said the water was heated by someone with an elements affinity?"

"Goodness!" said the woman in the tub. "You really have been living in the middle of nowhere if you think everyone with an elements affinity is a mage."

"But surely..." I frowned. "Doesn't everyone have their seed activated, enabling them to wield the power of their affinity? I can't imagine why you wouldn't activate it!"

She gave me a quizzical look. "Naturally everyone is activated. And we all wield some power which is very useful in its way. A blacksmith who can hone his fire to the perfect temperature. A farmer who can harden his crops against blight." She gave a happy little sigh. "A maid who can ensure the bathwater is always at the perfect temperature. But for all their usefulness, those are limited skills. Only those who complete apprenticeships under the Mages' Guild can claim the title of mage. And only those with seeds of sufficient power win such apprenticeships. Mages can perform far greater feats than this."

"And know their own worth too well to waste time on such a task—unless it's for themselves, perhaps," the woman on the bench butted in to add.

The woman in the tub nodded her agreement, the two of them exchanging a knowing look. Clearly mages were widely considered to have an overzealous awareness of their elevated status. That such a status existed confirmed some of our Father's teachings as accurate, at least. He had always said that of all the guilds, the Mages' Guild was the most prestigious and wielded the most power.

"Proficient," I murmured, trying to dig a memory from my tired brain. "Sutton said Hayes is a proficient. But also that he's a mage. What is a proficient, then?"

The woman tutted. "You really must have been living alone not to know such a thing. Those who apprentice to someone in the Mages' Guild graduate with the rank of proficient. Some will stay proficients forever, while others possess sufficient power to pass the mastery exams and gain the rank of master. They have schools that teach such things in every town and village in the kingdom, my dear. You really should have been enrolled in one."

"No doubt you're right, madam," Airlie said, in the polite tone she only used when she wanted to fob someone off. "Unfortunately our parents did not see matters in the same light."

Her strategy worked, the woman's face melting back into lines of sympathy at Airlie's casual sacrifice of our parents' characters.

"Yes, indeed, you poor dears. But I'm sure you'll learn quickly now you're here. I'm only passing through town, but I have many friends here, and I would be happy to ask around for you. There may be a place still in one of the local schools, despite your age. My husband is a scholar, and he always says we are never too old to learn." She beamed at us both.

"That's very kind," Airlie said. "But I've been newly apprenticed myself."

"Well, then." She sounded pleased at this evidence that all was as it should be. "You will soon have the information you need, in that case."

Another two women entered the room, looking surprised to find all three tubs occupied. They slowly paced over to join the woman against the wall, prompting her to clear her throat with significant volume.

With a reluctant sigh, I forced myself out of the water, plucking the top towel from a fluffy pile of white. Airlie followed me, patting herself dry with quick, efficient movements.

While I had been scrubbing every inch of myself in the tub, someone had slipped in and left a pile of clothes beside the baths. When I glanced questioningly at Airlie, she nodded.

"Evermund said he would send something clean for us."

I picked up a plain but serviceable dress in roughly my size and raised an eyebrow. "Had them in his pack, did he?"

She rolled her eyes. "He's the Royal Mage, remember? I'm sure the innkeeper was more than willing to fetch him anything he requested."

It was a reasonable point, and I certainly didn't intend to quibble further. I had been dreading putting my filthy rags back onto my delightfully clean body.

But I felt less amenable when we arrived back at the front of the inn to be greeted with the sight of two carriages.

"Surely we don't mean to leave immediately?" I looked between Evermund and Sutton. "The raiders can't threaten us here. Can they?"

"We are not in danger in such a large community—or so near the capital," said Sutton. "The General is not active in this area. But that is no excuse to tarry. King Marius will need a full report."

While I could imagine it would be of interest to the king to hear of such a brazen attack on his Royal Mage, Sutton's eyes lingered on Airlie not Evermund. A sideways glance at my sister showed she had also noticed his attention on her. But the proposition of meeting the king did nothing to diminish her usual confidence. Having burned our accommodation down to attract the attention of his Royal Mage, she had likely anticipated this outcome.

I ground my teeth together, unable to suppress the stab of betrayal. For two years, it had been just Airlie and me. I had thought us the closest of companions, but apparently I had known nothing.

My anger propelled me into the carriage in silence, but it couldn't uphold me for long. I had gone too many hours without sleep and with great physical strain. Despite the instructions of my increasingly foggy mind, my body would no longer be gainsaid.

Before we had turned off the street, my eyes drifted closed and my head lolled to the side to rest against the wall of the carriage. It might be full day now, the sun well above the horizon, but sleep had finally come for me.

I awoke with a jolt as the carriage rolled into an enormous courtyard. We came to a stop, and someone opened the door from the outside. I nearly fell out, still groggy from my sleep, and was steadied by a curious groom. He didn't ask any questions, though, merely helping me find my balance before turning back to assist Airlie. She, of course, alighted in a much more dignified manner.

I ignored them both, too busy gazing around me in astonishment. After the many happenings of the previous night and day, I hadn't given a great deal of mental attention to our destination. But the hazy thought that we were bound for Evermund's home had lurked somewhere in the back of my mind.

From the way the groom bowed and smiled, greeting Evermund by both name and title, it seemed we had indeed reached his dwelling place. But it wasn't exactly a house.

Stretching away to my left rose an enormous building of

gray stone, complete with towers, turrets, and several wings. A wide wall of the same stone encircled it, including several generous courtyards within its protective folds.

The courtyard where I stood wasn't the main one, although from my position I could see it, stretching between the front gate and the great doors of the castle. Instead we faced a side wing—detached enough from the castle to give the impression of a separate structure altogether.

The same gray stone as the main castle had here been shaped into a boxy horseshoe and limited to a modest two stories. The three equal stretches of building surrounded a manicured garden which faced the gate we had just passed through.

"Where are we?" I asked, foreboding filling me.

Even the town had been uncomfortable for me, but I had been too sleep deprived while there to do more than dully register the strange feeling of pressure from being surrounded by so many buildings and people. It seemed unnatural to press so close to so many other people. But a castle? I could only imagine the crowds who must live and work here.

"You're at the Training Academy, of course," an amused voice said from my right. "Were you expecting to find yourself somewhere else?"

I turned slowly to face the new arrival. A startlingly attractive young man stood a few steps away, an easy smile on his face.

I swallowed slowly. Was I still sleep addled or did his golden skin really glow in the setting sun? His warm brown eyes certainly seemed to shine as they laughed at me in the friendliest of ways.

"What's the Training Academy?" I managed to ask.

His grin broadened. "The Mages' Guild, I should say. The Training Academy is just an affectionate nickname bestowed by the most lowly of us who dwell here."

When I gave him a bewildered look, he chuckled and gestured at himself.

"Apprentices. It's what we call our small corner of the Guild."

"Oh. Of course." I knew I was floundering, but I couldn't seem to stop. Had anyone ever made a worse first impression? If only my brain would catch up with the fact that I was now awake.

Airlie stepped up beside me, directing a questioning look toward the young man. I flushed, realizing I hadn't even made it as far as an introduction.

He stepped into the awkward silence without hesitation, however, giving us both an elegant bow.

"Zekiel at your service, ladies. Although my friends call me Zeke." His smile suggested we could already consider ourselves among their number.

"I'm Cadence," I rushed to say, before my sister could introduce me like a child.

But I needn't have bothered. Although he smiled in my direction, his attention was clearly on Airlie as she gave her name.

I sighed, turning back toward the carriage. Boys who looked like Zeke tended not to notice me once they had seen Airlie and her golden-brown curls. Especially since he looked closer to her eighteen than my sixteen.

I patted my own chestnut waves. At least they were clean which was a vast improvement on twelve hours ago.

A groom emerged from behind the closest wagon, a pack in either hand. I lunged toward him.

"Those are ours!"

He gave me an odd look. "I'll see them to your room, Apprentice."

I shook my head. "I'm not an apprentice, and I don't have a room. I'll take mine." I grabbed my pack from his hand and reached out for Airlie's as well. "And that one, too. It's my sister's."

The groom relinquished both bags, putting up his hands in a gesture of surrender and hurrying back around the carriage, muttering under his breath the whole way. I flushed again but didn't loosen my grip on either bag. I had made it through capture by brigands with my pack, and I wasn't letting a mere groom take it away now.

"Zeke!" Evermund's amused voice made me turn back toward the other two. The Royal Mage strolled over to stand at Airlie's shoulder. "Why do you always seem to appear wherever events of interest are transpiring?"

Zeke gave Evermund the same easy smile he'd given me. "Would you believe me if I said I'm merely the most fortunate of apprentices?"

"Not for a second," Evermund said promptly, the amusement still in his voice.

"In that case, I certainly shan't say it."

Airlie chuckled, apparently as charmed as I had been. I shook myself. There was probably nothing so very special about Zeke. I was just reacting to the fact that I rarely had the opportunity to meet boys my own age. No doubt I would soon have the chance to meet a host of apprentices, and I would realize Zeke was merely one in a thousand.

I snuck another glance at him, already disbelieving my own false bravado. I had visited enough villages to know that his face would always stand out.

I shook myself. I was merely responding to the nerves of the moment. I was about to move into a building as large as the villages I was used to visiting. But this was the moment I had been dreaming of for years. I couldn't fall apart now, no matter how stressful the journey had been.

"Master Evermund!" A loud voice called across the courtyard, a group of people spilling from an entrance in the left wing, the one closest to the palace. Some wore official livery, but the majority were dressed in a variety of elaborate robes that looked more expensive than anything I'd seen on the townspeople we'd passed.

Their voices echoed across the stone of the courtyard, bouncing off the buildings as their words overlapped. And as the first of them reached us, several eyes turned my way.

"Is this the girl?" one of them asked.

Evermund stepped forward, drawing Airlie with him. "This is Airlie, my new apprentice."

If he had intended to introduce me as well, the opportunity was lost in the babble of talk that exploded at this announcement. Behind me, the carriage moved, the hooves of the horses clopping against the stone as they were led away toward the carriage house and stables. Even my refuge was disappearing, leaving me to stand awkwardly alone in the middle of the courtyard, weighed down with two heavy packs.

"Evermund!" A new voice boomed over the noise, and the others fell silent. A tall, imposing figure emerged from the same door the others had used, striding toward us. The small crowd parted for him, giving direct access to Evermund and Airlie.

The newcomer's close cropped, tight curls were almost completely white, contrasting with the dark brown of his skin, and adding an air of wisdom to his attitude of command. Although they looked completely different, something about the way he held himself reminded me of Evermund.

"Master Drake." Evermund smiled a greeting at the much older man. He turned to Airlie. "This is my own old master, and the current Master of the Elements—head of all elements mages in the kingdom."

He glanced toward Drake. "And this is my new apprentice, Airlie."

The Master examined Airlie minutely, as if her appearance

70

could offer some clue as to her character and the strength of her ability.

"Your name has preceded you, Airlie. A rare feat for a new apprentice—especially one discovered only a day ago."

"An unfortunate circumstance," Evermund said darkly. "It is not only the Guild that has had word of her." His voice dropped, and I barely heard his final words. "The General."

The Elements Master frowned, deep lines appearing on his forehead. "Not here," he said in a quiet voice. "Come."

He gestured toward the building, sweeping Evermund and Airlie before him, a trail of people creating a train behind them as the others—elements mages, I assumed—pressed close.

I sighed and hefted my pack over my shoulder. I had better follow behind before I lost them.

But when I reached for the other pack, it was gone.

"Allow me to assist," Zeke said from behind me.

I spun around to find him already carrying Airlie's pack, a smile in his eyes that seemed especially for me.

"You didn't think you were forgotten, did you?" he asked. "Us apprentices have to stick together."

SEVEN

"Actually," I said reluctantly, "I'm not an apprentice."

He raised an eyebrow. "Not yet, you mean?"

I frowned, not having had time to consider the matter. "I suppose...perhaps? I'm only sixteen."

"There you go, then," he said, as if the matter was decided.

While I appreciated his confidence, I didn't consider the issue so easily settled. But neither did I want to get into a discussion about it with someone I'd only met five minutes ago.

"You've been assigned a room in the apprentice wing, at any rate," he said. "I can show you the way."

"I suppose that's because of Airlie. She's an apprentice now."

Not wanting to seem rude, I restrained my curiosity as to how he knew anything about us and our arrival—let alone our room assignments.

"Oh, no." He led the way across the courtyard, making for the furthest, central wing of the building. "Masters have their own suites with a room for their apprentices attached. Some of them have so many they need bunks to accommodate them all. But Master Evermund's apprentice room usually sits empty, of course. His whole suite is empty often enough, given how much he travels, so your sister will have plenty of space to herself."

I stopped. "What? Where are you taking me, then?"

He halted a stride ahead of me, looking back over his shoulder. "As soon as we graduate and become proficients, we're entitled to start activating apprentices. But proficients don't qualify for a whole suite. So their apprentices share a collection of rooms wedged between the elements wing and the healing wing." He pointed at the corner where the left wing joined the middle section.

"No, no, no." I shook my head. "Airlie and I have to stay together. She'll insist on it."

He raised his brows. "I'm afraid apprentices don't do much insisting around here." His gaze crossed to where Evermund, Drake, and Airlie had disappeared into the building, a speculative look in his eye. "But then, I hear your sister is a very unusual sort of apprentice."

"Yes, everyone keeps saying that," I said shortly.

He turned back to me, seeming to consider his next words. "Shall we deposit these packs in your assigned room at any rate? They can easily be moved later."

I hesitated before nodding. What else could I do? Airlie had abandoned me in the courtyard which hardly lent much credence to my claim that we couldn't be separated.

I frowned as I followed Zeke the rest of the way. His questions about my future swirled heavily in my mind. Apparently Airlie's activation was note-worthy enough to bring both master mages and a notorious band of brigands running. So where did that leave me?

Seeds of glory and ruin.

I pushed the echoing words from my head, but they weren't easy to dislodge. Despite her melodramatic declaration after my near death, Airlie was nowhere to be seen. Now that she was activated, would she forget about me—the inconvenient weight holding back her glorious flight?

I shook my head. Now who was being melodramatic? More likely my abandonment was all part of Airlie's misguided notion that I would be protected by ignorance. I sighed and hoisted my pack higher, slinging it all the way behind me so I could fit through the narrow door tucked into the corner of the building.

Whatever I had been expecting, it wasn't what greeted me. When I thought of castles, I thought of vast halls and elegant columns, of rich murals and bright tapestries, like in the pictures of my mother's favorite book.

The corridor in front of me was narrow, the flagged stone floor chipped and scuffed, and the level worn down noticeably in the middle. No adornments graced the dark wooden walls, only doors that appeared at such regular intervals that I shuddered to think how narrow and poky the rooms behind must be.

But the physical surroundings were nothing to the writhing mass of people that rushed away from us. Even as I stood in the entrance, too shocked to move, at least three doors were flung wide. In each case, the person inside the room threw themselves heedlessly into the maelstrom of people. One of them collided with a young man hurrying down the corridor, but he didn't stop—merely calling an indignant protest over his shoulder as he scurried on.

Zeke glanced back and saw that he had lost me. As he strode back in my direction, he received three pats on the back, five calls of greeting, and a beguiling smile from a particularly attractive young apprentice with long, lustrous black hair. I might not belong in this chaos, but clearly he was at home here.

When he reached me, he paused, turning to survey the scene as if he was trying to see it through my eyes. I glanced at him sideways. Had anyone ever taken the time for such a thing before? Not that I was aware of.

"It is a little overwhelming, isn't it?" he said ruefully. "Apologies for the timing. The bell is about to ring for the evening meal, and no one wants to risk being late."

When I didn't respond, he gave me a conspiratorial smile. "There's a rumor the pastry chef is experimenting on a new creation, and the apprentices always get served the practice runs."

"There are so many people!" I said, still dazed.

He looked back at the crowd which was thinning now. "It's difficult to get an apprenticeship with a master. Most who aspire to become mages must content themselves with being activated by a proficient."

Somewhere in the distance a deep bell clanged. The remaining people in the corridor increased their speed, rushing away from us into the depths of the building. I remained stationary, sending Zeke an apologetic grimace.

"Will helping me mean you miss out on whatever treat is served?"

"While I appreciate your concern, you needn't worry. One of the pastry chef's apprentices will save some for me." He winked, and I suppressed a groan.

Of course they would. Given my own response to him, and the greeting he'd received from the mage apprentices, he was probably a favorite in the kitchens.

"Come on, your room is just down here." He started walking again, and this time I followed.

"Why are you doing this?"

He gave me a strange look. "Helping you? I'm just carrying a bag. Do I need a reason?"

"I think you do. I'm a stranger, after all." I drew a deep breath. "If you're hoping to somehow get to Airlie through me, then—"

"Airlie?" A small tornado that might have been a person

whirled down the empty hallway and slid to a stop in front of us. "Are you connected with her?"

"This is Cadence," Zeke said to the petite, dark-haired girl. "Her younger sister."

"She has a sister?" A new voice drawled the words, the speaker sauntering down the corridor toward us. "No one mentioned a sister."

I sighed. Of course they hadn't.

The second of the new arrivals came closer, and my breathing stuttered, my eyes growing wide. Gulping, I tried to school my expression. Maybe my hermit life really had sent me crazed—it seemed more logical than the coincidence that I had just met two boys in a row both attractive enough to knock me off balance. But however much I blinked, he didn't disappear, and when I looked sideways at Zeke, his face had lost none of its appeal.

I shook my head a little. The two were opposites in coloring —this boy golden-haired and blue eyed—but they possessed the same broad shoulders and air of command. Both looked as if they would be at home at Evermund's side, despite their current presence in the apprentice corridors of the Mages' Guild.

"A sister sounds very promising," the golden-haired newcomer said, his eyes making a thorough assessment of me, as if he could determine my worth with a glance.

I stiffened. Good looks weren't everything.

"What's your affinity?" he asked.

"I...I don't know." I wished I didn't sound so unsure. "I'm still sixteen. I haven't been activated yet."

He frowned at me. "What does that matter? You have been tested, haven't you?"

"You haven't?" The girl pushed past the boy who had taken up position slightly in front of her. Unlike him, she sounded excited at the possibility, rather than judgmental.

I shrugged. "I don't think so? Would I know?"

Sutton had said something about healing mages testing children. Perhaps Hayes had already checked.

The boy snorted. "Of course you would."

"Nik!" The girl spoke with unexpected force, and even more surprisingly, the boy subsided with only the hint of a sardonic look.

I gave the girl a closer look. At first glance the two looked nothing alike given her tiny stature and tight curls of dark brown. But they had the same blue eyes—not just in color but in shape—and the same determined tilt to their chin. Now that I examined them, side-by-side, it was clear they were siblings.

"No doubt you'll be tested the moment they finish with your sister. Imagine if there are two of you!"

I gulped. Whatever they were hoping for, I was fairly certain I wouldn't be able to deliver.

As if she sensed my unease, the girl turned a beaming smile on me. "I'm Gia by the way, and this is Nikolas. Welcome to the Training Academy."

"So tell us, how did she do it?" Nikolas asked. "We'll hear the truth soon enough, so you may as well tell us now."

"How did who do what?" I asked.

His expression turned haughty and sneering, and he took an almost menacing step forward. I stood my ground, but my heart beat too fast, and my palms started sweating. I didn't know the rules of this place yet, and I had no idea how much power he had to make my life difficult.

But I had forgotten Zeke at my side. With a half step forward, he angled his body so as to draw the brunt of Nikolas's menacing approach. My breathing eased as Zeke spoke, his voice still friendly and light.

"As I understand it, they're both entirely untutored in matters of power."

I nodded. "I'm not trying to be difficult. I just have no idea what anyone is talking about most of the time." I frowned. "In fact, I'm getting more than tired of it."

"Of course you are!" Gia's ready sympathy flowed over and around me. "Ignore Nikolas. He's just grumpy because we were supposed to be activated today. And now who knows how long we'll have to wait?"

I raised both eyebrows. "Did I mention not under-standing…"

"Oh! Sorry! Silly me." She laughed. "I've just never met someone our age who didn't at least know—" She cut herself off, throwing a guilty look at Zeke as if he'd sent her a silent reprimand.

"If we have to conduct a lesson, is it really necessary to stand about in the corridor?" Nikolas asked in bored tones.

"I'm just showing Cadence her room." Zeke hefted Airlie's pack as if it weighed nothing, using it to gesture further down the corridor.

"Is she going to stay here?" Gia asked.

I couldn't tell from her tone if she approved or disapproved. Maybe she thought someone who wasn't a true apprentice didn't belong in the apprentice section. But then, from what she'd said, she and Nikolas weren't apprentices yet either. Would they be asked to move out until their activation could be rescheduled?

"So, if you were both to be activated today, does that mean you're twins?" I asked, slowly putting it together as we all followed Zeke down the hall.

Nikolas turned to me with raised eyebrows, but Gia put a restraining hand on his arm.

"I know, we don't look much alike. People comment on it all the time. But we are, indeed, twins."

"Actually, I think you look quite similar."

"You do?" She turned to scrutinize her brother. "I'm not sure whether that's a compliment or an insult."

He smiled, as if he couldn't help himself, and it was the first endearing expression I'd seen on his face. When he grinned like that, without the guarded look in his eyes or the sneer on his lips, it was hard to remember my train of thought.

"Don't be fooled by size," Gia added. "I'm the older one."

A look crossed Nikolas's face that wiped out the earlier affectionate amusement. I looked between the two of them, but whatever had caused his change in sentiment, it no longer showed on either face.

"Here you are." Zeke pushed open a plain wooden door and gestured into the room beyond with a flourish, as if delivering me to a royal suite.

Only a pale blue handle distinguished the door. And given the rainbow of handles that lined the walls, I should probably try to memorize the shade. Instead, I peered inside.

A long, narrow room ended in a window that must look out on the other side of the building to the garden and courtyard. The room's length meant it was larger than I had imagined, the front section set up as a small study, with desk, chair and small bookcase, while the narrow bed sat under the window, a wash-basin and trunk beside it.

"It's...lovely."

My own words surprised me. I wouldn't be staying here, but I hadn't anticipated feeling a pang over that fact. I had never had my own space before, having always shared a room with Airlie, and the prospect was unexpectedly alluring. Especially given how much easier it was to breathe in here than in the crowded public spaces.

"They gave Cadence one of the large ones." Something in Nikolas's tone suggested that the information should mean more to me than it did.

I bit my lip. "It's not supposed to be someone else's room, is it?" I looked between them. "Not one of yours?"

"Ours?" Nikolas gave a contemptuous laugh, only cutting off when Gia kicked him in the shin.

Zeke cut in. "It's been empty since one of the senior apprentices graduated to proficient last week. You need feel no qualms about staking your claim."

I smiled my thanks at his reassurance. I was already a stranger here, without even the rank of apprentice. The last thing I wanted was to be making enemies on my first day. They might have agreed to house me for Airlie's sake, but clearly she wouldn't be spending every moment at my side.

Zeke placed my pack on the closed trunk and took a seat beside it while Gia pulled me down the room to sit on the bed beside her.

"It must be exciting not to know your affinity. I can't remember a time when I didn't know I had an elements seed. What about you, Zeke?" She gave him a curious look.

He nodded. "It's the same with me. Not that anyone was surprised. Both my parents are plant mages."

"So it's hereditary, then?" I asked. Did that mean I had an elements seed like Airlie?

"Yes, but it's not always direct. And just about everyone has all three affinities somewhere in their line, so sometimes there's a surprise." She threw Nikolas a closed look while she said it, and he turned away to look out the window.

"She's talking about me." He sounded bitter.

I gave Gia a questioning look, but she just rolled her eyes, waving a dismissive hand toward his back. I glanced at Zeke instead, and he shook his head slightly, so I let it drop.

"Is it true you lived alone in the wilderness?" Gia asked. "Were you raised by a pack of wolves? I've always thought that would be romantic."

"Romantic?" I eyed her. "It sounds smelly and uncomfortable to me. What would you eat? Raw meat?"

Zeke laughed. "And that, dear Gia, completely quashes that

romantic notion." He grinned at me. "Don't worry, Cadence. Gia wouldn't really run off to join a wolf pack."

Gia shook her head. "Of course not! But it's fun to dream." She sighed a little wistfully.

"Foolish, more like," her brother muttered from the window, but we all ignored him.

"I wouldn't say I lived in the wilderness." My words came slowly, my thoughts wary.

It would be all too easy to get swept up in Gia's friendly volubility. She was a force to be reckoned with, although she slipped in under your defenses in a way her brother never would.

"Our house was just remote," I continued. "We did visit local villages occasionally to trade and the like, but mostly we kept to ourselves. My mother died when I was a small child, and my father died two years ago. After that it was just Airlie and me." I threw Gia an amused look. "No wolves were needed at that point. We managed to feed ourselves, thankfully. Cooked meat only."

She sighed. "I suppose it's for the best."

"Now that I understand a bit more about activation, I think my father intended to activate both of us himself. But he died before we were old enough."

"And apparently he might have saved the kingdom in the process," Nikolas said with a bitter tone.

"Saved the kingdom?" I stared at his back. "What do you mean? What could my father's death possibly have to do with the kingdom?"

He turned around to face me, no sympathy on his face despite the topic of discussion. "Thanks to his absence, a stroke of good luck has meant your sister was just activated by one of our most powerful mages."

It had been more design than luck, but I didn't intend to tell anyone here that.

"Evermund is so powerful, then?" I asked instead.

"Of course." Nikolas looked back out the window. "He wouldn't be Royal Mage otherwise. It's a position of even greater honor than head of an affinity."

"He's very young to hold such a post."

Nikolas nodded once. "And thus we are back to our stroke of luck. Evermund is the only one of his generation to equal the strength of old Drake."

I frowned. "But perhaps there are others who haven't grown into their full power yet? Sutton mentioned Hayes is still studying for his master exam, and he must be a decade older than—"

"Which just makes Evermund all the more remarkable. None of his peers will be able to match him. It's impossible."

"Or it was," Zeke said quietly. "Until suddenly everything changed."

I looked between them.

"Airlie?" I whispered, unable to help a feeling of dread.

Gia nodded enthusiastically. "You obviously know about affinities and activation, but maybe not about the limits of strength? All of us are born with different strength seeds to start with, but that isn't the only decider of our future power. As well as our natural limitations, we're affected by whose influence we come under. No matter what the strength of our seed, our power will never exceed that of our influencer."

"Influencer? Evermund said something about that. You mean the person who activates you?"

I frowned, trying to remember the conversation in the field. The subsequent events had driven some of the details from my mind.

"But Evermund said there wasn't thunder at his own activation." I tried to remember his exact words, but they slipped away from me. He had definitely thought the thunder significant, though—and so had the General and his raiders.

"Precisely." Nikolas sounded tense. "At the time of activation, the seed responds, demonstrating both the affinity and the level of strength possessed. Someone with an elements affinity affects the air around them. But thunder...I checked the records. Thunder hasn't been recorded at an activation since the Master of the Elements two generations before Master Drake. And thus, we can no longer present ourselves to Drake for activation. *Everything has changed.*" He said the final line as if quoting someone he resented.

I looked helplessly at Zeke, and he responded to my unspoken plea with a more comprehensive explanation.

"I'm sure you can see the inevitable result of such a limitation on power. Slowly, over time, the strength of mages is decreasing. Already we're incapable of the sort of feats that were routinely performed a century ago. And so King Marius is left to wonder how long before his mages can no longer heal the kingdom's ill and injured, protect the crops, and guard the borders. It's the sort of question that robs a ruler of sleep. So when the Royal Mage—the strongest mage of his generation—sends word that he has activated an apprentice, and that the initial signs suggest she will possess far greater power than he, well..."

"Powerful people declare that everything has changed," I murmured, my lips numb.

None of it made sense. How—why—would Airlie be such an impossibility?

Seeds of glory and ruin. My father's voice whispered in my ear. How I wished he were still here so I could demand answers from him.

Nikolas turned back around. "So you really don't know why your sister's activation followed none of the established rules of power?"

I shook my head. I had been longing for a clear explanation

since Evermund and his companions burst into my life. But now I had one, and still nothing made sense.

I looked from Gia to Nikolas, my mind catching on a different aspect of his words.

"You were going to be activated by the Master of the Elements?" If I understood everything they had said, that must be a high honor. Was it one purchased with gold or with the potential of the apprentice's seed?

Gia shot Nikolas a glare, as if he'd given away something she hadn't wanted revealed. I looked across at Zeke, my eyes narrowing in suspicion at the open amusement on his face.

A knock sounded on the door, and someone thrust it open without waiting for a response. A footman in blue and gold livery took one step inside. He looked irritated, and my heart sank. Had I done the wrong thing following Zeke here?

But his eyes passed straight over me, landing first on Gia and then on Nikolas. His expression smoothed, his emotions disappearing in an effort of will, and he bowed low.

"Your Highnesses, an extensive search has been underway. You are wanted in the testing room."

I stared at him for a long moment as my thoughts tried to make sense of his words. When the reality sank in, I swallowed.

Frantically I tried to recall everything I'd said as I turned slowly to look at Gia. She stood in a single swift motion, her demeanor utterly transformed. Gone was the friendly apprentice, replaced with a young woman who I would no longer describe as petite. Had she grown? Her air of regal command seemed to have added several inches, and I would have believed her capable of looking down her nose at anyone.

From the corner of my eye, I saw the amusement still lingering on Zeke's face. He certainly didn't look discomposed by Gia's transformation.

"How rude of me not to have properly completed my introductions," he said. "May I introduce Their Royal Highnesses,

Crown Princess Morgiana of Tartora and Prince Nikolas of Tartora."

I glared at him, but his eyes just twinkled back at me. After a beat of silence, I hurriedly rose and bowed in the direction of the twins. It seemed safer than attempting my first curtsy.

Gia—Princess Morgiana, I should call her—inclined her head in my direction to acknowledge the introduction.

"You may tell our parents we will be there directly," she said to the footman. "And we will bring Cadence with us."

For the first time, the footman's eyes focused on me. His expression remained inscrutable, however.

"Very good, Your Highness. Her presence has also been requested."

The princess nodded as if already aware of this fact, although I knew she had only discovered my existence in the corridor with Zeke. As the footman disappeared back down the hall, leaving an open door behind him, I slowly sank back onto the bed. My shock at Gia's identity was already being consumed by a new worry.

The footman had said they were wanted in the testing room —and that I had also been sent for. Apparently it was time to find out just how much—or how little—I resembled my remarkable sister.

CHAPTER

EIGHT

Gia grabbed my arm, tugging me back to my feet. When I tried to pull away, concerned that I shouldn't be touching royalty, she pouted.

"I knew you would find out sooner or later, but I was hoping it would be later."

Nikolas gave an exasperated grunt, as if he was an unwilling participant in his sister's games.

I frowned. I didn't like being toyed with, but I could hardly say as much to the crown princess. I looked surreptitiously between the twins. No wonder it mattered which of them was the elder.

Zeke stood up with an exaggerated sigh, gesturing dramatically toward the door.

"Shall we? Best not to ignore a royal summons, I'm told."

No one pointed out that he hadn't been summoned, and neither twin made any demur at his joining us as we left the room and turned back toward the courtyard entrance. As we walked, he found his way to my side.

"Don't worry," he murmured in my ear. "She doesn't mean any harm by it. It's hard to always be princess—especially when you're still required to complete an apprenticeship. So we made a pact. When it's just us, she's Apprentice Gia. When others are around..." He gestured at her upright figure several steps ahead of us.

"But she doesn't even know me. Why would she..."

He shrugged one shoulder. "I can only speculate, but I would say that her excitement and curiosity overcame her at first, and then..."

"Then?" I prodded.

"Then you didn't know who she was. When you've spent every moment of your life scrutinized by an entire court, it's heady to meet someone who has no idea who you are. You're not a part of her court—apparently you're barely even a part of her kingdom. I suppose you seem safe."

I gave him a sharp look, and his brows quirked, his return gaze curious and open. I looked away, saying nothing and forcing my breathing to remain even. He couldn't possibly know I was Calistan.

After a slight pause, he continued. "And maybe she liked the idea of having another girl to talk to. Delightful as I am, I'm told by reliable sources that sometimes my company is not enough."

"Never!" I clapped a hand to my chest in false horror.

He chuckled. "I like you, Cadence, even if you're the most ignorant apprentice the Training Academy has ever seen."

"Thanks for the compliment." I rolled my eyes.

"I guess Gia likes you, too." He shrugged. "Or maybe you're a compromise. She wanted to be Apprentice Gia to all the apprentices, now that she was going to join our ranks, but Nikolas was strenuously against the idea." His eyes lingered on the tight line of the prince's shoulders. "Nik doesn't approve of his sister's...less formal ways."

I watched the straight backs of the two royals. Clearly there were layers here I was far from understanding. What would happen if I turned tail and fled back to my new bed to rest my pounding head?

My steps didn't falter, however. No matter how strong the instinct for escape, I couldn't act on it. The feeling of being in over my head only made it more imperative that I measure each action. I couldn't let Airlie down now that I understood the true danger of our position.

Would Airlie be at the testing? A cowardly part of me desperately hoped so. For all I complained about her, my older sister had always been there to shield and protect me.

I followed the others back through the narrow door and into the early evening gloom. The central courtyard looked as it had before—several formal arrangements of garden beds with an occasional out of place riot of growth, and several fountains of varying sizes that didn't match at all.

"I think they're the ones that various royal family members have rejected through the generations," Zeke murmured in my ear, apparently having caught me eyeing the fountains. "I can certainly imagine the king's grandmother strolling through the large formal gardens on the far side of the castle, taking one look at that monstrosity, and declaring it be banished to the Mages' Guild."

He indicated a fountain of water that blasted from the mouth of what might have been a foal or perhaps a malformed deer. The weathered gray stone didn't assist in deciphering the artist's intention.

"It is particularly ugly, isn't it?" I whispered back. "But it can hold its head up beside that one."

He snorted. "No doubt it was intended that the fountain erupt from the dragon's mouth like fire."

"Which would be a vast improvement on the reality—however poorly thought through the substitution of water for fire." It was almost painful to watch the way the water trickled from the enormous lizard's nostrils, as if he had caught a particularly bad winter's cold. "Why wasn't it disposed of altogether?"

"I like to think it was designed by some non-artistic member of the extended royal family. Or perhaps a high-ranking guild member. Only affection or politics could explain its continued existence."

I chuckled. "I can see you've given the matter some thought."

He grinned back. "No self-respecting apprentice pays attention in all their lessons." He swept an arm around the horse shoe behind us. "And a great many windows look out onto this courtyard."

"Then perhaps you can explain that." I pointed at the garden bed we were passing. The low, carefully clipped hedge had crossed some invisible boundary and burst into riotous growth, tendrils stretching out over the path, ready to trip unwary feet.

Gia glanced back over her shoulder, a laugh in her voice. "Zeke isn't the only plants mage who doesn't believe in paying attention in lessons."

"Who says they weren't paying attention?" Zeke said. "I, for one, prefer it this way."

"Until you trip and break that perfect nose," I muttered.

"Why, thank you! It is perfect, isn't it?" He winked at me, running one finger down the feature in question.

I flushed and increased my pace. He had better hearing than I'd anticipated.

"That way." Gia led us right, approaching an elaborate double door. She paused in front of it and glanced at me. "This is the elements wing. Behind us is the plants wing, and that's the healing one."

She pointed at the section of building that joined the other two. Each wing looked almost identical, containing a matching grand doorway, all of which were firmly shut.

The princess pushed one of the doors open without knocking, and I half expected a butler to spring forward to greet us. The foyer inside was empty, however.

Gia didn't hesitate, leading us straight across the open space and toward a door in the far left wall. This time, when she opened it, we were greeted by a guard. He wore the same version of the blue and gold livery as the guards I had met with Evermund, a sword strapped to his waist. He made no attempt to intercept us, however, merely bowing when he recognized the twins.

Gia nodded to him while Nikolas ignored him entirely, his attention on the rest of the room. I followed his gaze and swallowed hard. Stepping backward, I nearly stumbled into Zeke who steadied me with a hand under one elbow. The contact lasted only a few seconds, but it strengthened me, and I stepped forward again.

The large room—almost a hall—held a number of people. Some I recognized, some I did not.

Airlie stood in the center, surrounded on all sides by middle-aged men and women who carried themselves as if they knew their own worth. She didn't look in the least discomposed, however, and some of her certainty flowed into me. They had brought us here because they were convinced she was special—that must surely afford us some protection, even if it felt alarming to think of having such attention trained on us.

Of the group, only Evermund appeared close to our age, but he hung back, a step beyond the circle that surrounded Airlie. Not that he looked in the least awed by the presence of a couple bearing royal circlets on their heads. It was more as if he didn't want to influence their assessment of his new apprentice. Perhaps he was considered too involved.

But just the sight of him further eased my anxiety. It was Airlie's face I had been hoping to see, but to my surprise, Evermund's felt comfortingly familiar as well. I had been kidnapped and held hostage while part of his traveling group, but somehow his presence made me feel safer. I hoped that boded well for Airlie's apprenticeship—and both of our futures.

"Ah, there you are." An older man with graying hair and tired eyes frowned in our direction.

He wasn't looking at me, though. Instead his gaze focused solely on the twins. Given the circlet he wore, I could only assume he was their father. King Marius. I knew that much about Tartora, at least.

Both Gia and Nikolas bowed slightly, from the shoulders.

"We came as soon as we received your message. Have we missed the testing?" Nikolas sounded regretful.

"You have." The woman at the king's side gave them a warmer look, despite the brevity of her words.

Unlike King Marius, Queen Celestine's eyes moved past her children to fix on me. They instantly brightened.

"And you've brought the sister with you. Excellent."

"I'm Cadence." I stepped forward and bowed more deeply than I had for the twins. The introduction seemed a futile gesture, but I couldn't help the small protest. I wasn't just Airlie's sister.

"It's a pleasure to have you among us, Cadence," she said in a rich, lilting voice. "Your sister is a mystery—but one of the most welcome kind. Given the hereditary nature of power, abilities often run in families. We are full of hope that you may prove a welcome addition to the Mages' Guild as well."

The prince stirred restlessly in front of me at her mention of the role of heredity. What was his affinity that he disliked it so?

"Before we begin the testing, I would like to ask a few questions," King Marius said in an unexpectedly deep voice.

"Of me, Your Majesty?"

I bowed again hurriedly in case the question was deemed impertinent.

"Of you," he said, but for the first time there was a spark of warmth in his eyes.

I relaxed slightly. Apparently our monarch wasn't quite as forbidding as he had first appeared.

"Please, join us." The queen gestured toward Airlie.

I walked over to my sister's side, the other three blending in to the circle around us. Again no one actively invited Zeke's presence, but no one protested it either. And only Airlie sent him a curious look. Apparently being a close friend of the twins imparted a great deal of access and trust. It made Gia's overtures of friendship to me even more surreal.

Airlie put her arm around my shoulders, the gesture one of unspoken support. But the sharp, subtle dig of her fingers conveyed a different message altogether. When I glanced sideways at her, she flicked a warning glance toward an older man with a shock of unruly white hair and a cheerful face.

Of everyone present, he looked the least intimidating. My insides tensed. Why was Airlie warning me about him?

Evermund stepped forward, intruding on the cluster of people in the center of the room. He smiled sympathetically at me, as if he had caught my air of concern.

"Cadence, this is Their Royal Majesties, King Marius and Queen Celestine."

I bowed a third time for good measure.

"And this is the Triumvirate. Colton, Master of Healing, Augusta, Master of Plants, and Drake, Master of the Elements."

I gave another bow in their direction. I was going to fall over soon with all this flopping around. But while Father had never gone into detail about the Mages' Guild, he had taught us the hierarchy of Tartoran society, in which the Triumvirate played a central role.

Kingdom life was ruled by the various guilds, and at the top of the guild hierarchy was the Mages' Guild. The Mages' Guild was ruled by the three affinity heads—collectively known as the Triumvirate. Together they were the voice of the people in the government of the kingdom. Which meant I was about to be tested by the five most powerful people in Tartora.

"You don't need to bow to us, child." Drake sounded amused. "We aren't royalty. I was born in the hut of a blacksmith, you know."

"Indeed you were." Augusta's brow creased as she turned a speculative look on her fellow master.

She appeared particularly diminutive beside the tall, broad figure of the Master of the Elements, but nothing in her bearing suggested she had ever noticed the discrepancy. She carried herself with vitality, her golden face unlined, despite the generous gray in her smooth, black hair which made her exact age hard to pinpoint.

"Considerable effort has been expended over the course of generations," she continued, "and yet we haven't been able to determine why some children are born with seeds that appear to defy the natural course of heredity. A family of healing mages can have a child with an elements seed, and a long line of blacksmiths who didn't even qualify as mages can have a son with the strongest seed of his generation. I fear we may be left with no clearer answer in this instance, either. Sometimes power determines its own course, defying the rules we have created to understand it."

"I fear you may be right, Augusta." Colton clasped his hands over his rounded belly.

"And yet..." Drake frowned, clearly less willing to abandon the search for answers. "This isn't just a case of someone born to the wrong family, as it were. This is something entirely outside of our combined experience—and the experience of the Masters we trained under. We have meticulous records on a century of Guild apprentices, and I would swear they include no mention of such a thing. No apprentice can be stronger than the mage who activated them. The rule is universal."

"Such debates are important, and I have no doubt will

continue for weeks if not years," King Marius said. "But for now we are here to test the sister."

Cadence, I thought, but this time I didn't say it aloud.

"If Airlie is a random anomaly as Master Augusta suggests," Evermund said, joining the debate, "then any expectations about Cadence might be unfounded."

"Never mind expectations." Drake slashed the air, as if to remove all further impediments. "Let us discover the truth. Colton?" He turned to the Master of Healing—the same man Airlie had warned me of.

Had she intended to warn me about the test? There was no way for me to avoid it that I could see, so the warning seemed useless.

But when Colton stepped forward, I felt no disturbance of the air or anything else to indicate a test was underway.

"Do not be nervous, Cadence," he said with the same friendly smile I had noted earlier. "Simply answer us truthfully, and all will be well."

Truth! I refrained from glancing at Airlie. That had been her warning. Despite his elevated rank, Evermund had relied on Hayes—a mere proficient—to detect truth from lie. It must be a skill associated with the healing affinity. Airlie had been warning me to choose my words carefully.

I nodded to the Master of Healing, but apparently he needed no agreement from me because he had already begun his first question.

"Do you have any idea why your sister's strength defies the known rules of power?"

"No." I said the word confidently. I hadn't even known what the rules of power were—let alone that Airlie defied them—an hour ago.

"Do you know your own affinity?"

"No," I repeated. "Most of what I know about seeds, activation, and influence, I learned since meeting the Royal Mage. The rules and ways of power were excluded from my education. I know nothing of Airlie's strange situation, and even less about my own seed."

I glanced at Evermund. He watched me, his expression hard to read.

"What of your father and mother? Were either of their abilities remarkable in any way?"

I hesitated for a moment before shrugging. "My mother died before I was old enough to wonder about such things. As for my father...he never spoke of his power, and he didn't like to answer questions on this topic. He cannot have had a substantial ability since I never saw him make noticeable use of it. I don't even know for sure what his affinity was."

Colton looked to the king. "She speaks the truth, Your Majesty. There seems little point in pursuing further questioning."

"Very well." King Marius sighed. "Let us proceed to the testing, and then perhaps our meal will still be edible when we make it to table."

CHAPTER

NINE

Colton looked back at me, and though he didn't speak, the air around us changed. Something emerged from him and stretched toward me, but the sensation of invisible movement didn't have the clarity that had accompanied Evermund's testing of Airlie. It was almost as if the hilltop air had been clear, while whatever moved toward me here did so through a thick fog.

It took all my courage not to shrink from the reaching tendril, but when it brushed against me, I felt no physical sensation. In fact, a moment later I felt nothing at all, the invisible connection between Colton and me severed.

I stared at him, as did everyone else in the room except Evermund, who instead watched me, the slightest crease between his brows.

"Strange." Colton frowned.

King Marius leaned forward slightly. "She is also unusual?"

Colton blew out a long breath before replying. "She is, Your Majesty, but not as we had hoped. I'm afraid I cannot even tell you the nature of her seed."

"You couldn't detect her affinity?" Queen Celestine asked. "How is that possible?"

"It is not unheard of, Your Majesty," Drake interjected. "While rare, sometimes in cases of very weak seeds it can be difficult to detect even its presence, let alone its nature..."

Only Evermund didn't react to this news...almost as if it wasn't news to him. Had Hayes already seen my weak seed while he was healing me? If so, Evermund had chosen to keep the humiliating information to himself.

Airlie's arm tightened across my shoulders. "I'm sorry, Cadence. I didn't know..."

"There you go, then." I forced myself to speak, hoping my voice conveyed a lack of concern I was far from feeling. "Perhaps that is the answer to the big mystery. Airlie received the power for both of us."

Augusta rocked toward me, her expression intrigued. "I had understood you to be a couple of years younger than your sister. Are you in fact twins? While there are no recorded instances of power passing between infants in the womb, it is perhaps within the realms of—"

"We are not twins, Master Augusta," Airlie said.

"Ah." She looked disappointed. "Then I do not see how such a phenomenon could be feasible. No, we must look for other answers."

I bit my lip. I hadn't expected my suggestion to be taken seriously.

"It may be possible to identify your affinity when you are closer to being ready for activation," Colton said sympathetically. "I'm sure one of the healing proficients would be willing to test again for you when some months have passed. I understand you are not that far off seventeen."

I murmured my thanks, trying not to dwell on the unspoken inference of his words. Unlike Airlie, I did not warrant any further time from a master mage, let alone an affinity head. Which meant I needed to seize my moment.

"What of my future?" I asked. "I've been assigned a room among the apprentices."

"What?" Airlie drew back, her arm dropping and her eyes darkening. "Nonsense. You must stay with me, of course."

"I'm afraid that is impossible," Drake said. "It is a requirement of law that anyone activated by a master mage must reside with their activator for the full two years of their apprenticeship."

"A law that is currently under debate," Augusta murmured.

"Meaning for now, at least, it still stands—as it has long stood," the king said in a voice that brooked no questioning.

Augusta inclined her head.

"But we're not talking about me," Airlie said, pushing the issue, as I knew she would. "We're talking about my sister. Why can't she stay with me? Evermund said he has no other apprentices."

Evermund cleared his throat. "It is rare for the Royal Mage to take even a single apprentice. The space is only equipped for one. But I suppose in the circumstances, it would be possible to make the necessary adjustments."

Airlie nodded, but I could see disapproval on other faces. Allowing me to live at the Mages' Guild at all was permitted only because of Airlie's great value—I was too young to be an apprentice, and even when I reached the correct age, I would clearly not be accepted as an official guild apprentice. My seed was much too weak for that. Giving me an honored place with the most favored apprentices would only further highlight how out of place I was.

I cleared my throat. "Actually, if it is permitted, I would prefer to stay in the room assigned to me."

Out of the corner of my eye I saw a look of approval on Zeke's face which was far preferable to the intense curiosity he had been regarding me with during the preceding conversation. And Gia actually grinned at me, although I wasn't sure if she approved of my staying in the apprentice quarters or merely my show of independence.

"Cadence!" Airlie, however, did not agree with them. "What are you saying?"

I ignored her familiar glare to focus on Evermund. He raised an eyebrow.

"You're sure?"

I nodded. "I would like to live with the general apprentices."

"Very well, then." Drake seemed ready to move on to other matters. "As a dependent of Evermund's apprentice, it is up to him to determine what provisions you receive. I'm sure the rest of us see no need to get involved."

Nods all around the circle confirmed this assessment. As if released, everyone drifted from their positions, forming into pairs or small huddles.

I slumped slightly, relieved to be free from the pressure of such high-ranked scrutiny. But I wasn't given a chance to relax. A hand grasped my arm, fingers digging painfully into my skin.

"Cadence!" Airlie hissed through her teeth. "What are you thinking?"

I glanced around, but no one had approached us. Taking a deep breath, I dropped my voice as low as I could manage through the tightness in my chest.

"Here you're special, Airlie. One of a kind."

"Exactly! They can't refuse my requests. They want me to work with them, to cooperate. We can stay together. You heard Evermund, he was going to—"

"No, you don't understand." I wrenched my arm free, and her face creased in confusion. "You're special, Air, but I'm nothing. I shouldn't even be here. Unlike you, I don't belong in the Royal Mage's suite, and I would prefer not to be reminded of that daily. This is going to be a difficult enough two years as it is."

Her face paled, her expression stricken. "Of course you're

not nothing, Cadence. You heard Master Colton. They'll test you again..."

Guilt crept in at her obvious concern, but I refused to budge. Now that I had pointed it out, Airlie felt bad, but she hadn't taken the time to consider my situation for herself. Which was exactly why I needed to make my own decisions.

She'd been making the decisions for both of us ever since Father died. No longer.

"Yes, I did hear him. Did you? A *proficient* will test me on the off chance they can determine my affinity. Although what good that will do me, I can't imagine."

"No." She shook her head. "This can't be right! You're not weak, Cadie. I know you're not. Father—" She cut herself off, biting her lip.

"What about Father?" I hated the eager note that crept into my voice, betraying the hope he had confided some secret in her—some secret that would reveal me to be as special as Airlie. "Did he say something about my seed? About my power?"

She cringed, and the hope died. "Father only ever said one thing about our seeds. You heard it as often as me. He would never explain it to me any more than he would to you."

"I guess we know who has the glory and who has the ruin now," I said flatly. "Perhaps it's a good thing no one will be eager to activate my power when I reach seventeen. Apparently even my weak ability has the potential to be dangerous."

She shook her head again. "Don't talk like that! We don't know that's what Father meant. All power has the potential to be used for good or ill. Mother always said that, and she was the wisest person I've ever met."

"I guess I was too young to remember."

I knew how Airlie felt about our long-dead mother, so I refrained from pointing out that the sentiment meant little given how few people either of us had met. Instead I forced myself to return to the topic of relevance to the moment.

"Regardless of what she used to say, I'm not living with you. They've assigned me my own room, and I'm going to stay there."

I turned away, resisting her efforts to stop me.

"This conversation isn't finished, Cadence," she snapped, not quite loud enough to be heard by the others around us.

"I'm sure it's not." I rolled my eyes, not looking back to her. Airlie had never known how to take no for an answer.

Leaving my sister alone in the middle of the room, I hurried over to Evermund. Zeke had joined him at some point, but I kept my focus on the master.

"Master Drake said I'm your responsibility. So I just wanted to check. What should I be doing?"

"Doing?" Evermund's blank expression told me as loudly as words that he hadn't considered the matter.

I sighed. "Yes, what should I do? Thank you for the room you arranged for me, but I can't sit in it for two years doing nothing."

"No, of course not." He threw a bewildered glance at Zeke, who slid smoothly into the conversation.

"You're staying in an apprentice room, so you should join the apprentice studies, of course."

"An excellent suggestion." Evermund nodded his approval, as if that finished the matter.

"I'm not an apprentice."

"You can read, can't you?" Zeke gave me a challenging look.

I glared back at him, in no mood for games. "Of course I can read."

"Well, in that case, you can study. You won't even be alone. Their Royal Highnesses have negotiated to start their apprenticeships on schedule, even though they won't be activated. The three of you can play pretend-apprentices together."

"Have they now?" Evermund frowned. "I hope they know Airlie's strength doesn't excuse her from the full two years. You heard the other masters. The law on these matters is well-established."

Zeke gave Evermund a knowing look, and he sighed, scrubbing at his face with his hand as though exhausted.

"Morgiana has been looking forward to being an apprentice for years." Evermund spoke in a resigned voice.

"You needn't guard your words on my account," Zeke said cheerfully. "Gia is perfectly aware that the Triumvirate and her parents are only allowing it because they believe she'll get sick of playing ordinary apprentice within weeks. They no doubt think this an excellent opportunity to get it out of her system before her true apprenticeship begins."

It wasn't hard to read Evermund's agreement with this assessment on his face.

"And Nikolas follows wherever his sister leads," he murmured, his gaze turning to the prince who was now speaking with his parents and sister.

"But always with great reluctance, of course." The laugh in Zeke's eyes belied his solemn tone.

Evermund laughed and clapped Zeke on the shoulder. "I'm glad you came to the Guild, Zeke. You're good for my young cousins."

Cousins? I looked at Evermund with new eyes. He was nephew to the king and queen? Was that how he had gained such a prestigious appointment at such a young age?

It was still an impressive feat, though. The Royal Mage was required to have power as great as that of an affinity head—a necessary requirement given he was the official liaison between crown and Triumvirate, needing to be respected by both.

Gia detached herself from her family and bounced over to us. Throwing her arms around me, she exclaimed, "We're going to be non-apprentices together!"

I stiffened, taken off guard by the unexpected gesture. I had never had a friend to exchange hugs with.

"Slow down there, Apprentice," Zeke said. "Us commoners don't tend to be quite so affectionate with strangers."

She dropped her arms and gave me an apologetic look. "Too much?"

"Ah..." I stumbled over my words, unsure if I was allowed to tell a princess her greeting had been odd.

She laughed at what must have been a pained look on my face. "Don't worry. Zeke is helping me learn."

Evermund groaned. "Do I want to ask?"

Gia threw him a sparkling look. "He's teaching me to become Apprentice Gia. I thought it was a great bore learning to be Princess Morgiana, but it turns out the lesson sunk in rather well. It's much more challenging becoming Apprentice Gia than I expected."

"With good reason." Evermund gave her a disapproving look. "You can't just turn off being royal. It's important to maintain—"

Her eyes took on a mulish cast. "Two years. That was the deal. They agreed I get two years."

Nikolas strolled over. "Don't waste your time, Evermund. If she could be convinced, one of us would have succeeded by now."

"If you're so against it, why did you agree to come with me?" she shot back.

"Someone has to make sure you don't do something we'll all live to regret while you're playing *Apprentice Gia*."

She shot him the kind of sibling look I recognized all too well before determinedly turning her back on him.

"It doesn't matter anyway," she said to me. "We won't be strangers for long. I think we're going to be good friends. After all, we're the only non-apprentices here. So that means we have to stick together."

"If you say so, Your Highness," I agreed.

"No—call me Gia. Like Zeke."

I sent him and Evermund a questioning look, and they gave almost identical shrugs.

"Very well...Gia."

She gave her brother a pointed look, and he responded with a deep sigh.

"Nikolas, if you must. *Not* Nik."

"Of course she must," Gia interjected. "She can't call me Gia while constantly bowing and Your Highness-ing you." She gave me an exasperated look. "He's so convinced I'm going to disgrace us all, or undermine the monarchy or something, that he barely leaves my side. I'm extremely sorry, but we're a package deal."

"Oh...I..." I looked at the prince who currently appeared pained at being forced to converse with me.

"I really am legitimately sorry," Gia said, enough worry in her voice that I couldn't help relenting.

"Of course. Gia and...Nikolas."

The prince and I both winced, but Gia pretended not to notice.

"So, do you have a room near mine?" I asked, eager to change the subject.

Zeke threw his head back and laughed, wiping imaginary tears of mirth from his eyes.

"Oh, Cadence, you don't think Gia is *that* eager to be a regular apprentice, do you?"

"Zeke!" Gia's mortified exclamation only backed up his claim. "It wasn't my choice. You heard what they said about the laws. We were supposed to be activated by—"

"Master Drake," Nikolas interjected.

She gave him a look. "*I* was supposed to be activated by Master Drake, and Nikolas was supposed to be activated by Master Augusta. The three members of the Triumvirate each get two apprentice rooms, so Nik and I both have a room to ourselves in their suites."

"The suites of the Triumvirate members are equivalent to the royal suites in the main palace," Zeke explained for my benefit. "It's not what you would consider poor accommodation."

"Which you would know." Gia narrowed her eyes at him. "Zeke is apprenticed to Master Augusta himself, so he shares those quarters."

Zeke was apprenticed to one of the head mages? Was that why he seemed to know everything that was going on at the Guild? Perhaps it also explained his closeness with the twins. Master Drake's history suggested that strength mattered far more than anything else inside the Guild.

"Ah yes, but I'm not royalty," he said. "So I share the second room with her two other current apprentices, while Nikolas here gets the single room to himself."

"Really, children." Evermund grinned at them. "What will Cadence think of all this squabbling?"

Gia sent him a wrathful glare. "You may be Royal Mage now, but you're also family, so don't think you're safe from—"

"What's going to happen with your rooms?" Zeke asked. "Given you weren't activated." He assumed an exaggerated expression of innocence. "Not that I'm wondering for any particular reason."

Nikolas chuckled. "I seem to remember you had Augusta's single room before today, didn't you? I'm afraid to say our accommodation arrangements remain the same."

"It's an awkward situation," Evermund murmured, and I had a feeling he wasn't talking about room assignments.

His earlier mention of Airlie's apprenticeship, as if it was linked to the twins, made me uncomfortable. But despite Gia's insistence on informality, I didn't think I could demand to know why their apprenticeship plans were somehow dependent on hers.

Thinking about Airlie drew my eyes toward her. She

continued to stand alone, her gaze trained on our cluster. Even from the distance I could read her narrowed eyes and taut muscles. She was still angry with me.

A brief smug feeling radiated over me. Here I stood, laughing with my new friends—most of whom were royalty—while she stood alone. But I immediately squashed the ugly emotion. It wasn't Airlie's fault she was special, any more than it was my fault I had a diseased seed.

"Let me introduce my sister," I said to the twins, beckoning Airlie over.

For a moment I thought she would refuse, but after a second's consideration, she relaxed, joining us with a smile. I was fairly sure no one but me would be able to tell it was strained.

After the general introductions were made, and Airlie had curtsied with the sort of presence I lacked, Evermund stepped in.

"You've seen your new room, Cadence, but Airlie has yet to see hers."

"Thank you," Airlie said quickly. "You'll want to see it, too, Cadie." It wasn't a question.

"I've ordered food to be delivered to my suite," Evermund added, ensuring my support of the plan, despite the conflict brewing in Airlie's eyes when they rested on me.

Within moments, we were traveling through a long corridor that bore little resemblance to the one in the apprentices' section of the building. Here, the scrubbed pale gray stone reflected the warmth and light of the regular lanterns, the monotony of stone and wood broken up with bright tapestries on the walls. Underfoot, a lush red carpet ran down the middle of the hall.

"This is nice," I said.

Evermund threw me an amused look. "This is one of the

more public areas of the building—and thus of more importance to the Guild. Our status and reputation must be maintained."

"Do all the masters have suites here?" Airlie asked.

"This is the elements wing, so the elements masters do." He gestured at a number of doors of polished wood. The distance between them suggested the suites were made up of rooms of generous size. "The floor above is the same. But our suite is on the end."

Ahead of us, the corridor ended in a door more elaborate than the ones before it. In the middle of the wood, a polished metal plaque contained Evermund's name and title.

"Drake has the same above us," he said, pushing the door open. "And each of the other heads have such a suite in their own wings."

"Why is the Royal Mage's suite in the elements wing?" I asked.

"Officially or unofficially?" he asked.

"Both, of course," Airlie said promptly.

He threw her an amused look. "Officially it's because this wing is closest to the palace, and my role takes me there on a regular basis. Unofficially it's because elements is widely regarded as the strongest of the affinities, and the Royal Mage is usually an elements mage."

"Widely regarded..." Airlie said shrewdly. "You don't agree?"

Evermund shrugged, speaking over his shoulder as he stepped through the door.

"Brute strength might be showy, but it's not always the most effective solution to a problem."

I followed behind him, forgetting the thread of the conversation as I looked around me. Long curtains suggested large windows on both the left and far walls. During the day, the enormous room would be flooded with light. A round table large enough to comfortably seat four stood in the window corner, with a long sofa beside it. The other side of the room held bookcases, and several reading chairs.

"That is my bedchamber." Evermund pointed at a door in the right wall. "And that is your room, Airlie." He pointed at a second door not far from it. "I'm afraid I've been using it as a study, so it will take a little time to have it returned to a proper state for an apprentice."

"You needn't be concerned on my account," Airlie replied. "I've never even had a room to myself before."

"At your insistence," I grumbled quietly.

I had suggested she move into our parents' room after Father's death, but she had been the one to insist we stay together. Shooting me a warning look, she strode over to peek through the door.

But when she tried to turn the handle, it wouldn't budge. "It's locked." She looked back at Evermund.

"Oh good. I requested it be permanently secured." He rubbed the back of his neck as if uncomfortable. "While it is traditional—required even—for apprentices to live in close proximity to their masters, it seemed in this particular circumstance that..." He trailed away, as if unsure how to finish the thought.

Both Airlie and I stared at him in confusion until Airlie suddenly flushed, looking almost as flustered as him. I glanced back and forth between them, comprehension dawning.

Evermund was not a normal master mage. While I hadn't met every master in the Guild, the members of the Triumvirate all looked old enough to be grandparents. And from what the others had said, in normal circumstances, there would be multiple apprentices sharing a master suite. I didn't know if Evermund was thinking of Airlie's comfort or was protecting them both from gossiping tongues, but either way, it demonstrated a pleasing level of consideration.

"I'll give you a key for this door." Evermund led the way out an unadorned door in the far wall that opened into a small, pleasant segment of garden. Several steps along the same wall, we reached another door which he unlocked before presenting the key to Airlie. "This is yours now."

Unlike mine, the room beyond was a normal square shape, with large windows on two walls. Plush carpet in deep green blended well with the garden beyond the glass, but the luxurious fittings and furnishings were rather lost in the crush of furniture.

"As I said, we'll have it sorted soon." Evermund grimaced. "They hurried to move the bed back in, but as you can see, they haven't moved my office furniture out yet."

"I think the bigger problem might be the books," I said, a little awed. "Moving-wise, I mean. Obviously books aren't a *problem*."

"Bookcases aren't a problem either." Airlie's voice held a wry note.

My sister had always been one to love order, so I could only imagine her horror at the stacks of books, parchments, and scrolls that covered both desks, every chair, and half of the available floor.

"You'll get on well with the Guild steward," Evermund said. "He's told me the same thing in much less polite language many times."

"Never mind," Airlie said briskly. "I'm here now, and as your apprentice it should fall to me to keep your personal library organized."

I snorted. "By which she means your life is no longer your own. It's hard to say no to Airlie."

"On that topic," she said, her voice too sweet. "Would you help me unpack my things, Cadie?" She glanced briefly in Evermund's direction. "If you'll excuse us, that is?"

"Certainly!"

It might have been my imagination, but his retreat seemed to be conducted in unseemly haste, leaving me fully alone with my sister for the first time since she burned down our hunting lodge.

CHAPTER

TEN

I regarded Airlie warily as soon as the door closed behind Evermund.

"You don't want to unpack, do you?"

"Of course I want to unpack." She started pulling items of clothing blindly out of her pack and strewing them across the bed. "My things need to be unpacked, and someone has to do it. Sometimes you have to do things you don't want to do, Cadence. You can't just float through life doing whatever you want."

"Are you sure we're talking about clothes?"

She flung a boot on the bed with unnecessary force and turned to face me, her arms crossed.

"What were you thinking, Cadence?"

"Father isn't here anymore, Airlie, and through no fault of mine, it seems we've left our home for good. I was thinking that maybe—for the first time in my life—I could make my own decisions. Of course *you* wouldn't understand."

"Me?" Her teeth audibly clacked together, her jaw tensing. "Of course I wouldn't understand *anything* about not being free to make my own choices."

I flung my arms wide. "Well, I certainly haven't been

making decisions for you! I don't even get to make them for myself!"

"Cadie!" She paused, and all her antagonism dropped away, leaving her shoulders slumped and voice tired. "All I want is to keep us both safe. We need to stick together." Her voice dipped lower. "It isn't safe for us here, or have you already forgotten?"

I shivered, more swayed than I wanted to admit by her new posture. There was something terrifying about seeing my confident sister so shaken. But I had declared my intention to take the apprentice room in front of the king himself. I couldn't give in now.

"I haven't forgotten." I sat on the bed and patted the spot beside me.

Airlie gave a frustrated groan but pushed her haphazard pile of clothing aside and sat beside me.

"You're thinking about it wrong," I continued. "We're not in the wilderness anymore. I'm not in danger of encountering a wild boar without you and your bow around. You've just broken it to me that we're different—in a dangerous way. So it seems to me that drawing attention to ourselves is the last thing we want to do." I snorted. "Not that you can help drawing attention to yourself, of course. But we don't want to give anyone any extra reasons to think there's something strange about us."

She gave me a stubborn look, and I sighed.

"I don't belong here, Airlie. I already told you that, and if you're honest with yourself, you know it's true. The best thing for both of us is for me to stay out of the way as much as I possibly can."

She gave me a considering look, and I tried to appear wise, as if my decision was motivated by nothing but a logical consideration of our circumstances. When she threw an arm around me and dipped her head to rest on my shoulder, I knew I had succeeded.

"I suppose you're right, Cadie. I just hate the idea of us

being separated the minute we get here. It makes me wonder what the point of it all was. I already miss you."

I froze, trying to process her words. Was it possible *Airlie* felt as lost and alone and out of her depth as I did? It hardly seemed likely. She had always been so sure she had the answers.

"What's going on, Airlie?" I asked. "What *is* the point of it all? First you said we couldn't leave our house to join a village, then you decided we should spend months carefully planning a trip to the capital...and then you threw all those plans away in the blink of an eye. Why?"

She sat up, shaking her head emphatically. "We couldn't just join one of the villages."

I waited for her to explain further, but instead she stood up and resumed unpacking, moving more calmly this time.

"That doesn't explain the rest of it." I watched her with narrowed eyes. "I know you didn't suggest the capital because of my pleading. Did you know you needed someone powerful to activate your own powerful seed? Is that why you then reacted so drastically when you saw Evermund? I thought everyone was excited because it didn't matter for you, you're not bound by your influence."

Her hands stilled, but she didn't turn to face me. "Father didn't tell me anything about my ability. I already told you that. I didn't know I would be so unusual."

"What did he tell you, then?" I put my hands on my hips. "No more secrets, Airlie."

"He told me to keep you safe. And that's what I'm trying to do." She upended her pack, letting the last few items spill out onto the bed. "Evermund said there would be food. And I, for one, am starving. Shall we go see if we can find it?"

"Airlie! Do you really think I'm that easily distracted? Father obviously told you more than that!"

She drew a deep breath, as if reaching for patience. "You're right. You shouldn't eat with us. You said you wanted to be one of the ordinary apprentices, so you should go find their dining hall. You wouldn't want anyone to see you eating in the Royal Mage's suite."

I stood up. "Are you sending me to my room without food? Seriously?"

"This has nothing to do with me. You're the one making all the decisions now, remember."

I huffed out an angry breath. "Fine! Don't tell me anything. But don't go reassuring yourself that I'd understand if I only knew your circumstances. I'm sure Father made you swear an oath on his deathbed, or something. But he's gone now, and maybe your biggest loyalty should lie with me—your last remaining family member."

I stormed toward the door. Just as I reached it, she called my name. A large part of me wanted to continue out without a backward glance, but I couldn't help pausing and looking back. For all she infuriated me, she was still my sister.

"My loyalty is with you, Cadence. Please believe that. It's always with you. We promised, remember—that we'd always look out for each other."

I sighed.

"I remember. And when you finally realize how silly all these secrets are, I'll be waiting." I stepped out the door before turning back a final time. "I might be banished, but I'm taking food with me. And if there are any cakes, I'm taking yours as well as mine. Fair warning."

Her soft laugh chased me out into the garden and across into Evermund's enormous sitting room. He looked up as I entered, and if there was the slightest disappointment in his expression when he saw I was alone, he hid it quickly.

"I'm not staying," I said. "I've been banished."

He raised both brows. "Banished?"

I shrugged. "It's a sister thing. We'll be fine in the morning.

Can I take a plate of food with me, though? I can't remember the last time I ate."

"Of course." He picked one up off the table and began piling it high with food. When he got to the small delicate cakes, iced in pink, I told him to add extra.

"You have good taste." He grinned at me. "These are my favorites."

The chef must have known it, too, because someone had sent enough that Airlie wouldn't miss out, despite my greed. My irritation had subsided enough for me to be glad. We both needed something sweet after the day we'd had.

Thanking Evermund, I fled back across the garden, ignoring the strange looks from the handful of apprentices I encountered before I could reach my room. As soon as I closed the door behind me, I gave an enormous sigh of relief. My entire life had been upended in the most astonishing of ways. But I had a refuge all my own. I'd never had that before.

Maybe, somehow, we'd manage to muddle through this after all.

***

Despite my sleep on the carriage ride, I had no problem sleeping again on the soft mattress of my new bed. My room might be less luxurious than Airlie's, but the mattress still had fewer lumps than the one I had grown up with.

I woke early, however. Pushing my window wide, I enjoyed the fresh morning air while I emptied my pack. My clothes went into the trunk beside my bed, along with the few memories of my childhood I had brought with me.

I lingered over those, especially the two books. One had been a gift from my father, but it was the one from my mother that held me the longest, as I turned the thick, rough pages to look again at the pictures of an elegant palace and beautiful landscaped gardens.

Finally, with a sigh, I tucked it safely away. Did reality ever match up to our childhood dreams? Maybe not, but maybe it could be just as good in a different way. There was something approachable about the reality of gray stone around me that was missing from the pictures in that book.

Soon only a few practical items like my flint remained in my pack, souvenirs from our hunting and gathering trip. After a moment's hesitation I left them there, tucking the whole thing away in the bottom of the chest. Everything had changed too quickly to trust it wouldn't change again. Better to have the items on hand in case of future need.

By the time the sun had fully risen and a bell sounded across the courtyard, my stomach had begun to gurgle, having apparently already forgotten the feast of the night before. I slipped out of my room and followed the stream of people moving away from the garden door.

After the peace of my small haven, the shock of such a crowd made me tense, the press around me dense and over-whelming. I pushed through the feeling, however, forcing myself to move normally. The sooner I got used to my new situation, the better.

The living river carried me around a bend and through a set of double doors into the largest room I had yet seen. Round tables covered the floor, many of them filled with groups of talking people.

I had expected most of those present to be a similar age to me, but men and women of all ages mingled on the wooden seats. No wonder the room was so large—it must cater to the entire Guild.

I took hesitant steps inside, aware of the flow of people still pressing in behind me. But every time my eyes latched on an empty table, someone else beelined straight for it.

"Cadence! Cadence!"

From the corner of my eye, I caught a frantically waving arm. Turning, I spotted Gia smiling and gesturing for me to join her and Nikolas.

Relieved, I weaved between tables, heading for the one they had claimed. Gia looked delighted to see me, and I wondered if it had anything to do with the wide berth of open space around them. Apparently the rest of the apprentices were unaware of her Apprentice Gia campaign.

A moment before I slid into the empty seat at her side, another figure emerged from the crowd. Zeke balanced two breakfast trays as if he had spent years as a server in a tavern.

Taking the seat on my other side, he slid one of the trays my way.

"No one should have to brave the serving table on their first morning," he said in response to my surprised look.

I twisted around to regard the scrum of people on the far side of the room. It certainly looked intimidating.

"Or you can get up earlier and collect your food with us," Nikolas smirked. "You should have seen the crowd melt away."

"Nik!" Gia glared at him. "Don't look so pleased about it. We're supposed to be blending in."

"That was your idea, not mine."

"You'll learn it's best to change the conversation when they get like this," Zeke said in a clearly audible aside.

Nikolas glared at him, but Gia merely laughed, tucking into her breakfast with gusto. I joined her, starting with the steaming porridge, loaded with cinnamon and some other spice I didn't recognize.

"This is delicious!" I said around a full mouth.

"It's porridge." Nikolas sounded bored. "If you think the porridge is amazing, wait until you get to the cinnamon bun. You might pass out from joy."

"What is wrong with you?" Gia hissed, and from Nikolas's expression, I suspected she had kicked him under the table.

I was too pleased with my breakfast to take offense, however. "My father was a good cook, but he only had access to a small variety of herbs and spices. And after he died, it seemed wisest to stick to simple dishes."

I wrinkled my nose, remembering some of Airlie's early attempts in the days after his death.

"So you're telling us you're not a skilled chef?" Zeke tore apart a bun, stuffing half into his mouth. "Shameful."

Gia laughed. "Have either of you boys even attempted to cook something? Ever? I haven't. When I was five, I got it into my head I had undiscovered talent as a pastry chef. I kept trying to sneak into the kitchens."

"What happened?" I asked, polishing off the last of my bowl.

"I finally made it in one day and immediately upended an entire sack of flour over everything. When the actual pastry chef discovered me, I thought he was going to have a heart attack from the pressure of restraining his temper."

"I haven't heard this story before," Zeke said, "but I have an immense sympathy for your chef. Did he succeed in this superhuman effort of restraint?"

She nodded. "He kept his temper with me, but he informed my parents that he could only work in a princess-free kitchen... So that was the end of my baking career."

"That particular pastry chef makes Mother's favorite iced cakes," Nikolas said. "Which is naturally of far greater worth to her than her daughter."

"The pink ones?" Zeke waited for Nikolas to nod agreement before he nodded himself. "Most understandable on her part. The chef in question is a royal treasure."

"Ooh, pink cakes?" I smiled reminiscently. "I had three last night. They were the most delicious thing I ever tasted."

"Don't tell me it was better than porridge!" Nikolas muttered quietly. "Shocking."

I felt the heat pool in my cheeks as I blindly tore up the cinnamon bun he had earlier praised. I wished I had the courage to point out that they had been the ones to attach themselves to me. I had hardly foisted my presence on him.

But I kept my mouth closed. Gia had warned me that the arrogant twin came with the friendly one—and had all but pleaded with me not to be turned away by his attitude.

"Actually..." Gia hurried to fill the breach with a side glare at her brother as she did so. "It was just a convenient threat to ensure my compliance. Mother had already forbidden me to enter the kitchen before my misadventure, but the threat of no more iced cakes was a more effective deterrent than her lectures about proper behavior for a princess."

I quietly finished my breakfast as the twins launched into a debate about some event from their past that I couldn't quite follow. How opposite their childhood had been from mine—and yet how similar in some ways.

My closeness with my sister had come from physical isolation. With no other playmates, confidantes, or assistants, we had been forced to rely on each other. It made us close, but it also meant we had a long history of hurts, offenses, and irritations always ready to rear their heads again.

Gia and Nikolas were the exact opposite—constantly surrounded from early infancy, never alone, always bearing the pressure of watching eyes. But it was easy to see what a similar effect such intense scrutiny had on their relationship. Always on a stage, separated from those around them by the invisible barrier of royalty, they had only had each other.

I watched them out of the corner of my eye. Naturally I would like to think that between Airlie and me, I was the Gia of our sibling relationship. But I was fairly certain she would think the same thing about herself.

Seeds of glory and ruin. The echo inserted itself into my thoughts, souring the topic. I no longer wanted to consider which of us was the friendly sister, and which the bitter one.

"What are you all doing here?" I asked Zeke, as I remembered Evermund and Airlie's meal the night before. "Aren't you all illustrious affinity head apprentices? I thought the heads got food delivered to their rooms."

Zeke raised an eyebrow. "So Evermund's the sharing sort, is he? Us poor plants apprentices are forced to seek our sustenance with the masses."

His attempt at a downtrodden expression failed miserably when the beautiful apprentice I had noticed the day before called a greeting to him, the two girls at her side echoing both her words and her smitten expression.

"But just think," Gia said with a straight face. "If Augusta shared, you would deprive the rest of the Mages' Guild of your glorious presence."

"You make an excellent point," he said. "It would be a prospect not to be borne. And on that note, I can see someone trying to get my attention. I shall see you around, children."

He sprang up from his seat, flicking his fingers in a careless gesture of farewell before strolling toward an older man who must surely have finished his apprenticeship years ago and be either a proficient or a master. As Zeke joined him, I couldn't help but note the conversation included two others—one a glamorous young woman in a deep blue silk dress. Like the man who had signaled to Zeke, she must surely be past graduation —although not by many years in her case.

"Consider this your first lesson as a pretend-apprentice," Gia said gravely. "Zeke is never to be taken seriously."

I flushed again, quickly picking up a glass of water to hide my reaction. Had she noticed me eyeing off the strange woman and thought I needed a friendly warning?

"So we're to come up with our own lessons, then?" I asked.

"As pretend-apprentices. Or has someone worked out something to do with us overnight?"

"The library." Nikolas didn't sound impressed.

"Sorry?" I looked between them.

"He means we're to report to the library for independent study," Gia explained. "That's what all the apprentices do with their mornings anyway, so it's a convenient way to get us out from underfoot. Of course, the apprentices are assigned topics of study by their masters. Whereas we'll have to come up with something for ourselves."

I bit my lip. Clearly the powers that be in the Mages' Guild had every expectation of tucking us out of sight and out of mind. Thanks to Zeke, I knew they expected the twins to last mere weeks—in fact, the mages were probably under instruction to make their time as boring as possible with that end in mind. I, on the other hand, had two long years of this to look forward to. My heart sank.

Still, there was no point putting it off. I stood, pushing away my empty tray as Zeke had done.

"Lead the way to the library, then."

CHAPTER
ELEVEN

Lots of other apprentices moved in the same direction, although all of them gave us a wide berth so that we moved down the corridor in a strange bubble of empty space.

"I'm surprised they don't set up group classes for the apprentices," I said. "It seems more efficient."

"Efficient, yes," Nikolas replied. "But also illegal."

"Illegal? Classes would be illegal?"

"It's an old law," Gia explained. "One that some people think is outdated. There's debate going on at the moment about whether it should be changed. Given the way power is declining, it would obviously be expedient to—"

"Based on her confused expression, I don't think your student finds anything obvious about it," Nikolas drawled.

Unable to help myself, I shot him a look. He met my gaze, his face empty of the contempt I had expected to see.

"Gia's always been like this. You'll get used to it. My sister has a great deal of information in her head but a tendency to forget which of those pieces of information her listeners possess. It makes her a very confused storyteller."

"It's true, I'm afraid," Gia said, totally unabashed. "Whereas

Nikolas likes to explain topics in as few words as possible—factual and efficient." She grinned. "Which makes him an even worse storyteller."

"Also true." Nikolas shrugged. "I take that as a compliment. And I'll therefore take over this particular lesson. Otherwise Cadence will still be trying to sort out the tangled story when the lunch bell rings."

Gia didn't protest or try to retain her mantle of instructor. They might pick at each other, but they also seemed comfortable in their differing strengths.

"Many, many generations ago," Nikolas began, "people would pay master mages to activate their children. That way the children gained the full measure of power their own seed would allow. The mages would activate the children and move on, often without providing any training at all. Chaos ensued, with many people possessing more power than they safely knew how to wield."

"Like giving a toddler the power to lift a cow," Gia interjected.

"Not at all like that," Nikolas said, only to pause. "Actually," he said grudgingly. "It was a bit like that. Although they weren't actually toddlers, of course."

Gia shot him a triumphant look. Shaking his head, he continued.

"The mages grew rich from the practice and also powerful, since many parents tried to curry their favor. The king at the time naturally disapproved and decided something had to be done about the situation. He passed a law that every time a member of the Mages' Guild activated someone, they took that person on as an apprentice. And even the strongest mages were required to personally house and train their apprentices for a full two years."

"That was a clever strategy," I said, thinking through all the implications. "From the king's perspective, at least. That would have greatly limited both the creation of new master mages and the wealth and influence of those who already existed. And, at the same time, it ensured those with significant strength received the training to properly wield it."

"Yes, it was an excellent strategy," Nikolas agreed. "At the time. Back then, strong abilities abounded. Now, with each generation growing weaker, many argue we need the master mages to be activating as many as possible."

"That makes sense. So, what's the argument against changing the law?" I asked.

"Some say there's no point overturning our established ways when the damage is already done. Currently we test all youngsters and send those with strong seeds to the Mages' Guild. As it stands, the Guild already accepts those who two generations ago would have been rejected as having insufficient potential. There's no value in being activated by a master if your seed is weak, so those rejected by the Guild have no need for such a thing."

I stared at the ground in front of my feet, hoping neither of them noticed anything odd in my expression. No doubt my seed was far from Nikolas's mind when he made the comment.

"At least that's the official line," Gia said, distracting me from my self-pity. "But they're also scared that if they remove the law, some of those with strong seeds would seek activation by a master but reject an official guild apprenticeship."

Nikolas gave her a sharp look, and I suspected he hadn't intended to give me any unofficial information. But when Gia grinned impishly back at him, he sighed and expanded on her point.

"Official mages—that is those who have completed a guild apprenticeship—are not only bound to the Guild and its leadership, they're also guaranteed to have received sufficient training. There could be a danger to the kingdom in having people

124

with strong abilities running around without either of those protections."

"I see," I said slowly, now able to understand why the law hadn't yet been repealed.

"But while the Guild wants to maintain control of all future mages, that doesn't mean they want to be tied to their apprentices every moment of the day." Gia pointed dramatically at the doors in front of us. "Thus—the library!"

Enormous double doors of dark wood, scratched and worn from countless generations, projected strength despite their age. My heartbeat increased, my fears for the future temporarily forgotten at thought of the wonders behind those doors.

"Independent study." Nikolas sounded disgusted.

"A couple of proficients are assigned to the library on a rotating basis," Gia explained. "To answer questions and ensure the apprentices maintain proper library decorum. So it's the closest the Guild can get to a class."

As she finished the sentence, the library doors swung slowly open. The small crowd that had gathered in front of them pushed back momentarily, only to surge through the opening as soon as it had grown large enough.

We filed through in our turn, entering a large space that resembled Evermund's study. I stopped mid-stride, gaping at the books. So many books. Long shelves stretched out of sight in every direction, their shelves bulging with books, double stacked in places, with more books piled sideways along the top. Even more books piled on every visible surface, although I could see no gaps in the shelves to indicate where they might have come from.

Gia tugged me sideways, out of the flow of apprentices, rescuing me from creating a pile up.

"It's a bigger collection of books than even the palace library." She sounded proud, despite her own connection to the palace.

"But..." I stared around, still shocked. "How does anyone find the one they want? It's...chaos." Even as I said the words, I winced. Apparently Airlie had rubbed off on me more than I realized.

Gia giggled. "It is a tad chaotic. Very different from the palace library. Maybe that's why I like it so much."

The other apprentices spread throughout the vast room, most disappearing quickly from sight. A handful sat beside piles of varying neatness with a proprietary air that told me they had created them. How many waves of apprentices had been through here, leaving behind the chaos I saw now? I shook my head.

"Come on, let's find a place to sit," Gia said.

In a daze, I followed her across to the far side of the room and then down one of the rows of shelves. Halfway along, a gap in the shelving revealed a large alcove—more a small room—that opened off this side of the library.

I stopped, my eye instantly drawn by the contrasting neatness of the space. Whatever topic of study was stored in this section must have little interest to the apprentices, because not a single book was out of place.

"Appealing, isn't it?" Zeke asked, appearing from nowhere and making me start.

I nodded. "Let's sit in here," I said to Gia who had realized I was no longer following and backtracked to join us.

"It does look like there's more room for us in there," she said with a laugh.

Stepping forward, I noticed a low wooden fence separating the section from the rest of the library. Given it was only knee height, the gate in the middle seemed superfluous. Ignoring it, I lifted one foot, intending to step over. But a voice behind us stopped me.

"Breaking into the forbidden section on your first day. Bold!"

I swung around to find the black-haired apprentice who had greeted Zeke in the dining hall watching me with laughing eyes.

"I can only assume it's Zeke's influence." Her gaze moved to him.

He clasped a hand to his chest. "I am—as always—entirely innocent."

She didn't respond, having caught sight of the twins. Dropping into an elegant curtsy, she nodded first at Gia, then at Nikolas. "Your Highness. Your Highness."

For once Nikolas wasn't looking superior, scornful, or bored. And I couldn't blame him. Zeke's friend was as beautiful as she was elegant.

"Haven't you heard?" Gia asked brightly. "We're apprentices now, too, Karielle. And while we're in the Mages' Guild, that makes us equals. Please, call me Gia."

Karielle's eyebrows rose, but she inclined her head in acquiescence.

"If the Guild intends to treat you as regular apprentices, then you may need to make your efforts less...direct." She nodded toward the tidy section of the library, the laughter back in her eyes.

Gia and I both looked at Zeke, who was clearly trying to hide a laugh of his own. "It's something of a rite of passage among apprentices to attempt entry to the forbidden section of the library."

Gia put her hands on her hips. "And you were going to tell us this, when?"

He grinned. "I wouldn't have needed to say a word—no one can set a foot beyond the fence without the master librarian appearing to send them on their way."

"There are librarians?" I looked at the haphazard pyramid of old scrolls beside my feet.

"Only two," Karielle said, "which apparently isn't enough."

"Especially since one does nothing but guard the forbidden section," Zeke agreed. "According to apprentice lore, he even sleeps there."

I peered doubtfully in the direction of the tidy shelves. The area was just large enough that I couldn't see all of it from where I stood, but it seemed unlikely someone could actually live in there.

"Despite the rumor," Karielle said, "night is the favored time for attempting entry."

"Do many succeed?" I took two more steps away, not wanting to incur the wrath of the unseen librarian.

"Many *claim* success," Zeke said. "But none have yet provided proof. So I'll leave it up to you to decide how common it really is."

"Surely it would be foolish to remove evidence from the section. If it really is so very forbidden," Gia said.

I chuckled. "By that logic, entry wouldn't be attempted at all. You have to think like someone desperate for fame and notoriety among their peers."

She frowned but didn't argue. Such a thirst for recognition must be an entirely unfamiliar emotion to someone raised as a crown princess.

"Thank you for the warning, Karielle," she said instead. "I wouldn't want to earn a reprimand on my first day."

I could see a spark in her eyes that set off a twinge of unease in my belly, however. Just how much did Apprentice Gia want to set herself apart from Princess Morgiana? And would I be dragged into her schemes? It seemed far too likely—and also likely to draw just the sort of attention I was trying to avoid.

"I actually came looking for you, Zeke," Karielle said. "Master Augusta wants us."

"In that case, we shouldn't keep her waiting." He threw a wink at Gia and me as he offered Karielle his arm. "Don't do anything exciting without me."

The two strolled away, and while Karielle refrained from speaking to him in our hearing—perhaps constrained by the royal presence—I could read her response in her eyes.

You shouldn't waste your time baiting the first years, Zeke.

Since Gia and Nikolas hardly qualified as worthless newcomers, I could only assume the superior dismissal was meant for me. I sighed. I couldn't fault any aspect of her overt behavior to me, and I could hardly fault her underlying disinterest either. The only reason any of the older apprentices might be interested in me was my sister—and I had no desire to be courted for Airlie's sake.

"Lady Karielle is the daughter of one of our mother's friends." Like me, Gia was watching the two of them walk away. "But she was the only one of her siblings to be accepted for activation by the head of their affinity—something which is considered a great honor. She's in the second year of her apprenticeship, like Zeke."

She cast a sly look at her brother. "A circumstance I would have thought would resign you to being one of Augusta's apprentices, brother dearest."

"Royals are elements mages," Nikolas said stiffly. "Karielle's affinity is neither here nor there."

Before Gia could needle him further, I took Zeke's earlier advice and hurried into speech.

"Since we can't go in that section after all, we should find another space to make our own."

I cast a wistful glance back at the tidy area as we moved on. But perhaps, instead of making new piles, we could create our own tidy haven somewhere in the depths of the library.

When I suggested the idea, Gia approved, taken with the idea of claiming ownership of a small portion of the room. She even helped me select a promising location—a distant corner with windows in both walls overlooking the gardens. We spent the whole morning sorting and tidying everything within its sphere, ignoring the odd looks from the occasional apprentice who wandered past.

The end result well rewarded our morning's work.

"I'll confess," Nikolas said, surprising me by using a pleasant tone, "it's much more appealing to imagine large amounts of time spent here now."

Since his one bit of assistance had been to drag over a third chair to join the existing two, positioning them in a small semi-circle facing the windows, the compliment wasn't entirely barb free. But both Gia and I accepted it graciously.

"It's turned into a very pleasant space." I turned back from the windows to survey the shelves and sighed. "I just wish I knew what we're supposed to do here."

A bell sounded, resulting in a flurry of sound from all directions.

"Lunch!" Gia jumped up, giving me a cheery look. "And another day before we have to actually read anything. I call that fortuitous timing."

I let her tug me out of the library and back toward the dining hall, but the question didn't leave my mind so easily.

"What about the afternoons?" I asked. "What do all the apprentices do then?"

"They train with their influencers," Nikolas said. "It's the practical part of their study. They have to work to build up their control and precision."

"Like a mental muscle," Gia added. As we took our seats at a table near a window, her face fell. "The bit we can't do as pretend-apprentices."

"Mother predicted you'd last a month, but I'm going to lose my mind if we're here more than a week," Nikolas muttered.

Gia pretended not to have heard, although the faint color in her cheeks told me otherwise. Instead she began to chatter about the menu for lunch and her opinions of the Guild cooks.

Perhaps feeling guilty, Nikolas offered to brave the serving bench and fetch enough food for us all. He came back with aromatic bowls of stew and enormous chunks of soft, fluffy bread.

I accepted my share with gratitude, almost inhaling the food. Whatever other stressors the Guild might prove to contain, the food went a long way to making everything worth it.

But even as I shoveled the stew down, a niggling feeling of discontent assailed me. At first I couldn't identify its source, but after my second sweeping glance around the room, I realized where it came from. Without Zeke, the table felt incomplete.

It made sense he would usually eat with his senior apprentice friends. That was completely reasonable, and I would expect no less. But the sensible pronouncements of my brain did little to ease my lingering chagrin.

My eyes made a more ordered search of the room, only to fail at finding their target. Something inside me eased. Zeke hadn't rejected us—he was absent altogether. As was Karielle. Augusta must still be keeping them occupied.

With that discovery, it suddenly became easier to listen to my own internal lectures. Zeke was still almost a stranger to me, and I had no claim on his time. If he sat with us at all, it was no doubt on account of the twins.

"What do you intend to do this afternoon?" Gia's question broke through my distraction.

I chewed the large piece of bread I had just stuffed into my mouth slowly, giving me time to think. An echo of my lingering feeling of unease remained. And it wasn't due to Zeke's absence. I had never gone so long without seeing Airlie.

Despite her reticence the night before, it felt strange not to be near her. On impulse, I spoke.

"I'm going to find my sister. Maybe I'll be allowed to sit in on her lessons. At least I can check on her, if nothing else."

"That's a good idea." Gia pushed her empty bowl away. "We'll come with you to Evermund's suite."

"Oh. I—"

"Unless you'd rather go on your own, of course." Gia spoke brightly, but she was worrying at her lip.

I hesitated. I wouldn't have any chance of private conversation with my sister if they came. But how could I say no? My time at the Guild so far would have been very different without Gia's open welcome. And it likely wouldn't matter anyway. Being alone in Airlie's room hadn't inspired her to answer my questions—I had no reason to think a night's sleep had changed her attitude.

"Of course you should come," I said. "I'd love to have you."

Gia's smile burst across her face, making me instantly glad for my decision. Nikolas looked less pleased, but neither did he offer any resistance. Perhaps he was glad to be visiting Airlie's lesson given his odd determination to receive elements training despite having a plants seed. Either way, my experience so far suggested he would accompany his sister on her determined path whatever his own feelings.

CHAPTER
TWELVE

A pang of doubt assailed me when we actually arrived at the garden door to Evermund's sitting room. But a glance at my companions gave me courage. Not even the Royal Mage could take umbrage at my bringing his royal cousins with me.

I peered in the window as I knocked on the door, hoping to find them inside. Thankfully a familiar figure came into view, although he wore a disapproving expression as he crossed the room and swung open the door.

"Cadence." Sutton didn't look or sound pleased to see me. His eyes traveled past me to the twins, his expression growing no warmer. "And Your Highnesses."

Before Gia could speak, he continued. "Don't ask me to stop using your titles or any other such nonsense. It isn't residence in the palace that makes you royalty, so the fact you're now temporarily living in the Guild doesn't have any bearing on the matter."

"See." Nikolas sounded smug.

Gia glared at Sutton. "We came to see Evermund and Airlie, not you, Sutton."

I wasn't surprised to discover pre-existing animosity

between the two. A royal who wanted to abandon formality and tradition must be anathema to Sutton. It was a dilemma for him, though, since those very values demanded he respect her position, if not her person. I tried not to snigger as I imagined the headache it must cause him. No wonder he didn't like the princess.

"Is my sister here?" I asked, keeping my less diplomatic thoughts to myself.

"Cadence?" Airlie appeared behind Sutton.

When she caught sight of me, her face broke into a delighted grin. Someone, at least, was pleased to see me.

When Sutton didn't immediately move aside, she squeezed past to wrap me in a tight embrace.

"It was so strange not to see you all day!" She let me go, gesturing for us all to come inside.

"That's exactly what I was thinking." I grinned back at her.

"Sister minds!" We said in unison, as we always did in such situations.

Gia trailed in behind us, looking wistful. "I always wanted a sister."

"So sorry to disappoint," Nikolas muttered.

Gia paused in the middle of the room to throw her arms about his waist. "Not that I don't love you, Twin. You know I do."

"Someone has to reach things on the top shelf," he muttered, but his eyes softened.

Gia pulled back, chuckling. "You know nothing of the affliction of being short."

"Is there a reason you're here, disturbing my lesson?" Sutton asked, his irritation still in full force.

"She's my sister," Airlie protested. "She doesn't need a reason."

"Your lesson? I thought Evermund had to teach her?" I looked around but could see no sign of the Royal Mage.

"You may recall we were on official business when your... situation changed our plans." Sutton frowned. "King Marius already considered the incursions of the General and his raiders to be significant enough to warrant sending the Royal Mage to investigate. The fact they were bold enough to attack us directly only increases the urgency of the situation. Surely you don't expect Evermund to sit around the Guild for the next two years playing tutor?"

"I...perhaps I misunderstood. I thought it was required by law."

"The head of each affinity, as well as the Royal Mage, is granted seconds because of their demanding roles. Seconds are proficients within their affinity, and they assist with training the apprentices of the masters—among other important duties, such as standing in for them in their absence."

"Sutton is Evermund's second," Airlie clarified.

"We don't take apprentices of our own," Sutton said, "since our role as seconds keeps us busy."

"So Sutton is to be my teacher in reality, not Evermund." Airlie sounded completely neutral, but I knew her well enough to read her slight disapproval.

It made sense that after centuries, the Guild had found every possible chance to stretch the laws limiting them as widely as they could. And each instance I had so far encountered made sense. The Guild—and especially its leaders—needed to function, despite their necessary training role.

"If it's such an important role, why not make a master the second, instead of a proficient?" I asked.

Sutton swelled visibly, and Airlie gave me a look that was half remonstrance, half amusement. No doubt she had been wise enough not to antagonize her tutor with such a question.

"It's an active, practical role," Gia jumped in to explain in a moment of tactful diplomacy. "With a little too much administration to suit most of the masters—many of whom are older.

Instead it's used as a training ground for promising proficients on their way to mastery. Almost every mage who ends up winning a position as head of their affinity at some point served as the second for a previous head."

I stifled a smile at the way Sutton's expression softened the further into her speech she got. By the end he was almost smiling.

On a personal level, I was disappointed, though. I had been harboring visions of unofficially joining Airlie's afternoon lessons. But that wasn't likely to happen if Sutton was her teacher. And even if he allowed my presence, I wasn't sure I wanted to be there to be battered by his constant disapproval.

"I suppose since you're here, you should stay," Sutton said, as if reading my mind.

I gulped. Mind reading wasn't within the capacity of an elements mage, was it?

"We will be starting today with some of the basics of affinities and influence. You may as well hear the information as well, Cadence."

He glanced fleetingly toward the twins. "And I'm sure there's always value in revision—even for the most exalted among us."

Airlie dragged me over to the sofa, plonking down beside me. I didn't complain, completely understanding her desire for closeness. How many times as children had we sprawled together on the sofa in our family's sitting room, listening as our father told us tales by the firelight? Although I suspected his tales—always fantastical and impossible sounding—were a lot more interesting than anything we would hear from Sutton.

"I have just finished explaining some of the finer details of each of the affinities," Sutton said by way of beginning. "And I was moving on to the question of influence. In particular, cross-influence."

His attention was focused on Airlie, but at his final words,

Nikolas stiffened. The twins had each chosen armchairs, settling in to listen willingly enough. But the prince now looked as if he was rethinking his presence at the lesson.

Given his manner, it almost seemed as if Sutton had invited us to join them for some underhanded reason. I glanced between the twins. Even Gia looked a little on edge, shooting glances at her brother as if she expected him to do something dramatic.

I sat up straighter, my existing interest heightened, while Airlie's eyes flicked around the room. Having had almost no contact with the twins, she was even less able to read the strained undercurrents of the room than me. Sutton, however, continued on as if oblivious.

"I've already explained how the overall strength of a new mage is affected by the strength of the mage who activates them. The influence on the new mage's ability goes beyond mere strength, however."

"Do you mean there's a connection between them forever —beyond the legal bond of their two-year apprenticeship?" My nose wrinkled. I didn't like the idea of being bound to another person—especially given they might be someone I barely knew.

"Between the individuals involved? No."

Sutton answered readily enough, not even criticizing my interruption. Perhaps he took it as a sign I was paying attention.

"There is no lingering connection between the influencer and the new mage in the sense that you likely mean," he continued. "They can't draw on each other's power or sense each other's presence or any such romantic nonsense. The influence affects only the one who has been activated. Let us use Evermund and Airlie as an example. Because Evermund's power reached out and activated Airlie's seed, its influence is stamped onto her ability. That is why his strength is relevant to her own —or would be in the usual case. But since his power is flavored with his own affinity, her power ends up tangled with traces of his affinity as well."

"Evermund is an elements mage, the same as Airlie, so that seems a meaningless distinction." I glanced at her.

Shouldn't it be Airlie who was asking the questions? Or was she only feigning ignorance on the topic in order not to attract ire for trapping Evermund? She had left me to answer the question about our training in front of Hayes, so likely she was. I suppressed a sigh. At least it worked in my favor on this occasion.

"Certainly in her unique case, it's hard to judge what impact —if any—the shared affinity has had," Sutton agreed. "Perhaps Airlie was a poor example to pick. Let us consider the prince and princess instead."

Nikolas stiffened again, a thundercloud growing on his face which Sutton ignored.

"Zeke has a plants affinity and is apprenticed under Augusta," I said, trying to break the tension between them. "And Gia has an elements affinity and is to be apprenticed to Master Drake. It certainly sounds as if the normal way is to pair apprentices with mages of the same affinity."

"It is the normal way with the three heads," Gia agreed. "But it's not always the case with the other masters, and certainly not with the proficients. There's an element of practicality to the matter—those with a weaker seed will accept any place in the Guild they can get—as well as personal preference. Some mages prefer to work with apprentices of their own affinity, others do not."

"The most powerful mages take apprentices of the same affinity for the good of the kingdom." Sutton's tone chastised Gia, as if he disapproved of the suggestion such important matters were left to the mages' whims. "If you want to gain the full measure of your potential power, you must be activated by someone of your own affinity. It ensures all of your power is directed toward controlling those aspects of the world that fall within your affinity. Given the overall decline of the Guild's strength, we must maximize the power of the strongest among us."

He turned and fixed a stern look on Nikolas, not bothering to mask his unspoken message this time. Had the king and queen asked the senior mages of the Guild to watch out for opportunities to repeat this lesson to their son?

At least I now understood why he was being forced to apprentice under the Master of Plants. No doubt the royal family all had seeds of great strength.

What I didn't understand, however, was why Nikolas would be resistant to the idea. He didn't strike me as someone interested in weakness.

"So why isn't everyone activated by someone from the same affinity, then?" I carefully looked away from Nikolas. "Why would anyone actively want weaker apprentices?"

"Weaker is a matter of opinion." The prince leaned forward, glowering at Sutton. "In terms of brute strength, yes —a pure elements mage manipulating the elements will have more power than they would have done with a cross-influence. But a great deal has been accomplished across the generations by those who were cross-influenced—feats that would never have happened if everyone stayed within their own affinity."

Gia sat forward as well, nodding. "There's a creativity to it that's always appealed to me. It's so difficult to predict how it will impact the ability of any specific individual, and it encourages valuable flexibility of thinking. That's why the Guild still permits it, and why the royal family approves of their doing so, despite the current struggles."

Nikolas sat back and crossed his arms. "Except in their own family, of course."

Airlie, who had been frozen beside me, let out a soft breath.

Obviously she had just caught up with the unspoken issue behind the debate.

"Strength is the hallmark of the royal family," Gia said. "You can't blame Mother and Father for continuing as our family has always done. And given the current state of things, I can hardly blame them."

"Easy to say when you possess an elements affinity." Nikolas stood. "I am done being lectured by a mere proficient."

He strode out the closest door—the main one that led to the hallway—letting it slam behind him. For a moment, silence gripped the room, and then Gia leaped to her feet.

"Please accept my apologies on my brother's behalf, Proficient Sutton." Her voice carried a note I had only heard once before, when she addressed the footman who had come to my room. Apparently her brother's offensive behavior required a royal response.

Sutton huffed. "Sit down, Your Highness. I'm the second to a Royal Mage who is actually royal himself. I hope I am close enough and loyal enough to your family not to take offense at the hotheaded words of its youngest member."

Gia sank into the chair, looking relieved.

"Besides..." For the first time I saw an actual twinkle of amusement in Sutton's eye. "I did choose to broach the subject."

"At my parents' instigation, no doubt." Gia sighed and then glanced at Airlie who wasn't trying to hide her interest in the proceedings. "There's no point attempting to conceal that my brother opposes the plan to have Master Augusta activate his plants seed."

"Prince Nikolas has a plants seed?" Airlie looked at Sutton in surprise. "I thought the royal family were elements mages?"

"The rest of them are," Sutton said.

"And there lies the problem." Gia sighed again. "He's one of those rare cases where heredity produces something unexpected. Mother and Father consider it most important that he maximize his strength, so they have decreed that Master Augusta activate and train him. But Nikolas has the ridiculous idea that to be accepted as a true royal, he has to be an elements mage. And since he can't change his seed, the next best thing is to be activated by Drake and be a plants mage cross elements."

"I will concede there is value to be had in cross-influence," Sutton said. "We have a number of elements mages who come under the plants influence and are thus able to manipulate earth as well as air, water, and fire."

Airlie raised both eyebrows. "A useful skill."

Sutton nodded. "But not one worth crossing Their Majesties to achieve. The prince would do well to fall in line."

"Actually…" Gia spoke reluctantly. "Airlie's arrival may have worked greatly in his favor."

Sutton gave her a long, careful look before shaking his head. "Is it true, then? They think to delay your activation for so long?"

Gia shifted uncomfortably. "Nothing is decided, of course. But there has been some talk that perhaps it's not necessary to wait until Airlie's apprenticeship is complete. We could all study under Evermund together."

"You mean under me." For the first time Sutton didn't sound enthusiastic about the idea of extra responsibility.

"Wait. Me?" Alarm sounded in Airlie's voice. "Are you telling me the king wants *me* to activate his children? And to do it soon?"

Gia grimaced. "I probably wasn't supposed to say anything. But it did strike them as providential—news of your existence arriving when it did, just before we were to be activated. There is even some speculation that perhaps your unique capacity is something that your influence could bestow on others."

"You mean they think that if Airlie activates you, you might end up more powerful than she is, just as she's more powerful than Evermund?" I stared at Gia in disbelief. "Surely that's not possible!"

She shrugged. "Who can say? Airlie's own ability is impossible, so..."

"So Nikolas might get his wish to be activated by an elements mage after all," Sutton murmured. "I suppose in the circumstances it might be possible to convince the Triumvirate to agree to such an irregularity."

"Hold on!" Airlie held up both hands. "My ability was only activated two days ago! I'm not ready to be activating other people. I don't even know how to do so."

"No one is suggesting you do it today." Sutton gave her a reproving look, as if her words were a statement of doubt in him as her teacher. "Their Majesties would certainly need to speak to Evermund about it at the very least, and he is no longer in the city."

He had mentioned that fact earlier, but I had been distracted by other aspects of the situation. Now it hit me that Evermund had left to chase dangerous criminals.

"Will he be all right?" I asked. "I hope he took more guards with him this time."

"Not just guards," Airlie assured me. "He had a number of other mages with him, as well. From all three affinities."

"I should be with them, of course," Sutton said. "If circumstances hadn't necessitated that I remain here."

"I'm sorry about that." Airlie sounded unusually contrite. "I really didn't know what havoc the situation would cause."

"Naturally not." Sutton gave us both a superior look. "If you had, you would not have been dealt with so leniently, I assure you."

I swallowed, carefully not looking toward Airlie. She seemed almost unnaturally calm, given our situation, but could Sutton read the tension on my face?

He didn't even seem to notice me, however. Standing, he

142

stretched and declared he needed a hot drink before he did any more talking. But as he twisted the handle on the door, he paused to look back in our direction.

"I'll find the prince along with refreshment and represent to him the desirability of returning. If there is any possibility of his studying under Evermund, he must prove to me that he is capable of accepting my tutelage."

He disappeared out the door too fast to hear Gia's snort. "Good luck with that. Nikolas has never had much time for Sutton."

"I would have thought the two a natural fit," I said. "Nikolas seems much more interested in royal protocol and correct behavior than you. He and Sutton are alike there."

Gia chuckled. "Yes, but you're forgetting the great size of Sutton's own self-worth. Despite his love of protocol, it makes him willing to correct us. As you heard for yourself. Thus ensuring he is not Nikolas's favorite person."

"I had no idea my arrival would cause so much upheaval," Airlie said. "I truly didn't intend for it. And I'm sorry it's caused delays to your own apprenticeship."

Gia waved away the apology. "If there's even the slightest possibility you can pass on your unique attributes, I understand why Mother and Father have to take it. And Nikolas will even accept Sutton if it means being activated by an elements mage." Her mouth twisted. "I just hope the Triumvirate doesn't insist we wait until you graduate."

"Surely they wouldn't—"

Splintering glass cut off the rest of my sentence. All three of us leaped to our feet, turning toward the largest of the windows.

It was gone—shattered completely—and shards of glass sprayed across the floor in all directions.

Two men, dressed head to toe in black, sprang through the jagged opening.

CHAPTER

THIRTEEN

For half a second, all five of us stood frozen, staring at each other. Then everyone moved at once.

Airlie and I acted in unison, both racing for the princess. Gia scrambled for the hall door at the same moment, while both of the men pursued her, knocking over anything in their path.

Gia reached the door first, attempting to wrench it open. But something stirred in the air around us. A half-second later, a jet of highly focused wind shot past me, slamming into the door and pushing it closed.

"That wind's too strong!" Gia cried over her shoulder at us. "I can't get it open."

Airlie threw herself sideways, tackling the man closest to her.

"Don't let them touch her!" she shouted at me as she did so.

I hesitated. Every instinct told me to run to my sister's aid, but that would leave the second man free to attack Gia. I didn't know what would happen if he touched her, and I didn't want to find out.

I pivoted toward Gia, who was shrinking back against the

door. Apparently now that her avenue of escape was cut off, she had frozen.

I threw a chair into the path of the remaining assassin, but he dodged around it, his fingers stretching toward Gia.

Outrage and fury gripped me as memories of my capture by the raiders washed over me. Screaming a wordless cry, I pulled the dagger from my boot and charged.

My shout broke his concentration, and his head turned in my direction. Spinning on the balls of his feet, he whirled to meet me. A blade of his own appeared from within the folds of his black clothing.

"No! These two we need alive," the other called from across the room. He had managed to pin Airlie's arms behind her back, but she was still fighting hard.

The man facing me grunted, the sound giving little indication of whether he intended to honor the warning or not. My pulse sped up, my breathing coming in ragged gasps.

I tried to remember my father's instructions, his steady voice calming me from across the years. *Center your balance. Drop your weight. Steady your hand.*

"Cadence!"

Despite myself, my eyes flicked sideways to my sister.

Her assailant had hauled her to her feet, gripping her roughly by her arms which were now firmly behind her back. Her round eyes met mine, and I could read the fear in them—all of it for me, no doubt. Airlie had never given much consideration to her own safety.

A look of intense concentration twisted her features, and the gluggy air in the room thickened and swam. A loud wind, half tornado, half gale roared into existence. Sweeping in a rough circle, it sent books, plates, cushions, and every other loose item flying.

I staggered, as did my opponent. When Airlie's wind encountered the jet of air, it swept it away as if it were nothing.

"The door!" Airlie cried. "Get out of here—both of you!"

I started, dashing to join Gia at the door. She grabbed the handle and swung it wide. But we both hesitated, neither willing to be the first to flee. As one, we turned back toward Airlie.

Recognizing the source of the threat, our attacker had temporarily abandoned us, bearing down on his companion and Airlie.

I shouted a warning to her as he pulled an object out of his clothing. Roughly the size of a small apple, it looked more like an enormous chestnut, glossy and smooth. I didn't recognize it, but everything in his stance told me it was a weapon.

Airlie's head snapped around, and she screamed, a wealth of horror and indignation in the cry. The object burst into flames, the flickering red and orange burning higher and higher.

The man holding it dropped it, leaping back. But the damage was already done. His clothes had also caught alight. The flames danced, their movement unnatural as they leaped across the distance to attach to the other attacker, leaving Airlie untouched.

He dropped her arms, backing away even faster than his companion had done. But swathed all over in material, the fire engulfed him within seconds.

My sister watched them both, her face pale and her eyes glassy.

"Airlie!" I screamed, repeating her name again when she didn't respond. "Airlie!"

She gasped, my shout breaking her from her daze. With a shake of her head, a curtain of water erupted from the ceiling over the two places where the men stood. Like Evermund's waterfall back at the burning shack, it extinguished the flames with ease. But still it continued to pour down as the men flailed and sputtered, until I wondered if it was possible to drown standing up.

Rushing over to my sister, I placed my hand on her arm. She flinched away from me, and I pulled back, shocked. But a second later, she shook herself and flung both arms around me.

"Are you hurt?" she asked in a muffled voice.

"No. But those men..."

I could hear my unease reflected in my voice. If she stopped her watery onslaught, what would they attempt to do?

Running feet sounded from the corridor a second before the door was thrust the rest of the way open with extreme force. Gia, who had been standing behind it, went flying, landing in an undignified huddle on the floor.

Four guards poured into the room, Sutton, Zeke, and Nikolas on their heels. Instantly the water pouring from the ceiling cut off. Both men staggered, one of them stumbling to his knees.

The guards converged on them, hauling them onto their feet and out of the room in response to Sutton's terse commands. Nikolas raced straight to his sister, helping her to climb up off the floor, while Sutton and Zeke moved toward Airlie and me.

"Are you injured?" Nikolas asked Gia roughly. "What did they do to you?"

"Nothing." She gave a shaky laugh that sounded close to tears. "You were the one to knock me over when you opened the door." She turned toward us. "Airlie and Cadence protected me."

Nikolas gave us a sharp bow. "My family is indebted to you."

I drew an unsteady breath, my legs shaking now that the danger had passed.

"Are you all right?" Zeke asked in my ear. He spoke in a tone

I hadn't heard before, softness overlaying steel, without a hint of amusement.

I nodded. "It was Airlie. I just distracted them momentarily. Airlie was the one to save us."

Gia's head bobbed up and down in agreement. "She was incredible. I've never heard of anyone doing something like that only two days after they were activated."

Everyone turned to look at Airlie who had released me and now stood alone, her expression forbidding. After a moment, she relaxed, however.

"I couldn't let them hurt either of you." She glanced toward Sutton. "How did you know to come?"

"You weren't the only one to be attacked."

At Nikolas's grim pronouncement, Gia gasped, clutching at him.

"It was a very good thing I went looking for the prince," Sutton said, his expression dangerous. "And that he had encountered Zeke in the corridor before I arrived. It took the combined effort of all three of us to turn back the assassins."

Gia squeaked at his final word. "So they truly were assassins?"

"There can be no doubt about their intentions." Sutton's brows lowered. "Why? What happened here?"

"Certainly they were assassins," Airlie said quickly. "And at least one of them is a healing mage. I…" Her expression grew confused. "I smelled it on him."

The twins both looked equally bewildered by this pronouncement, but Zeke's eyes tightened with interest, and Sutton dropped back a step, his mouth falling open.

"You smelled his affinity? Are you sure?"

Airlie shrugged. "Perhaps scent is not the right sense. But the matter is easily tested, I assume. It should be a simple matter for the guards to identify both of their affinities. Either way, it seemed wise not to let him close enough to the princess to make contact."

Both of the twins shuddered. "Certainly not." Nikolas put a protective arm around his sister's shoulder.

"Why?" I asked, struggling to follow the conversation. "Obviously we wanted to keep as far away from them as possible, but is there some significance...?"

"Healing mages need physical contact to use their power on someone," Zeke explained. "And once they have that contact, their ability isn't limited to healing. Healing mages would better be described as those with an affinity for breathing creatures of all types." The ghost of a smile flitted across his face. "However, not even the head of an affinity has the arrogance to go around calling himself the Master of Life. So the ability is labeled healing. But power to disrupt the natural process of the body can be used both to heal and to hurt."

"Cadence would give me all the credit," Airlie said, sounding proud. "But she's the one who threw herself between the assassin and the princess, holding him off long enough for me to work out how to access my power. And she did it without even understanding why it was so crucial not to let him near."

I shrugged, uncomfortable. "You said not to let him touch her. That was enough in the moment. There wasn't exactly time for explanations."

"Your trust in your sister does you credit," Sutton said. "And I'm sure you will find Their Majesties most grateful."

"Our parents will be furious." Nikolas's lips were white. "Not with any of you, of course. But such a brazen attack? On the Guild itself, and in the middle of the day, no less! It's unthinkable."

"The escalation is certainly unprecedented." Sutton glanced unsubtly toward Airlie, reminding us all that it wasn't the only unprecedented thing to happen lately. Although why my sister's new ability should provoke an attack on the royal family was less clear to me. It did, however, remind me of one other important aspect of the attack.

"They weren't just after Gia," I blurted out. "They wanted Airlie, too."

Sutton raised his brows. "They wished to assassinate Airlie?"

I shook my head. "They wanted to assassinate Gia and abduct Airlie. Just like the raiders tried to do on the road here."

I ignored Airlie's furious face, confident I had done the right thing in disclosing their second purpose. She might not want everyone to know the truth, but I wasn't willing to keep it a secret. From the monarchs to the Guild, these people had no problem using Airlie's gift—so the least they could do was ensure she remained safe while they trained her.

"Ah." Sutton nodded. "We know the General and his raiders to be enemies of the crown, so perhaps they sought to take down two birds with one stone, so to speak. Airlie's presence may have been what tipped them over into taking the risk."

"One that did not pay off." Zeke's voice threatened danger to anyone who made a future such attempt.

"What happened to the assassins who attacked Nikolas?" I asked. "They didn't get away, did they?"

"They did not," he said shortly.

"They're dead." Sutton didn't attempt to soften the words. "So it's a good thing you were able to capture yours alive. With the help of a healing mage of our own, we may yet gain some valuable intelligence from this incident."

A mage who could tell lies from truth would certainly be of value in an interrogation. And now that Zeke had explained the full nature of the healing affinity, it made more sense why healers were the ones to possess such an ability. Did they sense minute changes in the body that accompanied a lie?

"We called for backup from the palace, so more guards will be here any moment." Nikolas looked at Airlie. "If the attack was also aimed at you, then I think you had better come with us until we can determine a way to ensure your safety. No doubt my parents will also be interested to hear your account of the battle."

Sutton nodded his agreement, but absentmindedly, his gaze scouring the room. It looked as if an explosion had taken place—shards of glass sprayed across the floor, every movable object upended, and black soot hammered into the sodden carpet.

I half expected him to scold us on the destruction, but he merely shook his head.

"An apprentice two days from her activation with no practical training whatsoever. Extraordinary, truly extraordinary." He glanced toward Airlie. "With training, you will find the effort easier. And you will be able to control your use of power in order to direct it more effectively."

"You don't intend to lecture me for destroying the Royal Mage's suite in his absence?" she asked with a weak smile.

"Certainly not. No destruction can be considered too great in the protection of the princess and yourself. And I have read accounts from the past—some as much as two hundred years old—which speak of great damage wrought by fledgling apprentices. It was one of the reasons for the establishment of our current system. You cannot be blamed for the strength of your ability or for being untrained."

"So two assassins went after Nikolas, and two after Gia and Airlie." Zeke's forehead was creased.

"No doubt they would have sent more if they had thought Airlie able to control her ability already," Sutton said. "Their concern that she might learn such control probably drove them to move too quickly and make foolish mistakes."

He exchanged a glance with Zeke. "I can only assume their

possession of a neutralizer means they feared she might gain some level of control on the journey back to the General."

"A neutralizer?" Gia had regained her equanimity. "Was that the object the assassin tried to use?"

"What object?" Sutton gave her a sharp look. "One of your assassins wielded an object?"

"It was round, about so big." She made the shape with her fingers.

"It looked a little like a giant chestnut," I said. "I've never seen such a thing."

"I would think not!" Sutton shuddered. "Where is it? Quick now! We must—"

"It's there." Gia pointed at a pile of ash lying between the two soggy patches of carpet.

Sutton and Zeke exchanged a lightning fast look I couldn't interpret.

"You burned it?" Zeke asked Airlie slowly, as if wanting to be sure he didn't misunderstand.

She looked as if she intended to speak, but after a moment she simply nodded wordlessly.

"It just burst into flame," I clarified. "And after the assassin dropped it and leaped away, the fire spread to both him and his companion—thus the water when you walked in."

"Both of our combined efforts," Sutton muttered in a dazed voice to Zeke, "and still we barely managed to destroy one...And she burned it. Just like that."

"It wasn't just like that," Airlie snapped, lacking her usual composure. "I was terrified."

"I suppose the fear might explain it," Sutton acknowledged. "The fear combined with your extraordinary strength, that is."

I met Airlie's eyes, my own drawing together. She had been afraid, but not for herself. I had revealed the assassins' interest in her to the others, but it seemed she had no intention of doing the same for me.

Drawing close, she put a comforting arm around me.

"Promise me you won't say anything," she whispered in my ear. "As far as everyone else is concerned, the assassins were only after me."

When I didn't reply, she turned to me, pleading in her eyes. "Please, Cadence!"

Reluctantly, I nodded my assent.

Several guards appeared at the broken window, a captain barking orders as they filed into the room and took up defensive positions around the prince and princess.

"Come, Airlie," Sutton directed. "We should accompany them."

Airlie—apparently still determined not to draw attention to me—nodded and joined him without looking in my direction.

Gia, however, met my eyes. Had she heard the assassin's words identifying their interest in me as well as my sister? It was hard to be sure in the panic of the moment. There was every chance she hadn't.

With a small nod, she followed the directions of the captain and exited the room without comment. If she knew I was more involved than Airlie and I were letting on, she was keeping my secret. I just wished I understood why it had to be a secret. Or even why the assassins wanted me in the first place.

It would be so simple to assume it was because of Airlie, but I hadn't forgotten the words of the woman who shot me. Of all the aspects of my new life that I didn't understand, this was the one that produced the most anxiety.

At the door, Airlie looked back, hesitating.

"I'll look after her," Zeke said, placing a hand on my shoulder.

Airlie gave him a grateful look before Sutton called her away.

"Did you want to go with them?" Zeke asked, as soon as we were alone. "It's not too late to catch up..."

I shook my head. I had no desire to relate my part in the strange and terrifying events of the afternoon to the king and queen. What I wanted, more than anything, was my bed.

"I just want to go to my room."

"That's easily done." His smile warmed me, helping put strength back in my legs. "You look like you've just been through an ordeal, and don't particularly want to undergo another one—of the royal variety—right now."

I smiled gratefully. He understood exactly.

Together we left the destroyed room behind, walking through the corridors of the Guild. A small part of me felt guilty for not attempting to clean up, but the rest of me was too exhausted to care.

The memory of the assassins leaping in from the garden made the inside of the building feel safer, and once again Zeke seemed to instinctively understand. He led me back to the apprentice section on a longer route that didn't involve stepping outside. When we arrived at my door, he hesitated.

"Will you be all right on your own? I could stay, if you like."

I considered the offer.

"Thanks, but I think I just want to go to bed." I smiled. "Don't worry, I'll lock the door."

He nodded and pointed at the window. "If you look outside, you'll see the royal guard are now patrolling the Guild grounds. I don't know what the long-term arrangements will be—since the Triumvirate represent the people, they have to maintain their independence from the royal family—but I'm sure the guard will remain for tonight at least. You'll be safe."

A small knot of tension in my chest eased, and I thanked him again. But as I slid into bed a few minutes later—having firmly locked the door, guards or no guards—I couldn't stop thinking about Airlie walking away and leaving me. Had she known about the patrols when she orchestrated the situation so

I remained behind? Given no one had mentioned them, I didn't see how she could have.

Which meant that even though we had just faced down assassins intent on abduction, Airlie considered me safer alone in the Guild than brought to the attention of the king and queen. Was it just because we were Calistan? Or was there more she wasn't telling me?

CHAPTER
FOURTEEN

When I stepped out of my room the next morning, Zeke was waiting for me. He was leaning against the narrow gap of wall between my door and the next one, his arms crossed, and his eyes half lidded, as if he was almost asleep. When my door swung open and I appeared, he started.

"Have you been there all night, sleeping standing up?" I asked, only half joking.

"That would have been valiant of me, wouldn't it?" He sounded wistful.

"Tales of your romantic feat of heroism would be retold across the kingdom for generations." I strode forward in the direction of the dining room, Zeke trailing behind.

"Merely around the Training Academy would do for me," Zeke said meekly.

I laughed. "Yes, of course. The female apprentices are a much more interesting audience for such a tale than your grandchildren."

"You understand me so well, Cadence," he said appreciatively. "And since you don't know exactly how long I was outside your door, you could feel free to leave the exact time-frame vague…If it should happen to come up in conversation."

"If it should happen to come up, I shall certainly do so."

Stepping into the dining hall, I realized that for the first time, the crowded space didn't intimidate me. Maybe after the attack of the afternoon before, the small mass of people was actually comforting.

Whatever the reason, I pushed toward the serving table without a second thought. After loading a bowl with porridge and taking two cinnamon buns, I surveyed the room. Zeke was still beside me, but I told myself not to assume he would sit with me. Especially since even more people than usual called greetings to him, many casting curious glances at me as they did so.

The heightened buzz of conversation in the room was noticeable, and I concluded that if anyone in the Guild hadn't heard of me yesterday, they had now. I could see no sign of Gia or Nikolas among the diners, however. A sinking feeling stole my hunger. Had the attack caused the king and queen to put an early stop to their children's apprenticeship experiment?

Spotting an empty table, I made for it. I didn't say anything to Zeke, not wanting to pressure him after everything he'd already done for me. But within two strides, he'd caught up. And as we weaved between the tables, he maneuvered me toward a different goal—this table half full of self-assured apprentices. Second years, presumably, given Karielle sat in their center.

"Zeke!" she called. "There you are! Sit down at once and tell us everything." She smiled at me. "You too, Cadence."

For a moment I blinked in surprise, but the slightest touch on my back propelled me forward and into the closest chair.

"It seems too impossible to be real," Karielle said, the barest hint of a question in her words.

"Unfortunately, the attack was all too real." Zeke looked

serious for once, tearing up a bun with quick, sure movements but not putting any in his mouth.

"And is it true that your sister killed two assassins using only her ability?" The boy on Karielle's right looked avidly in my direction.

I frowned. "She didn't kill anyone. She just disabled them until the guards arrived."

The apprentice on his other side nodded gravely. "Master Colton was out half the night questioning them."

"You didn't tell us that, Bryce." Karielle turned reproachful eyes on him.

The apprentice in question shrugged. "There wasn't anything much to tell. You can't imagine he shared any of his findings with us apprentices, surely?"

She turned her gaze on Zeke. "What about you? Have you heard anything? Don't think it escaped our notice that you were gone all night. Were you there for the questioning?"

"Me? Hardly. Why would I be included? It's no use looking to me for answers."

All night? I stared at him, although his eyes remained steadily on his plate of breakfast. Surely he couldn't actually have been outside my door all night?

Bryce, who was presumably one of the Master of Healing's apprentices, nodded. "Even we wouldn't have known about it, except Hayes warned us all not to wake Master Colton on our way out this morning."

"Hayes?" The name broke through my thoughts about Zeke.

Bryce nodded. "He's Master Colton's second."

"Hayes is the second for the Master of Healing?" I frowned down into my porridge.

"Why? Do you know him?"

I looked up to find Karielle watching me with curiosity.

"He was traveling with Evermund when they found us," I said, wondering how much they knew about Airlie's activation.

Several heads nodded.

"He goes with the Royal Mage sometimes when the Triumvirate want their own representative included," Bryce said. "The three heads are getting too old to be doing much travel themselves."

Karielle nodded. "They all trust Hayes. Master Augusta says he's the best second Colton has had in years."

"He's certainly skilled," I said. "I thought I was going to die before he healed me, but he did it like it was nothing."

"Die?" Karielle stared at me with wide-eyed interest. "I didn't hear you were injured in the attack yesterday."

"Oh." I bit my lip. I'd spoken without thinking.

Was the attack on the road supposed to be a secret? Too late, if so.

"Actually it was when we were attacked on our way here."

"So it's true this was the second attack?" Bryce regarded me with as much interest as Karielle had done. "I heard rumors, but it was hard to fathom such a blatant attack on the Royal Mage. Of course now..."

"Clearly the General will stop at nothing to get his hands on the Royal Mage's new apprentice." The slightest hint of envy tinted Karielle's voice, and I saw her slip a covert glance under her lashes at Zeke.

Did she covet the distinction of being so sought after? She wouldn't have felt that way if she'd been there to face the assassins. I pushed my bowl away, my appetite soured.

The boy who had asked about the fate of the assassins glanced around to check who was near us before leaning forward and lowering his voice.

"I heard the assassins carried neutralizers." Over the chorus of indrawn breaths, he added, "Plural."

My eyes flew to Zeke. Just below the table, I could see the tension in his clenched fist. But his expression remained relaxed as he scoffed.

"Where did you hear such an outlandish tale?"

Karielle leaned forward as well, speaking in an equally low voice.

"Is it so impossible? Master Augusta herself taught us about them last year."

"As a historical curiosity." Zeke shrugged dismissively. "If any still exist, they are in the locked vaults of Calinara. How would an item from the depths of the fallen kingdom have found its way into the hands of assassins in Tarona?"

The tension around the table eased as everyone acknowledged his words with varying levels of disappointment. The apprentice who had made the report looked defensive.

"You can't blame me for giving some credence to the tale. Nothing seems impossible after an attack like that."

"Precisely why ridiculous rumors will be flying in every direction." Zeke flicked me the briefest of warning glances, but he didn't need to worry. I had no intention of playing a part in a conversation I clearly did not understand.

"How long can we expect to have royal guards here, watching our every move?" a girl from further around the table asked.

"Would you rather be surprised by assassins?" Bryce raised his brows.

The girl tossed her hair. "Us elements apprentices can take care of ourselves. Our newest member proved that."

She looked proud, as if the whole of the elements affinity could take credit for Airlie's success.

"Don't be a fool, Carissa," Zeke said without heat. "Both the prince and I would likely be dead right now if we hadn't had the good fortune to be with Sutton—a mage who will no doubt pass the mastery exams sooner rather than later—at the time of the attack. It took all of us working together to take down two assassins."

The girl screwed up her face, looking like she wanted to argue, but Karielle jumped in.

"Does the attack mean Their Majesties will rethink allowing their children to apprentice at the Guild?" She voiced the question that had been worrying me since entering the dining hall.

"How can it?" Bryce asked. "Our future monarch must be a mage, and mages must apprentice at the Guild. The royals are the ones who set the laws requiring apprentices live with their masters."

"Which means they can change those laws," Karielle replied. "Because Carissa's right—they can't leave royal guards here indefinitely."

"Certainly not."

Most of the table jumped at Nikolas's cool voice behind them. Only Zeke smiled a welcome and gestured toward two empty seats. Gia slid into the one closest to him, and after a brief pause, Nikolas took the other.

"Your Highnesses." Bryce gave an awkward, seated bow, and the rest of the table followed suit. "We're relieved to see you both well this morning."

Gia yawned. "I think I could sleep for a week, but I'm very grateful to be no worse off than that." She beamed at me. "Which is all thanks to Cadence and Airlie."

"Mostly Airlie," I said quickly. "I don't think my hunting knife would have held them off for long."

A ripple passed over Zeke, but when I looked at him, his gaze remained focused on Gia, his usual half smile on his face.

"When do they intend to remove the guards?" Carissa asked again, this time of the royals.

"They're already gone," Nikolas replied.

"That was fast." Zeke looked at me, a speculative gleam in his eyes. I sent him a quizzical look back.

"Father thought it would take a few days, at least." Gia paused to yawn before continuing. "But Airlie stayed up half the night practicing, and Sutton pronounced her competent first thing this morning."

"Airlie?" I stared at her. "What does my sister have to do with the royal guards?"

"The masters will work out additional protections of their own, of course," Nikolas said, "but what convinced our parents to allow us back was Airlie's new ability."

"Her new ability?" I wasn't the only one interested in the question, judging by the faces of the apprentices around the table.

Gia focused on me, however. "Do you remember yesterday, how she said she could smell that one of the assassins was a healing mage?"

I nodded.

"She smelled his affinity?" Karielle looked confused. "What does that even mean?"

Carissa, however, seemed to understand, her eyes growing round. "But that's—"

"An elements ability that hasn't been seen in two generations," Zeke finished for her.

Carissa nodded. "Because no one has the strength for it. I suppose...I suppose it makes sense—if what they're saying about her is true."

"It is," Zeke said, a strange smile playing around his lips.

I tried to suppress a pang, focusing my mind on the new information rather than wondering if perhaps Zeke had spent the night helping Airlie rather than guarding my door. Given his lack of surprise, I didn't believe his earlier protestations of ignorance, and it would have been a far more sensible use of his time.

Understandable, too. Airlie was closer to his age, as well as being unique and powerful. Anybody would be excused for finding her more interesting than me.

"Does someone want to explain for the rest of us who

haven't studied historical abilities of the elements affinity?" Bryce asked impatiently.

"Those with a very strong elements ability can detect information about others in their vicinity from the air around them," Gia explained. "They call it smelling because those who could do it always swore the closest way to describe it was as a unique scent. But it's not really being detected by the nose—and the information seems to be understood instinctively. Like how Airlie used the ability for the first time yesterday but understood immediately what it was telling her about the assassins."

"So he was a healing mage?" I shivered.

Gia nodded, her face grave. "And she was able to detect other things about them once Sutton tested her ability."

"It does sound like a useful sort of skill," I said. "But how does it help us keep the Guild safe?"

"Can you feel a slight breeze in here?" Nikolas asked, out of nowhere.

I frowned, too distracted to have noticed anything about our physical environment for some minutes.

"A light one," Karielle answered for me. "What of it?"

"That's Airlie." Gia sounded admiring. "She's sent a breeze circulating in an endless loop around the entire Guild. It brings her constant messages. Sutton is satisfied from his testing that she'll be able to recognize the presence of any more assassins."

Zeke nodded with satisfaction. "You can't hide from the air."

I stared at them. "We've been here for two days, and Their Majesties trust Airlie to keep us all safe?"

Nikolas shrugged. "She proved herself yesterday. And it's not as if anyone else could do the job instead of her—she's the only one with the necessary capability."

I frowned. Of course Airlie would have agreed to the scheme. She couldn't resist assuming responsibility for anything and everything. I shouldn't have been so selfish after the attack. If I'd gone with them all, at least there would have been one person there who cared about what such a task might do to Airlie.

And what if she missed something? Would she be held responsible?

I was glad I hadn't eaten much of my breakfast because my stomach was now churning. While I'd peacefully slept, exhausted from an ordeal less severe than Airlie's, my sister had been awake practicing a new skill so she could take on a responsibility that should never have been given to her. And from the look of it, the twins had stayed up with her. Was it only me who had spent any time in bed last night?

By now everyone had finished eating, and the hall was emptying around us. Gia, who had eaten quickly, scraped her bowl clean and bounced to her feet.

"Come on, Cadence. The library awaits."

I stared at her. "Today? Really?"

"Of course." She gave me a stern look. "This is what apprentices do every day except rest day. And since no one is going to keep us accountable, we have to do it for ourselves."

"Or you could go to bed," I suggested. "You look like you need it."

"Really, Cadence?" Gia gave me an impish look. "Did you just tell a princess she looks dreadful?"

I flushed. "I didn't mean—"

"She does look dreadful," Nikolas said bluntly. "But royals don't spend the day lolling in bed any more than apprentices do."

"Besides," Gia stressed the word, giving me a significant look. "The library is an excellent place for talking."

"Oh...right. Of course." I hurried to my feet, the last one to leave the table.

Zeke chuckled, waving at us all. "Have fun, children."

I rolled my eyes at him. "We'll do our best, old man."

I tried not to think about his light-hearted farewell as we walked to the library. Did he really think of me as a child?

At home I had often complained to Airlie that we were no longer children, to hide away in our isolated house. But since we had come here, I had started to doubt myself. I felt like a child in this place full of people I didn't know and things I didn't understand. It seemed like no matter the conversation, I was always missing some necessary element to make it comprehensible.

And as soon as we were settled in the corner we had claimed as our own—a corner that remained just as tidy as when we had left the day before—Nikolas's words confirmed my insecurity.

"No one gave us permission to talk to Cadence about any of this. Just because her sister was part of the discussion—"

Gia interrupted him, wrinkling her nose. "Cadence is just as involved in this as the rest of us. You weren't there, Nik. She threw herself at that assassin to protect me." A fierce note entered her voice. "Why? Are you going to report me to Mother and Father?"

Nikolas held up a hand in a placating gesture. "Of course not. I'm hardly going to start doing so after seventeen years. Tell her whatever you like." He sat back and turned his head toward the window, as if absolving himself of responsibility.

I looked worriedly between him and Gia. "Please don't tell me any royal secrets."

Gia laughed. "Hardly. Don't listen to Nikolas. He's always getting worked up about silly things. This is about the attack. You of all people deserve to know what's being done."

I sat up straighter. Information about how the raiders were going to be kept at bay interested me even more than Gia could realize. And that was before Airlie's new involvement in our protection.

"Father insists they've gone too far, and we have to send out a force large enough to wipe them out once and for all."

I gasped. "War?"

Nikolas looked back toward us, apparently unable to resist joining the conversation.

"Hardly. They're a band of brigands, not a sovereign nation."

"Of course not. I suppose I just thought...Their leader is called the General, after all."

"That's just a name he calls himself," Nikolas said sharply. "It's not an actual rank. Who would have bestowed it on him? The nomads don't have an army, and we aren't missing any generals."

"No, of course not." I sighed. I should have thought the matter through more carefully.

"So when is the force leaving?" I asked.

"Not for a while," Gia said. "Given their willingness to attack us here, Father wants to be sure our defenses are solid before he sends anyone out. Once Evermund and his force return, he'll be sent out again with reinforcements."

"Including an actual general," Nikolas added.

Questions niggled at me, but I didn't know how to ask them after Nikolas's earlier response. Where had the General and his people come from? His raiders seemed far more organized and effective than the occasional group of brigands we had heard tell of in the border villages. Those bands had always been dispersed by royal forces as soon as they grew large enough to provoke a complaint to the king. And nothing as significant as a battle had been needed to achieve it.

So who were these raiders to attack the royal family behind their own wall? And what were they trying to achieve with such extreme recklessness? If it was merely gold and a life of ease they hadn't earned, they would hardly be risking incursions into the Mages' Guild. What did they think Airlie could do for them?

"How long until Evermund returns?" I asked, instead of the many more burning questions.

Gia shrugged. "No one is sure exactly. A few weeks."

"Weeks?" I stared at her. "We're just supposed to sit around waiting for weeks?"

"You'll be sitting around for longer than that," Nikolas snorted. "Were you expecting to be sent with the attack force? Now you're starting to sound like Gia. I promise they won't be sending any apprentices—especially not *pretend*-apprentices."

"Why shouldn't we go?" Gia exclaimed in an impassioned voice, and I realized I had stumbled into the middle of an existing argument. "This whole thing has more to do with us than anyone. Of course we want to see it through to the end."

"Crown princesses get to see things through from the comfort of the throne room," he said in a sour voice. "You know that as well as I do."

"What sort of ruler leaves other people to march into danger while she keeps herself safe? And what kind of person would want such a life?" Her voice sank. "Not me."

Nikolas rolled his eyes. "A wise ruler who understands the disruption to the kingdom if she should be killed by a stray arrow or the touch of an enemy mage. As well as any sensible person. I may be your twin, but I will never understand why you want to foolishly throw yourself into danger, Gia."

"It's not foolish to want to protect the people you love. And I'm hardly the first person to want a little adventure before I have to settle down to a stable life." She sighed.

"At least you get to be Apprentice Gia," I offered tentatively. "And so far I imagine that role's proved far more exciting than anyone anticipated."

Gia laughed, her whole demeanor transforming. "Very true! I like having you around, Cadence."

I smiled back at her. "Thanks! Although I'm still not sure why we have to wait so long to respond to the attack."

"According to Father it will be time well spent by those preparing for the campaign."

I bit my lip, once again gripped by the feeling this was war by another name. But it sounded like it was going to be fought far from Tarona, meaning there was nothing I could do but be glad I wouldn't have to spend the rest of my life looking over my shoulder for another assassin to appear.

"What, no chair for me?" Zeke appeared from between the shelves, making both Gia and me jump.

"Don't sneak up on me like that!" Gia glared at him, but he just laughed at her.

"I'm doing you a favor. You need to keep your senses sharp." He strolled over to one of the windows and leaned against the sill.

His pose was casual, but the way his eyes roved over our surroundings, checking for anyone close enough to hear his words, I could tell it wasn't a mere social visit.

"Someone's been talking out of turn," he said softly.

FIFTEEN

He instantly captured all of our attention. Even Nikolas abandoned all pretense that he wasn't involved in the conversation.

"Talking out of turn about what?" he asked, looking ready to jump up from his seat.

"Somehow a rumor has gotten out that the assassins had neutralizers."

"What?" Gia cried loudly, only to clap a hand over her mouth, her gaze darting to either side. "Sorry," she said in a quieter voice. "But how? Who?"

Zeke shrugged. "I did what I could to quash it among the apprentices, at least, but you had best let your parents know."

My eyes darted between each of them as they talked. Were they really surprised at the leaked information? Given how open Gia had been with me—a virtual stranger to her—and how Zeke seemed to charm his way into everything going on at the Guild, they weren't exactly a tight ship.

Not that I blamed any of them for trusting Zeke. In the short time I'd been here, he'd shown himself to have more than earned it. And I only had to look at what was happening with

Airlie to see that strength and loyalty were enough to earn anyone a place of importance here, no matter their background.

Zeke must have felt my eyes on him because he smiled at me. "Well done on not saying anything at breakfast, Cadence. I was afraid you were going to blurt something out, but I didn't dare give you any kind of warning."

"I hope I'm not as oblivious as that! It was glaringly obvious I needed to keep my mouth shut."

Zeke's brows drew together, and Gia turned concerned eyes on me.

"Oh, not obvious to the others, I don't think," I clarified. "Zeke played it off very well. I think the other apprentice ended up embarrassed to have believed the rumor. But they didn't have the advantage of having been there yesterday."

Zeke relaxed. "Hopefully we've gotten to it early and nipped it in the bud. There hasn't been much time for it to spread."

"But what is a neutralizer?" I asked. "And why is it such a grave concern that the assassins had them? Airlie seemed to destroy it easily enough."

"Yes, how did she do that?" Nikolas asked. "I thought they were supposed to be incredibly difficult to destroy. You and Sutton certainly had enough trouble destroying ours."

"They're incredibly resistant to damage." Zeke sounded worried. "Which tells you the fire Airlie sparked was no ordinary fire. It must have been burning unimaginably hot."

"The assassins' burns certainly concur." Gia wrinkled her nose. "It took two healing masters to restore them to health."

"Have they revealed anything of their purpose?" I asked, gripped by a new fear.

Why had it not occurred to me that the assassins themselves might reveal my secret? Had some hidden part of me hoped they would—if it meant I might finally get some answers?

"They talked readily enough." Nikolas sounded frustrated rather than pleased. "Father was furious. They're not bandits at all but assassins from Tarona—bought and paid for with tainted gold."

"So it's been confirmed?" Zeke tensed. "About the gold?"

Gia nodded. "The head of the Goldsmiths' Guild arrived in the early hours. He says there can be no mistaking it."

Zeke groaned. "Then it becomes all the more important that no word of either the gold or the neutralizers gets passed around. Can you imagine the reaction?"

"No," I said promptly. "I haven't the least idea what you're talking about. Again. It's getting rather tiresome, in fact."

"For once, we can't blame your education," Gia said. "Not many people know about any of this."

"And for good reason," Zeke said. "People don't need more reasons to be afraid. And neither do treasure hunters need encouragement to go charging into Calista to lose their lives."

I gulped. I didn't feel like I needed more reasons to fear either. But I couldn't stop myself from asking the question.

"Why should we be afraid, exactly?"

Zeke stilled, giving me a long, considering look. After a number of seconds ticked by, he spoke.

"Neutralizers are an ancient device made using...methods that are no longer available. Physically it's the nut of a tree that doesn't grow in Tartora, but that's just the storage device. When broken open, it is able to deaden someone's ability for a time—essentially like tying their hands behind their back, but neutralizing their power."

"But that would be..."

"Incredibly powerful? Yes it is. But every aspect of their creation is lost to us. It was Calista that knew how to create them, and their treasury now contains the only remaining examples. Or so we thought."

My father's fireside stories about the Calistan capital of Calinara rushed through my head. "But no one can access the Calistan royal treasury. I thought no one had even made it into Calinara at all since the local people fled after the invasion? Aren't there supposed to be powerful protections put in place by the dead Calistan ruler?"

Zeke rubbed the back of his neck. "Precisely. If our ancestors had known what would be triggered by the deaths of the royal family, they would no doubt have handled the situation differently, and we wouldn't now live next to a dangerous wilderness, brimming with uncontrolled power."

"And a haven for brigands," Nikolas said.

I looked down into my lap where my hands were clasped so tightly together they had gone white. With so many shocks and revelations, I hadn't put it together before now. The great-grandfather of my new friends had been the one to lead the invasion against my people. In fact, all of my new friends were my natural enemies.

And the General and his raiders were sheltering across the border in the fallen kingdom. Which meant they must be Calistans—at least if what Airlie had said about the protections was true. Did the Tartorans know that? Was it why they still despised Calistans so much, even all these years later? Had there always been remnants of my countrymen crossing the border to harry their neighbors?

My nails dug into my palms. It didn't feel real because I didn't feel Calistan. Airlie declaring it as fact mere days ago couldn't wipe out sixteen years of identifying with the Tartorans of the surrounding villages.

I looked up to catch Zeke watching me with concern. He and Gia had been nothing but kind to me—a stranger who had little to offer—and I couldn't hold ancient history against them. I could only judge off my own life.

The Tartorans had welcomed us—and in the case of Evermund and his traveling companions—put themselves at risk to protect me. The raiders who sheltered across the border in our old home, on the other hand, had attacked me twice now. Without my noticing, my hand pressed against the place on my middle where the arrow had hit. The equation was simple. The remnants of Calista had shot me, and a Tartoran had put me back together. I wouldn't turn away from my friends for an accident of birth.

"What's more concerning?" Gia asked. "The idea that the General has found a way to make neutralizers, or that his raiders have somehow found a way into the heart of Calinara and have all the resources of Calista available to them?"

Zeke spread his arms. "Take your pick. Either way we have to avoid a general panic."

"Which means we need everyone to see us living like normal." Gia straightened, as if relieved to have a role to perform.

"Whatever normal is," I muttered.

I hadn't meant the others to hear, but Gia gave me a sympathetic look, patting my leg.

"Don't worry, Cadence. We won't abandon you. You'll see. Coming here to the library every morning with us will soon feel like a normal routine."

I thanked her, but I couldn't help thinking how strange the idea sounded. Despite my desire to leave our home and join civilization, I had never imagined a daily routine that didn't include my sister.

Zeke left soon after, so it was just me and the twins when we entered the dining hall for the midday meal.

A quick glance around the room showed Zeke was already seated with Karielle and the other apprentices of the affinity heads. For a moment my eyes lingered on the sole remaining chair at their table, but when Nikolas led the way to an empty one some way down the room, I followed without hesitation.

As we ate, I couldn't help my eyes wandering across to Zeke's table, however. And as I watched the collection of the Guild's most powerful apprentices, a long overdue question occurred to me.

Where was Airlie?

I had yet to see her in the dining hall even once, although the Triumvirate apprentices ate there, along with the proficients, and even masters—everyone all mixed together. Was she eating at all?

My concern grew as the meal progressed until the bread tasted like sawdust in my mouth. Evermund had ordered food to his suite that first night, but he had been gone since then. And the suite had been subsequently destroyed in our battle. Where was Airlie spending her time, and who was making sure she received food?

As soon as the meal ended, Gia and Nikolas left to complete some sort of royal responsibility at the palace. I barely heard Gia's apologies, too busy stashing several rolls in a large napkin to take to Airlie.

My worries about her distracted me enough that I didn't feel the slightest fear as I dashed through the garden toward Evermund's suite. But I shivered as I ran. The days were getting colder. Soon I wouldn't be able to get away with even the shortest trip outside without my cloak.

I tried to remember those neglected geography lessons. Did it snow in Tarona?

At Evermund's garden door, I stopped, panting for breath.

For a moment, all looked normal, until I remembered how I had left the room. Pushing open the door, I charged inside.

"They've already fixed the window!"

"Cadence!" Airlie was already standing beside the round table, as if she had anticipated my arrival. "What are you doing here?"

"I came to check on you. And bring you these." I held out the wrapped parcel of rolls. "You haven't been in the dining hall at all, and I was worried..."

My voice trailed off as I saw the remains of a generous lunch.

"Well, never mind." My voice soured, embarrassment creeping in at my unnecessary concern.

"You shouldn't have been worrying about me!" Airlie bustled over, a frown on her face. "And you shouldn't have come over here."

"I'm sorry for caring." My words come out sharp. "Everyone else eats in the dining hall, even the masters, and no one told me you were being served here." I tried not to let resentment creep in. Apparently Airlie ranked higher than masters of many years standing.

"Oh, I didn't realize." She looked back at her empty plate before giving me a wry smile. "Their Majesties are most grateful for my efforts against the assassins."

I looked around the room, taking in the rest of it properly. My brows rose. "Most grateful!"

She gave a small shake of her head. "Remarkable, isn't it? It looks like nothing ever happened. It was like this when I got back this morning—all except the window. That was only finished an hour ago."

"Shouldn't you be sleeping?" I asked, memory of her overnight efforts softening my irritation over her lack of appreciation for my care and concern.

She yawned. "Don't say sleep, or you'll set me off again. I've barely woken up."

I looked around the room a second time. With everything back as it was before, it was hard to believe the fight had ever happened. It felt more like a dream than reality.

"Shouldn't that door be locked?" I asked uneasily, remembering the way I had been able to burst in without impediment.

"Why?" A smile quirked up the corners of her lips. "The assassins didn't come in the door, remember?"

"Airlie! That doesn't mean locks don't matter."

"Are you sure about that?" She tilted her head and waggled her eyes like she used to do when we were younger, a childish imitation of our father when he was in lecturing mode.

Despite myself, a laugh slipped out, and then another. Within moments, we were both clutching our sides, tears running down our cheeks. We collapsed onto the sofa, gasping for breath.

When our ridiculous mirth subsided, I mopped at my face. "I can't even remember what was so funny now."

"No, but I do feel better. Don't you?" Airlie flopped back against the cushions and stared up at the ceiling. "I think I needed the outlet."

She glanced across at me. "What's become of our life, Cadie? Can you believe that less than a week ago we were sitting at home discussing if it was the right time for a hunting trip?"

"It seems like another life entirely." I bit my lip. "I worry sometimes that my memories of home will slip away." My voice dropped. "Like the ones of Mother."

"Oh, Cadence." Airlie gave me a squeeze. "You were so young when she died. Home is different. You lived there for sixteen years. You won't forget it."

I sighed. "Maybe it would be better if I did."

She sat up, frowning at me. "What's that supposed to

mean? We had so many happy times there. Do you want to forget all of that? And Father? What of him?"

"Of course I don't want to forget Father, I just..."

"What is it, Cadie?" Her voice softened, coaxing me, and for a moment I resented it.

A petty part of me wanted to get up and leave—let her be the one waiting for answers for once. After all, she was the one who had upended my life.

But the thought passed, and I stayed put.

"Doesn't it bother you?" Even though we were alone, I whispered the words. "You say we're Calistan, but that means..." I glanced out the window at the peaceful gardens. Apparently it wasn't as easy to throw off the shadow of the past as I had hoped.

"That means these people were the ones who killed our family and drove us from our home." She sighed.

"I feel like I should be angry about it," I said. "But I can't seem to conjure the emotion. I don't feel Calistan. And I never knew any family members who were killed. It all happened so long ago not even our parents would have known them."

"It does make me angry sometimes," she admitted at last. "All those stories Father told about the beauty of Calinara and the power of Calista. There weren't problems with brigands back then."

"Apparently there were other problems, though," I murmured.

She frowned. "Yes, clearly so. I guess when I start to wonder about it all, I just remember that Father always spoke with respect of the people we encountered in the villages. And he never spoke with anger or hate toward Tartora. I can only assume he didn't want us to hate them either. Otherwise he would have raised us differently, I'm sure."

I looked around the room. "Is this really what he intended,

though? Did he mean for us to end up here? Can you tell me that much, at least?"

She stood up, her face closing off. "How can I tell you what he wants? He isn't here. There's just us." She frowned down at me. "And that's why you shouldn't be here. It isn't safe for you to be wandering around on your own. You should stick to the apprentice section of the Guild. I'm sure it's always crowded there."

I jumped up. "And never see you? Is that what Father would have wanted? For us to be driven apart?"

She flinched. "No, of course not. I'm not saying that." Her gaze strayed to the dirty dishes on the table. "I'll come to you. In the dining hall. How about that? Then you won't have to come here."

I put my hands on my hips. "And what am I supposed to do every day instead? I'm not a true apprentice like you, remember."

"But you will be soon." Her eyes narrowed as if she were counting something in her head. "Your birthday is early spring, so you might be ready to be activated in as little as two months."

"Why do you look so pleased about that?" I wrapped my arms around my waist, trying to stop the tremble I could feel in my hands. "You heard what happened at my testing. I don't qualify to be an apprentice at the Mages' Guild. No one here is going to activate me."

"Of course they will. Because I'm here. Those who don't win an apprenticeship with one of the guilds get activated by a family member. So if the rest of them want to be fools, I'll activate you myself."

"You're the one being foolish!" Her insistent blindness to my situation stung. "You heard the debate about you activating Gia and Nikolas. Apprentices aren't allowed to go around activating people. They're not even sure you're going to get an exemption for the crown princess!"

"Family is different." She sounded stubborn now, as if she expected the facts to bend to her instead of the other way around. "You have no other family to activate you, so they have to let me."

A set look overtook her features. "And who said we have to ask for permission? I'll have received enough training by then that we can just walk away if they try to cause trouble afterward."

I shook my head. She must know no one was going to let us walk away that easily. The laws that bound masters to train those under their influence went both ways.

"What if I don't want to be activated?" I could hear the defiance in my tone as I finally voiced my real concern.

"Not be activated! Of course you'll be activated!" Airlie stared at me. "*Everyone* gets activated by someone. Why would you say something like that?"

"Seeds of glory and ruin, Airlie." I didn't meet her eyes. "I think it's pretty clear you hold the seed of glory. You were activated four days ago, and you've already saved the crown princess and taken up protection of the entire Guild. So what does that leave me? It might be better for everyone if my seed stays a seed."

"No, no, no. It doesn't mean that."

She stepped toward me, but I stepped back, keeping the distance between us.

"There's nothing wrong with your seed, Cadence. I'm sure of it."

"How can you be sure?" I held her gaze. "Did Father tell you something?"

This time she was the one to look away. "I don't need Father to tell me you're not rotten inside. I know you, Cadie. We all have good and bad inside us, but you lean more toward the good. You always have."

She winced. "I think when he used to say that, he meant it as a warning to me."

I laughed, a single inelegant guffaw. "If you'd ever seen the way he looked at you, Airlie, you wouldn't say that. You were the child he always wanted."

She finally turned toward me, a glow in her eyes. "Do you think so?"

I turned away. Apparently she wasn't going to attempt any empty words about him loving us both equally.

"I don't want to be activated." I said the words as firmly as I could. "There's no great value in it if I'm going to be so weak anyway. And I'll stop coming here if you don't want to see me."

I started for the door, but she ran after me, catching me before I reached it. "You know it's not that. I just want you to be safe. I'll see you every day in the dining hall. I promise."

With a slight roll of my eyes, I nodded. I had no intention of abandoning the outdoors altogether, but since she hadn't thought to demand it of me, I could leave with a clear conscience.

"As for the other thing," she added. "We've got time to talk about that."

I groaned. "I'm not spending the next two months debating it, Airlie."

"No, of course not." She said the words breezily, propelling me back out the door.

I groaned again. That was the tone she used when she was entirely convinced she would get her own way.

And she generally did.

But as I wound my way through the carefully sculpted paths, determination settled in my core. She wouldn't have her way in this. I had been swept along by the last week, with little chance to make my own decisions. But this was different. This was about me and my life. No one would make this choice for me.

But any momentary relief from the firm decision soon subsided. Refusing to be activated did little to change my underlying situation. A situation I still didn't really understand.

Airlie wanted to keep me penned and confined, convinced I was in danger—but she wasn't willing to answer any of my questions. Instead I seemed to come away with more every time I spoke with her. So how was I ever going to take control of my own life?

CHAPTER

SIXTEEN

True to her word, Airlie turned up in the dining hall for the evening meal. She joined Gia, Nikolas, and me at our table, her eyes growing round as she took in the enormous room.

"It's so noisy." The look on her face reminded me of how I had felt my first time in here. It was strange to think of being more experienced than Airlie at anything.

"You get used to it," I assured her.

"Have you been able to maintain the monitoring?" Nikolas sounded genuinely interested rather than critical.

"It's...strange." Airlie wrinkled her nose, sniffing, as if testing the air around us. "It's hard to think straight with so much constant input. I'm getting used to it, though. Despite the differences in affinity, there's a sameness to the feeling of everyone from the Guild that makes it easy to tune them out."

She grimaced. "I'm glad the royal guard are gone, though. They were constantly setting my nerves jangling with their sense of otherness."

"It's a strange sort of ability." I swirled my spoon through my soup. "I can't really imagine it."

"Maybe you'll get to experience it for yourself once you're

activated," Gia said in a staunchly loyal voice—as if she was just as determined to bend the facts to suit her as Airlie was. "You must be old enough soon."

"I won't be seventeen until the spring," I said, warmed by her loyalty where Airlie's declarations had only irritated me.

I would wait until we knew each other better to break it to Gia that it didn't matter when I turned seventeen, given I'd decided not to be activated.

"We'll be seventeen in a couple of months." Nikolas made the declaration as if it was a minor point, but something in his tone made me glance between him and Gia.

He was proud of their age. Did that mean being ready to be activated early was a sign of strength?

"She joins us at last." Zeke slid into the seat on the other side of Airlie and smiled around the table.

I hoped my own smile didn't look strained. Perhaps it was coincidence his return coincided with Airlie's arrival.

Glancing at Karielle's table, it was easy to read the emotion on many of the faces. They wished they had the courage to join him. No doubt everyone was eager for a chance to talk to Airlie.

"Has Sutton run you ragged?" Zeke tore off half his bread roll in one go. "He has a reputation for being tough."

"Actually he gave me the afternoon off. He said we trained so hard overnight that I should take the day to rest."

"Goodness, he's getting soft in his old age." Zeke shook his head.

Nikolas snorted. "More likely he's convinced himself that with Evermund away, he's needed to help with all the logistics being planned today."

Airlie chuckled. "No doubt you're right." She sobered. "So the king still intends to go after the raiders?"

"What other choice does he have?" Zeke asked softly. "He can't allow such a strike at the heart of his kingdom to go unanswered."

She sighed. "No, I suppose not." She plucked at her bread roll, tearing off small chunks that she made no effort to eat.

I watched her closely. Was it concern for her training or for Evermund himself that motivated her dejection? Or just a general worry about the state of the kingdom?

Personally, I was relieved to think the king meant to permanently end the threat of the raiders. It was hard to relax knowing they were out there—and wanting me, for unknown reasons.

The conversation flowed on, and I returned to eating with a suppressed sigh. While Airlie did nothing to actively exclude me, somehow I found myself on the periphery of the conversation. As if her presence was so dominant, it left no room for me.

Gia nudged my arm as I finished the last of my soup. I looked up to find her beaming at me, completely ignoring the conversation still going on with the rest of our table mates.

"Tomorrow is rest day," she said. "What are you planning to do?"

"I don't know." I stared at her blankly. "I'd completely lost track of the days."

"I'd take you out to show you Tarona, but Father says we're confined to the palace and Guild until this whole business with the General is concluded."

I nodded. "Very wise."

"So I was wondering if you wanted to come on a tour with me? I thought I'd show you some of my favorite places—starting with the royal kitchens."

"The kitchens?" I grinned reminiscently. "I thought you were prohibited from entering them?"

"Ah!" She gave me a conspiratorial wink. "I'm not five anymore, and I've learned a thing or two in the years since then. I'll make it worth your while with payment in the form of pink cakes."

I glanced at Nikolas and Zeke, completely absorbed in their

conversation with Airlie, and extra affection for Gia blossomed inside me. Her interest in me didn't wax and wane depending on my sister's presence.

"How could I say no to company and pink cakes?" I asked. "I would love to."

Gia grinned and immediately began chattering about other places we might visit.

Only when we were gathering our dishes, ready to abandon the others to their conversation, did Zeke look up and give me the briefest of winks. I blinked, my hands fumbling my plate as I wondered if I'd imagined it.

Or perhaps Zeke wasn't quite as absorbed in Airlie as I had thought.

I shook my head as I left the table. Just more proof that Zeke followed everything going on at the Guild and knew far more than he should. But given the way people gravitated to him, it was easy to see why.

"Simple, yet effective." I shook my head at Gia, chuckling.

It turned out her secret wasn't complicated at all. The pastry chef had rest days off. His deputy—a matronly woman with an easy-going smile—hadn't arrived at the palace until Gia was eight, and she thought the princess sweet. And—more importantly—in need of fattening up.

We were both quite willing to listen to her fuss that we were wasting away in exchange for a plate full of pink cakes prepared for that evening's meal. The apprentices on duty bobbed quick curtsies or bows when we arrived, but otherwise treated Gia as if her presence was familiar.

She directed me to a small alcove in a tall window. It looked like it might once have housed some sort of cooking device that had long since disappeared, leaving behind a faded and slightly grubby bench that doubled as a window seat. We tucked ourselves onto it, out of the way of the bustle of the kitchen, and proceeded to gorge on cakes.

"Do the junior kitchen staff not get a day off?" I licked icing off my finger. "It makes me feel a little guilty, sitting here eating while they work."

"This is only a skeleton staff," she said. "The kitchen is much busier every other day of the week. They try to schedule only simple dishes for rest days, and the staff take turns being on duty. Those who have rest day duty today will take a different day off during the week, instead."

I settled back against the window. "Well that's all right, then."

She gazed out over the kitchen, but from the glazed look in her eyes, I wasn't sure it was the kitchen she was seeing.

"When I was ten, I asked my parents when princesses got to have time off."

I winced. "What did they say?"

"Never." She looked down at the plate, her fingers tightening around it. "That's when I knew I had to be Apprentice Gia. It's like I'm having all of the rest days for my entire life in one go."

I examined her face, hesitant to ask questions about such a delicate subject. But I still had no idea how she had managed to convince her parents given all the legitimate concerns I'd heard Nikolas raise.

"But never mind that!" Gia looked up with forced cheer, and my moment for questions passed. "Do you think if we stay here quietly for a while, everyone will forget we already had a plate of cakes and give us a second one?"

I groaned. "I might be sick if they did."

Gia shook her head slowly. "A pathetic showing! You just need to practice so you can build up your stamina. You'll see."

I groaned again before letting my head sink back against the window.

"What affinity do pastry chefs tend to have?" I asked idly. "Is there a particular one that gets precedence for the apprenticeships? I know blacksmiths are always looking for those with an elements affinity and farmers for those with plants."

Gia frowned thoughtfully. "They seem to be the full range here at the palace. But I think that's because the kitchen is so large. There are always staff with an elements affinity around to ensure the baking is done at the precise temperature the chef requests. In smaller establishments, the pastry chef and their apprentice might have to oversee that themselves."

"And I suppose the same applies to the cooks." I glanced behind me at the gardens. "An ordinary cook would do well with a plants affinity, but here I'm sure only the best vegetables are delivered, and the royal gardeners no doubt produce superior specimens in the herb gardens."

Gia nodded. "Whatever your affinity, it's prestigious to gain an apprenticeship in the palace kitchens."

A flurry among the pastry apprentices caught my attention. Someone new had walked in, and all work in the pastry section of the kitchen had stopped as everyone greeted the new arrival.

"How are the finest members of the palace staff today?" a familiar voice asked.

A good-natured chorus answered, and someone produced a plate of pink cakes. Gia looked up as well, snorting with indignation.

"That's as many as we got between us. And I'm their future queen! Who is Zeke, I ask you?"

"Too attractive for our good, judging by the looks some of those apprentices are giving him." The words leaped out of my mouth before I could stop them.

I wished I could reel them back in, but Gia went off into peals of laughter.

"I won't tell him you said that," she said when her mirth subsided, mopping at her cheeks with her shoulders.

"Please don't." I could feel the red in my cheeks.

Zeke gave no sign of having seen us, despite Gia's outburst. Instead he meandered around the benches, stopping to chat with most of the apprentices as well as the deputy chef. Only after he had submitted to her good-natured scolding did his steps turn in our direction.

He looked up—directly at me—and smiled, not a trace of surprise in his face. I bit down on my lip. I wished I knew how his smile produced such a reaction in me.

"Good morning, ladies." He hoisted himself up to sit beside us. "What a surprise to find you here."

"You heard us yesterday!" I accused.

"My ears are specially trained to hear the words pink cakes," Zeke explained with a serious expression. "It's taken many years of careful practice, but I've honed my skills to needle sharpness. No mention can slip past me."

When I rolled my eyes, he shrugged.

"Every apprentice has to be good at something. Or else how will we distinguish ourselves?"

"There's a supreme arrogance in that statement," Gia said thoughtfully. "You only say it because you know you're good at everything."

"Me?" Zeke looked wounded. "Far from it. For instance, I can't smell the presence of intruders in the air."

"Nobody should use Airlie as their comparison," I said, the words coming out much more glumly than I had intended.

Zeke threw me a look that was a little too knowing, but Gia saved the moment.

Jumping down, she shook her head at him. "Considering that was never a plants mage skill to begin with, you don't have me fooled. And it's time for us to be going."

"Are you giving Cadence the grand tour?" Zeke asked. "If I

promise to be appropriately meek and humble, will you let me come? I want to see her face when she sees the portrait of you as a child."

Gia gasped and declared him horrid, and they were still arguing when we left the kitchens. But it didn't surprise me at all that not only did Zeke accompany us for the rest of our exploration, but Gia reluctantly showed us the royal portrait gallery.

Overall the palace looked much as I had imagined it since arriving in Tarona—a larger, grander version of Evermund's section of the Guild. But it was a strange experience walking its halls because every time we encountered another person, Apprentice Gia melted away to be replaced by stately, regal Princess Morgiana. It was like a coat she could shrug on and off at will.

"Is it tiring?" I asked when we ducked into the empty portrait gallery and out of sight of a curtsying maid. "Being two people, I mean."

"Exhausting." Her face was turned away from me, toward the nearest portrait, so I couldn't read the emotion behind the single word.

"Such melancholy topics will fall from your mind once you've viewed the true highlight of the collection," Zeke announced into the silence.

Gia groaned but let him lead us down the long gallery.

"Ta da!" He presented the enormous painting with a dramatic flourish.

"Oh!" I stepped back several paces, trying to take it in. "It's..." My hand went to my mouth, trying to hold in a laugh.

"Don't bother," Gia said in a resigned tone. "Just let it out."

Gurgles of laughter instantly erupted from my mouth. "Were you really? I mean, surely you weren't..." The giggles took over, and I stopped trying to speak.

"No," Gia said, "I did not, as a child, look like some horrifying half-dead monster with that pale, sickly skin—and those eyes." She shuddered dramatically.

"Were you taller than your brother?"

"Of course not. Have you met us? But the artist took a dislike to me and insisted I stand on a stool behind everyone else."

"A dislike to you? But why?"

Zeke grinned. "I have it on good authority—"

"Nikolas's, of course," Gia interrupted him to say, using the same resigned tone as earlier. "It's always Nikolas."

"—that a young Princess Morgiana tripped during her portrait sitting and somehow managed to tip an entire palette of paint over the work in progress."

"It wasn't my fault," she wailed. "He had me in the most ridiculous pose. I couldn't keep my balance."

"And so he got his revenge in the family portrait? And your family hung it up!"

"That is most definitely the best bit," Zeke agreed with a nod. "I'm still pondering what that decision says about the royal family, the kingdom, and artistry in general. It's a matter that occupies me often during spare moments."

"It's my punishment," Gia said glumly. "Not that my parents will admit as much."

"I think it's a test," I said. "The king and queen can bring guests here and see how they respond—whether they comment on it or not. I'm sure it would tell them a lot about someone."

Zeke cocked his head to the side, looking from the portrait to me with a quizzical look. "I think you might be right."

"The good news," I said to Gia, "is that when you're queen, you can have the thing burned."

"But will I?" she asked wistfully. "It's such a very good portrait of the rest of the family."

I bit down on my tongue to stifle another round of giggles. "That does rather add to the pain, doesn't it? I would have thought the royal family of all people could ensure they don't end up with a spiteful portrait painter."

"You'll realize your mistake soon enough," Gia said with a sigh. "Being royal involves a lot less ordering people around than you might suppose. It's more like a diplomatic dance in which the only preference that doesn't matter is yours."

"Come now." Zeke shook his head. "That's an overly gloomy portrayal. Does anyone else get to raid the kitchen for pink cakes whenever they like?"

"Yes," Gia said promptly. "You, apparently. And, in fact, I'm limited to rest days while you can do it every day of the week."

I laughed. "She has a point, you know."

"Ah, but I'm a special case."

"I'm not sure how that's supposed to be reassuring to me," Gia grumbled before brightening considerably. "Unless you intend to teach me your tricks?"

"No, no, don't ask for that!" I exclaimed. "You're just giving him a chance to tell you that what he has can't be taught."

A distant bell rang.

"They're serving lunch back at the Academy," I wheedled. "That should cheer you up."

With some more grumbling under her breath, Gia allowed us to lead her back toward the dining hall. As we crossed into the Guild, her stiff posture softened, and her breathing relaxed. Zeke and I exchanged a conspiratorial smile, and a sense of homecoming washed over me.

I had referred to the Guild as the Training Academy without thought, an insider reference that had been incomprehensible on my arrival. How was it possible I had been here only days? Already I felt as if I belonged in a way I had never felt anywhere else.

Days turned into weeks, and life fell into a routine, just as Gia had promised. Airlie didn't always join us for meals, but she made at least one appearance every day. Zeke sat at our table when she was there, and sometimes when she wasn't, and I tried not to overthink it.

Together, Airlie and Gia developed a course of study for us non-apprentices that followed what she was learning. Some of the topics felt irrelevant, given my intention never to be activated, but at least they kept us occupied in the library each day.

And since we couldn't practice with our abilities, Nikolas arranged for a rotating series of guards to spar with us in the afternoons in order to keep our defense skills sharp.

Given the way Gia had frozen during the attack, I was surprised to discover she was just as adept with a sword as her brother. When she caught me watching her in confusion, she flushed guiltily.

"I know I disgraced myself during the attack," she said. "I've thought about it so many times since, and I can't explain why. I suppose it's one thing in training, but I'd never actually been in danger before."

"It was because you didn't have your sword," Nikolas said confidently. "If you'd had it in your hand, I'm sure you would have been a different person. All those instincts you've spent years training would have kicked in."

The captain assigned to our training that day ran a hand across his closely cropped hair. He had a grizzled appearance that spoke of long years of training and duty in all weathers. It took me a few moments before I realized why he looked familiar. He was the guard captain who had come to our rescue that afternoon.

"You might be right there, Your Highness. There's a reason we train our young recruits so repetitively. There's nothing like knowing your muscles will perform with or without your mind. It might be a wise idea for both of you to carry your blades at all times until this business is complete. And some hand-to-hand training might be a good idea as well, if you're interested."

The twins exchanged a quick look before nodding in unison.

"Very well, I'll request permission from your parents tomorrow morning."

Neither of the twins protested that they could make the decision for themselves. No doubt any guard would want official royal approval to deliver blows to the prince and princess—even in a training setting.

"We wouldn't need swords or our fists if we were activated," Nikolas muttered when the captain was out of earshot.

"Don't complain to me," Gia said. "I'm not the one saying Airlie isn't ready to be activating other apprentices yet."

"Then you'll support me to Mother and Father?"

I'd never heard Nikolas sound so eager. But his sister shook her head emphatically.

"I didn't say that. This is one battle you'll have to fight on your own. I already fought mine, and I don't have much sway with Mother or Father right now."

I turned away, resuming the practice moves with my knife, the hilt comfortable and familiar in my hands. One day I would find a way to ask Gia how she convinced her parents about her apprenticeship, but for now it was clearly still a sensitive subject.

E very time I saw Airlie, she reminded me to be careful—and then used all her own caution to evade any questions I might ask. But if she thought I would eventually abandon the search for answers, she was wrong. Instead of my interest waning, it only grew more intense.

At the same time, the weather grew colder and colder, snow eventually dusting the garden. I was used to snow, but another change accompanied the worsening weather that was new and far less pleasant. The air around me grew heavy until sometimes it felt as if a deep breath was impossible. And a tightness developed deep in my chest that seemed to thrum in time with the air around me.

Something in me was changing, and I was afraid of what it might be. I mentioned what I was experiencing to no one, but sometimes, on separate occasions, I would catch either Airlie or Zeke watching me with concern lurking in their eyes.

I defiantly kept my silence. If the change heralded what I feared, then I didn't want to precipitate conflict with my sister. And what if I was mistaken? The arguments would be for nothing.

It seemed unlikely I could be right, anyway. If being ready for activation early was a sign of strength, then I must surely still be months away.

Despite my reassurances, my anxiety grew.

While no one else complained of a gluggy feeling in the air, the general sense of tension increased with each passing week. The Guild had been given the choice of which mages joined the expedition against the raiders, and it had finally been decided who was to make up the group. But it turned out the period of waiting that followed the fevered hum of decision-making was even more fraught.

Evermund had delayed his return since he was already in active pursuit of the raiders when word of the attack in the capital reached him, and the potential to discover the location of their home base was too valuable to be abandoned. Occasional reports came back that he was pursuing the General through the countryside, and some of the more optimistic predicted that a larger force wouldn't be needed. But no one with significant knowledge of the raiders' size and organization indulged such positive thinking.

Sometimes the whispered conversations and constant

debate pursued me even into my dreams, and the questions that swirled in my head became louder and louder. Where had the raiders come from? And why were they increasing their attacks now? If they were dispossessed Calistans with neutralizers and other Calistan tools of power, why had they waited so long to make a move?

Sometimes the knowledge of my true heritage burned so fiercely in my throat, I feared I would open my mouth and send it spewing forth. It took all my self-control not to flinch each time I heard the name of my home kingdom on the lips of a nearby mage.

Airlie's compromise of meeting me daily in the dining hall made private conversation difficult—an intended effect, no doubt. And some topics were completely forbidden in such a public place. But I had gone over and over the events of the two attacks in my mind, and something stuck out to me in memory that I hadn't noted at the time.

My sister had reacted with fear to the neutralizer—as if she knew what it was. Her flames had gone after the object, not the assassin who wielded it. But what did Airlie know of an ancient Calistan weapon? And what did the General and his followers want with me?

With nowhere else to turn for answers, I scoured the library for information about Calista. I found nothing but a few dry, historical texts on trade treaties, agricultural yields, and physical features, alongside a small handful of modern texts that discussed the nature of the barriers which kept everyone out of the fallen kingdom.

But since each of those texts disagreed with the others, they didn't appear to be of great value. Certainly some of what they claimed I knew to be false from personal experience. Crops might not grow on Calistan land, but walking on it wouldn't cause a person to shrivel and die.

I told Gia I wanted information on Tartora's old neighbor

because I hoped to find something of use to Evermund. She endorsed the plan and enthusiastically joined me in the search. But when we surveyed our pitiful findings after days of dedicated effort, she shook her head.

"Before Calista fell, we had centuries of history as neighboring kingdoms. And the fact that Calistans can't be told apart from Tartorans on sight suggests there must once have been an open flow of people between the kingdoms. So where are all the records of that time? We have ancient texts in this library—both originals and duplicates carefully copied onto fresher pages. There is just no way these are the only records that discuss Calista."

Nikolas looked over, interested in our search for the first time. "There's only one explanation. Someone has removed them."

My chest contracted. Of course they had.

"How could that have happened?" I asked. "I know this place looks like chaos, but I saw an apprentice try to take a single book from the library last week. The head librarian appeared from nowhere and gave him a lecture that lasted a full ten minutes. How could someone remove every book on such an enormous topic without the librarians catching them?"

"They couldn't," Nikolas said. "Which means it was an official action. So we know what that means."

"Do we?" I asked, struggling to join the dots.

"The forbidden section." He shrugged. "The books must be there. I've always wondered what illicit topic could possibly fill so many shelves."

"But why?" Gia shook her head. "I'm going to ask Mother and Father about it next time I see them."

But she came back from her subsequent trip to the palace quiet and withdrawn. Apparently her information gathering mission hadn't been a success.

After so many days searching the library, my patience had

worn thin. Those books were my last hope of finding anything resembling answers, and their purposeful removal only fueled that hope. Why bar the public from accessing them unless they held something of interest?

Alone in my room in the middle of the night, I came to the only possible conclusion. I was left with one option. I had to find a way into the forbidden section.

CHAPTER
SEVENTEEN

I didn't believe the librarian actually slept laid out between the shelves, so night seemed the most promising time for the attempt. But I would still have to step carefully.

Given the apprentices' game of attempted entry, the librarian must have traps set up to catch them. And I couldn't afford to get caught. I didn't have the excuse of being an apprentice, and it could prove dangerous for both Airlie and me if anyone started asking too many questions about my interest in Calista.

That night I paced up and down my room, too on edge to be at risk of falling asleep. There was no preparation I could think to make, and therefore no reason to delay the attempt, but I kept thinking of excuses to do so. I refused to listen to them, however. The time had come for action.

When enough hours had finally passed for the Guild to fall quiet, I crept from my room and down the hallway. Every tiny creak of the ancient building made me jump, and when a mage appeared around a corner, I ducked my head low and scurried in the opposite direction, despite my having as much right to be out in the corridors as him.

By the time I reached the library doors, I was once again

second-guessing the entire operation. But the deep thrumming inside me drove me on. I couldn't let myself give up. Something inside me was changing, and I wouldn't be able to hide it forever. But how could I make decisions about my future when my past was a tangled mess I couldn't hope to understand?

Cracking open the library doors, I slipped inside. Darkness stretched away in every direction. The faintest glow—courtesy of moonlight through distant windows—illuminated the dim shape of shelves. I had brought a lantern with me, but now that I was here, I didn't dare light it. In the darkness of the cavernous space, it suddenly felt possible that the librarians might be lurking somewhere near, out of sight.

Placing the lantern silently down just inside the door, I continued on without it. The forbidden section contained a whole row of windows, so I would have to rely on the moonlight to help me find the titles I needed.

A creak of settling wood made me jump and freeze, holding my breath as I counted the seconds. No further sounds came.

I resumed walking, reminding myself that I had heard such sounds emanating from the ancient shelves during the day. Some of them looked old enough to be at risk of imminent collapse.

But when I stepped on a floorboard that creaked ominously, I froze again, straining my ears for an answering sound. Only silence reached me.

The tension inside my chest was mounting, my insides wound so tightly, it felt like something had to snap. My hands fisted around the straps of my pack—unearthed from my trunk as a receptacle for the books I intended to carry away.

While it felt horribly, impossibly long, in reality it took almost no time to reach the alcove with its small wooden fence. And, as I'd suspected, the moonlight was stronger here. I could move without fearing I was about to knock over a precarious pile of books.

I shook my head at the strange barrier, lifting my leg to step over it. Before I actually did so, however, I once again stopped.

Lowering my foot, I stared at the gate. Why have a gate? It seemed a foolish affectation in a fence even a child could step over. Unless it served some other purpose?

I crouched down and examined the wood. It was fresher than the wood usually used for crafting and building—almost green, as if it had only recently been stripped from its tree. I racked my brain, trying to remember if anyone had ever mentioned the affinity of the librarians. But it had never come up in conversation.

Which meant it was possible at least one of them was a plants mage. In fact, it seemed unlikely anyone but a plants mage could have crafted the fence from such raw wood. In which case, they might have built in other unusual features as well.

Staying low, I strained my eyes in the dim lighting. And, sure enough, I found what I was looking for. Crawling a short way along the floor, a thin vine disappeared away into darkness. The smallest thread of impossible green life connected this fence with someone or something far away. The head librarian, perhaps?

I sat back on my heels. If he had manipulated this vine into sensing whenever someone stepped over it and alerting him to their presence, then he must be a plants master. Which meant I needed to tread very carefully indeed.

Making my way back along the fence, I found only one section that wasn't threaded through with a vine. The gate.

I leaned back on my heels and shook my head admiringly. It was brilliant in its simplicity. What apprentice would ever make use of that gate? Not a one. Obviously those with permission to be here, knew the trick. And now I did, too.

The gate swung open on well-oiled hinges and closed with only the tiniest clink. I stepped forward away from the fence and examined the shelves before me. Beyond the barrier, they looked just like they had from the other side—ordinary shelves filled with ordinary books.

I glanced over my shoulder at the seemingly innocuous fence. Clearly these books were far from ordinary.

I had made it inside, and there was no sign of a vengeful librarian. But something still made me hesitate. Straining my ears, I once again listened for noises in the library around me.

I heard nothing.

And yet, still I couldn't bring myself to step forward. Despite the utter lack of evidence, I couldn't shake the sensation that I wasn't alone. A strange certainty that someone else was hiding here—not just in the library but in the forbidden section itself—overtook me.

As the seconds ticked by, nothing occurred to support the idea, so eventually I forced myself to override my instincts. Not attempting to mask the sound of my footfalls this time, I approached one of the windows. And although I watched out of the corner of my eyes as I moved, I saw nothing but deep shadows and darker corners.

When I reached the glass, I stood for a long moment looking out at the moon-washed landscape below. I hadn't spent any time at the rear of the palace, so in ordinary circumstances, the view would have interested me. But as it was, I could barely process anything my eyes were telling me, all my attention focused on my ears.

I waited and waited some more. The only game I had ever managed to consistently beat Airlie at was hide and seek, and I had therefore insisted we play often. Over the years, I had become adept at holding still and silent for extended periods of time. If there was someone else here, they would soon discover they couldn't outlast me.

Finally it came. The tiniest of sounds reached my ears—the

brush of cotton against cotton. And then again and again. Still I waited.

When I heard it a fourth time, I spun, moving as fast as my tensed muscles would allow.

The person behind me whirled to flee, his long cloak swishing through the air. Springing forward, I launched myself across the space to collide with his back.

We both went down—hitting the ground hard. My fall was broken by his large bulk, but his cape entangled one of my legs, twisting us together in a knot that defied my fumbling attempts to free myself.

"Cadence?" asked a rough whisper.

"Zeke!" I gasped back. "What are you doing here?"

"Never mind me, what are *you* doing here? It's the middle of the night."

"Well, it is the forbidden section. Night is the logical time to come."

I forced my voice to stay light although I was burningly aware that we lay on the ground in a strange sort of embrace—although it was the cloak, not Zeke himself, that held me in place.

Moving my fingers more slowly, I managed to untangle myself and roll off him. He regained his feet at the same moment I did, his hooded face tilted down toward me, although I could make out none of his features in the darkness.

"Well, then?" he asked. "What is this foolishness, Cadence?"

His whisper cracked through the air with no sign of the lightness I had tried to achieve. Instead his posture and voice reminded me of his seriousness during the attack. But whereas then he had been all solicitude, now he radiated anger.

My palms began to sweat, the relief at discovering his identity dissipating. Just how great a crime were we committing by being here? Had I catapulted myself into yet another situation I didn't really understand?

But even with my new misgivings, I wasn't going to let him dictate the conversation.

"I was the one to catch you, thank you very much. And you can start by telling *me* what *you're* doing here. And don't even think about saying I'd be better off not knowing. I am sick to death of people thinking they can decide what I do and don't need to know."

For a moment he hesitated, and I feared he meant to ignore me. But then he sighed. "I'm here looking for information on Calista."

I stiffened, despite my resolve to give nothing away, and he leaned forward. "You're here for the same purpose? That's a big risk to take, Cadie!"

Scowling, I reached up and pushed back his hood. If I was going to stand here exposed by the moonlight, then he could, too. He gave me an odd look but didn't pull it back up.

"You've never used my nickname before," I said irrelevantly. "No one uses it except Airlie."

He gazed down at me with a look I couldn't interpret. The intensity of his regard unnerved me.

"Do you dislike it?"

"No." I shook my head, proud of my steady voice. "You can use it if you like."

But it feels different from my full name, I added in my head. Here, in the darkness and the solitude, it felt different to hear him call me Cadie. It had an intimacy to it that our normal interactions lacked.

For a moment, I let myself pretend that he had also fallen under the spell of the night, allowing the name he used for me in his head to slip out.

A sound in the far depths of the library made his head snap around.

"We've made too much noise," he hissed. "Come on."

His hand took mine, warm and strong, and he tugged me toward the low fence.

"You need to..." My voice dropped away as he leaped the fence, directly over the gate.

Our linked hands pulled me stumbling after him, and then we were both running. The thought flashed through my head that we could run faster apart, but he didn't let go, and I didn't pull free.

A shout sounded from the depths of the library, no question now that someone pursued us. At the double doors, Zeke paused.

I took the opportunity to snatch up my dark lantern, straightening just in time for him to propel me out the doors, sliding them silently closed behind us. I raised my eyebrows.

"I set his vine to singing," Zeke explained in a whisper. "He gave up the chase to go back and look for intruders in the forbidden section."

"Impressive."

"We should still get out of here, though. Can I hide in your room for a while? It's much closer than Master Augusta's suite."

"For a price." I led the way down the corridor. "You can hide in my room for as long as you like if you use the time to explain everything. Thanks to you, I came out of there empty-handed. But you've been researching the same thing, so you can give me some answers."

He looked doubtful, so I gave him my sternest glare. "That's not a request."

When we arrived at my room, Zeke followed me inside, closing the door before giving me a long, measured look. "What do you want to know?"

"To start with, something has been bothering me about what just happened back there. I'm not a plants mage, but I managed to detect the librarian's warning vine. And then you were able to take control of it from afar when he was chasing us. If you can do that, how come every plants apprentice doesn't use their ability to suppress it in the first place?"

A smile curved up one side of his mouth. "Do you really want to know?"

"Of course."

His smile expanded. "I'm better than most plants apprentices—both stronger and more skilled."

"And a beacon of modesty, too." I rolled my eyes.

He shrugged. "You asked."

"I'll give you that one. I did."

"And I can't take all the credit. Neither of us would have made it across the fence without discovery if the librarian hadn't been...distracted."

"What's that supposed to mean? Did you have help?"

"Not directly, but my mother is a plants mage cross healing. She's made a study of how to imbue plants with extra healing qualities. In particular, she's spent a great deal of time growing a herb that when brewed will put an ill patient into a healing sleep." He gave me a cheeky look. "It has many medicinal purposes, actually."

"And some non-medicinal ones." I shook my head. "What do you do, slip it into his tea?"

Zeke snorted. "How exactly would I manage that? If I had, we could have saved ourselves all the running. Not even a sword fight in the middle of the forbidden section would have brought him running. No, I just burn a few leaves and send the smoke under his door. It has quite a pleasant aroma and encourages drowsiness. Given it's already the middle of the night, it merely deepens his sleep. Nothing nefarious, but it keeps him from sensing his secondary protections."

I grimaced as I imagined what would have happened if I hadn't turned up while Zeke was already there.

"I suppose I should thank you. But that doesn't get you off the hook for answering my questions." I looked around my room. "You might as well take the chair. Pull it up close to the bed, and then we can be comfortable. We might be here a while."

He grimaced but did as I instructed, leaving me to sit on top of my untouched coverlet.

"I want to understand what's going on with the raiders," I told him. "It's obvious it's all connected to Calista somehow, but I don't know enough about the kingdom's history to understand why or how." I could only hope he would believe my interest was general and not personal.

He sighed. "You're not alone there. Only the briefest history of Tartora and Calista is taught in schools."

"But you know more." It wasn't a question.

"My family has a...different perspective on the matter."

I considered his answer, watching him with careful eyes. Did that mean he was more sympathetic toward Calistans than most? Or less?

"Calista's problem was that they were powerful," he explained. "Too powerful."

I raised my eyebrows. "I thought their problem was that they were evil—or their royal family was, anyway. That's the official line, isn't it?"

"This isn't the official version. I already told you that." He shifted in his seat. "No, the root of their problem was power. The rumors of treachery and ill intent from their king only sparked their final downfall. His behavior wouldn't have brought on an invasion if they hadn't grown strong enough to scare their neighbors."

"Neighbors plural?" I frowned. "How were the nomads involved?"

"That much even the schools teach." Zeke watched me too closely for comfort, so I just shrugged.

After a moment, he went on. "Tartora and the nomad tribes

banded together to invade Calista and wipe out the threat once and for all."

"Massacre, you mean." I said it calmly, without emotion.

I couldn't let him see me display any personal connection with the story.

"Yes, it was." He matched my matter-of-fact attitude, but I detected a hint of regret, even anger, in his eyes. Was he ashamed of the actions of his great-grandparents and their generation?

"Of course, they didn't mean to lay waste to the entire kingdom," he said. "But they miscalculated badly, and now everyone is paying the price."

"The price? You mean the raiders?"

"They're a part of it, but it's much larger than that. Tartora convinced the nomads Calista's power was dangerous—but without Calista, everyone is weaker."

"Everyone?" I frowned. "You mean the decline of power? I thought that was generational—a natural process."

"Yes, it is, but somehow Calista counter-balanced it. If they hadn't, we would have lost virtually all power generations ago."

A piercing shaft of pure fear shot through me. If what he said was true, how long before someone drew a link between Airlie's ability and Calista? How long before someone guessed our history?

"And the Calistan people?" I asked. "Why did the invaders drive them all out if they didn't intend to destroy the whole kingdom?"

"They didn't drive them out."

My brows knitted. "What do you mean? Everyone knows Calista is empty. And every town and city in Tartora has Calistan refugees to prove it. Just because they've blended in, doesn't mean they're not there."

"It wasn't the invading army that drove the people out, it was—"

"The royal protections." I cut him off as my thoughts caught up. "Of course. When they killed the royal family, it triggered the protections."

Zeke's lip twisted. "If you can call them that."

I frowned. "Isn't that what they are? Protections designed by the Calistan royals to guard..." My voice trailed off as I realized how little sense it made. Why had I never questioned it before?

"Exactly." Zeke watched me knowingly. "What sort of protection only comes to life after those it seeks to protect are dead? And why would the protections poison the land itself? That hardly sounds like a protection to me. Something else is at work in the fallen kingdom, and I think using that label is merely a convenient excuse—a way to blame what happened on the dead Calistan royals instead of the invaders who unleashed it. The invaders convinced themselves that their safety required the death of entire families—down to the last child, but their atrocity released something no one understands. And it prevents anyone from living in Calista."

"Except the raiders. They shelter there, don't they?"

He leaned forward, his elbows on his knees and his hands loosely clasped. "But how? That's the central question."

The conversation seemed to energize him, as if he had found it difficult to keep all this information bottled up inside. His previous qualms at finding me in the forbidden section had melted away, replaced with the camaraderie of a fellow conspirator.

"How are the raiders able to safely traverse the fallen kingdom?" he asked. "The protections—for want of a better name—are changing, twisting and corrupting further. They're starting to reach across the border and threaten the border regions. So how are the raiders immune to them?"

His eyes were fixed on me, a light in their depths. He seemed to be willing me to understand something.

"It's getting worse?" Anxiety clenched my insides. "Why didn't I know that?"

"The king and the Triumvirate are keeping the information tightly controlled. Didn't you wonder why King Marius responded to an attack on a village by sending the Royal Mage rather than a squadron of guards?"

I didn't want to admit that in the whirl of everything that had happened, I'd never considered the matter. I shook my head, trying to force my whirling thoughts to fall into order.

Zeke had assumed my question was directed at him, but it had actually been rhetorical. Until recently, I had lived over the border in Calista. How could I not have known about a dangerous power swirling out of control through the area?

Airlie said it was because we were Calistans. And so I'd assumed the raiders must be Calistans, too. It certainly made sense, although it was an idea I had been trying not to think too much about. I didn't like having anything in common with people who had twice threatened my life.

I clutched at my head, as a headache began to form behind my temples.

"It's always the way," Zeke said softly, his voice turned sad. "One tragedy fueling the next."

I was silent a moment. But the pain of the ancient past couldn't quiet the questions that swirled through my mind.

"Isn't it because they're Calistans?" I blurted out, although I hadn't meant to speak the thought.

Zeke gave me a confused look, and I blanched. But it would only have attracted more attention to try to back out, so I elaborated.

"Can't the raiders live across the border because they're Calistans? Doesn't that make them safe from the so-called protections?"

Zeke's expression grew even more confused. "Most people believe them to be of Calistan heritage, certainly, but that wouldn't afford them protection. The people of Calista wouldn't have fled if so."

I stared at him blankly. "But...the land is barren. The animals are mostly gone, and they couldn't grow food...I thought..."

He shook his head. "Some at least of the refugees would be willing to live there anyway if they could safely do so. They could trade for food for themselves and their animals."

"I suppose that makes sense. Of course that would be true." I flushed. "I don't know what I was thinking..."

"It's not your fault," he said, his warm voice sympathetic. "If they taught the matter properly in schools, people wouldn't be left to come to all manner of erroneous conclusions. It only increases the superstition."

I nodded, accepting his kind justification, but it hadn't been a school teacher who failed me. Airlie had been the one to tell me our Calistan heritage protected us. And given the danger of our situation and her manner at the time, I couldn't believe she had been lying to me. Which meant she had been given false information by our father. But had it been purposefully done, or had he also been misled?

"I still don't understand most of it," I said, scrambling to fill a silence that was growing too long. "How was Calista so much more powerful than the other kingdoms? From the research I've been doing these last few weeks, distribution of strength among mages is roughly equivalent across Tartora and all the nomad tribes. Why was Calista so different?"

"According to the tales, they were storing power." His gaze turned sharp and keen again, the air between us heavy and thick as he watched the impact of his words.

"Storing it? That sounds like nonsense!"

From my study, I now had a much better understanding of the ways in which Evermund's analogy of reaching out and picking up a pack was a good one for power. Suggesting power

210

could be stored was like suggesting someone store the strength of their muscles each day so that after a month they could lift a horse. It simply didn't work that way.

He settled back into his chair. "That is what the tales say." He sounded faintly disappointed, despite a strange gleam in his eyes, and I had the distinct impression I had just failed a test I didn't understand.

"If it was possible, I can understand why storing power would have unnerved Calista's neighbors," I said. "Especially if they also possessed neutralizers."

Zeke nodded. "Add in persistent rumors that the new king intended to use that power to cull all mages from the neighboring kingdoms, and then have him dismiss both the Tartoran and nomad ambassadors from his court..."

"And you have incentive for a massacre," I finished for him. "It explains something of what was happening back then, but it doesn't help us much with the problems we face now. You said your family gave you this information, but how did they learn it if it's not taught in schools? Did they attend the Training Academy? Were books on Calista freely available in their day?"

"Attend here?" Zeke gave me an odd look. "Cadence, you know I'm from one of the nomad tribes, don't you?"

My mouth fell open, and I gaped at him. "You're...you're a nomad? I had no idea! How is it possible I didn't know that?"

"I'm not sure. I thought everyone knew." His mild concern suggested regret at the oversight but not shame or anxiety about his origins.

And he had no need for such emotions. His reception at the Mages' Guild suggested the Tartorans didn't care where he came from. I reviewed my first days at the Guild, trying to work out how I'd missed such a crucial piece of information.

"You were the first person I met when I arrived," I said. "So you were the one to introduce me to everyone else. I guess seeing me with you, everyone just assumed I knew your history."

"I'm sorry." His guilt deepened. "I wasn't purposefully keeping it from you."

"No, of course not."

Apparently the turn of the conversation in his direction was Zeke's cue to leave. Within a minute, he had said his good-nights, and we stood at the door of my room. But he paused there, looking down at me.

Something crackled between us, the opposite of the heaviness that had filled so much of the air lately. This was bright and heady—like a breath of fresh air to my tired lungs. Without thought, I swayed toward him. He went very still, his eyes focused on my face. For the briefest moment, his solid warmth surrounded me, and I was sure he was leaning in my direction.

Then he pulled back, murmured a final goodnight, and exited my room. I remained in place for several moments before I managed to stumble in the direction of bed. Exhaustion dragged at my limbs as I fell into it.

Zeke was a nomad. The concept was hard to grasp. And it made the universal goodwill in which he was held even more remarkable. Zeke was yet more proof that at the Mages' Guild power mattered far more than your origins. A convenient fact for Airlie, but a depressing one for me.

The thought weighed me down almost as much as my physical exhaustion now that the tension of the illicit excursion was behind me. Both my body and mind felt drained of all energy. I would have to process Zeke's revelations in the morning. For now, I needed to sleep.

CHAPTER

EIGHTEEN

The morning brought little in the way of clarity, although I was relieved that the anticipated headache failed to materialize. Instead I woke to a faint scent that was entirely Zeke, a lingering reminder of his presence, and a lightness I hadn't felt since I started my initial search of the library. While the night had produced as many questions as answers, at least we hadn't been caught.

Gia pounced on me as soon as I appeared for breakfast.

"I have an official invitation to visit the kitchens—and it's not even rest day!" she announced, a twinkle in her eye.

"Is the pastry chef ill?" I asked with a grin.

"Not at all—he's going to be presenting all his newest creations for me to taste." She rubbed her hands together at the anticipated delights.

"Goodness, what's the occasion?"

She gave me a look. "Our ball, of course! Don't tell me you've forgotten!"

"Oh, of course." I tried to look knowledgeable. Gia had been talking about the ball to honor her and Nikolas's seventeenth birthday for at least a week, but I'd been too distracted to listen to the details closely.

"You have to come with me, naturally," she said with mock solemnity. "I'll need a second opinion on selecting the items for the menu."

"And as your friend, I'm obligated to accept the role." I nodded pompously. "Difficult as it will be, I'm confident I'm up to the challenge."

Gia slung her arm around my shoulders. "I'm so fortunate to have you as my fellow pretend-apprentice, Cadence. Don't think I'll forget you once I'm in formal study."

"You can call me Cadie if you like," I said before my brain caught up with the end of her comment. "Wait, what do you mean? Formal study?"

Gia winced. "Hadn't you heard? I thought your sister would have told you."

I suppressed my instinctive response—that Airlie preferred lecturing me to actually giving me new information. It didn't matter if it was true, she was still my sister, and I wasn't going to speak ill of her to the royal family.

"She hasn't made it over for many meals lately," I said instead. "I think Sutton is pushing her training hard."

Gia scrunched up her face. "He probably wants to impress Evermund. As if it's his hard work instead of Airlie's."

"Is Evermund due back soon, then?" I was surprised I'd missed that bit of news. Apparently I'd been more bound up in my search than I'd realized.

"He's tracked the General and his people up to the border, so Evermund can't go any further. He should be back in time for the ball."

I shifted uneasily. "The raiders are hiding in the fallen kingdom?"

She nodded. "It's what we were expecting given their route so far. And since the snows are getting heavier in the border regions, they're not expected back until spring. So Evermund's on his way home. That's why Father said yes."

"Yes?" I asked, still distracted by the mention of the border.

"After extensive discussions with the Triumvirate, they've all agreed that once we're seventeen, Airlie can activate us. The Guild is just requiring Evermund's presence since Airlie's his apprentice."

I stared at her. The crown princess and her brother were going to put themselves under my sister's influence.

Our old life of isolation couldn't be further away. And never had the pressure of our secret origin felt so great. What would happen if the truth came out? The royal family would be furious at our deception, especially now everyone was so on edge from the raiders.

I swallowed. "What if Evermund disapproves?"

"He can't go against the combined wishes of the king and the Triumvirate."

"Not even in a matter regarding his own apprentice?"

She shook her head. "It would undermine his entire position. He's the mediator between them. He can't defy them all."

"So it's settled, then." I tried not to let the dread sound in my voice.

"Don't worry." She linked her arm through mine. "We can still study together in the library some of the time, at least." Her face brightened. "You can study the same things as me. Maybe Evermund will even let you join us and Airlie. We'll be our own little class—like Nik and Zeke are with Augusta's other apprentices."

My heart sank as I realized I would soon be the only non-apprentice at the Training Academy.

But before I could become too despondent, we arrived at the kitchens. And it was impossible to stay downcast while sampling the mouth-watering confections of the pastry chef.

After the kitchens, Gia produced a long list of other preparation activities for the two of us to complete. In the conversation with the head gardener, I got assigned the task of liaising with the team of royal gardeners over the flower arrangements for the ballroom. And when Gia dragged me along to her dress fitting with the royal seamstress, I was ambushed again.

Within minutes, I was being poked and prodded with pins myself. Gia declared my dress would be her early birthday present to me, so it would have been churlish to keep protesting.

Instead I let myself admire the materials the seamstress produced, eventually choosing a forest green silk. I even went as far as to give input on the cut. I had never attended a ball, or owned such an elaborate gown, but I had always secretly dreamed of floating onto the dance floor of my mother's stories in an elegant cloud of material.

Airlie's visits to the dining hall became less and less frequent. But when she did appear, it was with complaints about Sutton's arduous training regime, so I refrained from calling her to account for it.

And since I had been swept up into the whirlwind of Gia's preparations, it was easy to give in to the temptation to forget about Calista and the raiders and my sister's strange power, and instead let myself revel in anticipation of the ball. There didn't seem any harm given the raiders were out of reach for the moment.

We were so busy, I almost didn't have time to notice Zeke's absence either. He had only eaten a single meal with us since the misadventure in the library, but when we crossed paths, his smile held the same warmth it had always done—although Gia received the same smile, as did Airlie and Karielle.

When Gia caught me watching him across the dining hall the evening before the ball, she chuckled.

"Do you ever wonder how many hearts he broke when he left home for the Academy?"

"What?" I turned a startled look on her.

"Don't pretend you haven't noticed!" She put one hand on her heart and fanned her cheeks with the other. "No one should be that attractive and that charming at the same time. It's not fair to the rest of the world."

My eyes slid sideways to Nikolas of their own volition. His golden hair sat in perfect tousled waves, and his broad shoulders radiated strength. It was strange to remember I had thought him as good-looking as Zeke at our first meeting.

He smirked at me. "I don't need charm; I'm a prince."

Gia snorted. "I suppose we should be glad for the sake of the Training Academy that you don't have Zeke's way with people. One of him is quite enough."

I chuckled along, hoping the heat I could feel in my cheeks wasn't noticeable. Could Gia read my mind? Did she know that every time I imagined waltzing onto the ballroom floor in my new gown, I pictured myself in Zeke's arms? It had been natural enough since the only other boy I spent time with was the prince. But when I considered how many others in the dining hall might be dreaming the same dream, it seemed like a child's foolishness. In my room after the library incident, it had felt as if we had a connection, beyond the friendly smiles he bestowed on everyone. But in the light of reality, I couldn't point to a single fact to support the idea.

Some of my excitement for the coming dance soured, and once in bed that night, I tossed and turned before finding sleep. But when morning dawned, the buzz of anticipation among both the apprentices and the mages rejuvenated me. News of the twins' coming activation had now spread everywhere, and it lent an extra air of interest to the evening's event. Even those older mages who had no interest in balls huddled in eager clumps discussing Evermund's expected return.

Only now that it was lifting did I recognize the heavy cloud that had fallen on the whole Guild as the pursuit of the raiders stretched out. The attack here on their own grounds had rattled them, and no one complained of the fresh layer of snow on the garden or the bite in the air when everyone was conscious that it was the weather that gave us this breather from the raiders and their attacks.

Neither of the twins was at breakfast, of course. Given it was their birthday, I had expected as much, but after my self-recriminations the night before, I found myself strangely reluctant to join Zeke at Karielle's table.

So when Airlie appeared while I was still lingering by the door, I greeted her with relief. The brief flash of surprise on her face hit me hard. When had this distance grown up between us? Was this what it meant to live at the Guild—separate lives that only occasionally intersected until we became virtual strangers?

A deep ache radiated through my chest. I missed my sister and the easy familiarity she had always represented. It didn't matter how much I resented her at times, I never had to wonder what she really thought of me, or if I had presumed too much on our friendship.

"Would you like to get ready for the ball in the suite with me?" she asked, the tentative note in her voice exacerbating the ache.

"Of course!" My enthusiastic response made her smile, and I wished I could remember the last time she had smiled in that uninhibited way.

"I went out to the markets last rest day and purchased a dress," she told me as we served ourselves food and found an empty table.

"You left the Guild?" I stared at her. "I thought you said it wasn't safe."

"It isn't," she said, a little too quickly. "You definitely shouldn't leave the palace walls. Just like Gia and Nikolas."

"But you can? Because the raiders had no interest in you."

She rolled her eyes at my heavy sarcasm, and just like that, the familiar resentment came surging back, driving the ache away.

With an effort I fought it off. For one day we would wear pretty dresses, eat delectable treats, dance, and not think about Airlie's controlling tendencies or my disappointing failures.

***

"There! Perfect!" Airlie slipped the final flower into my hair, stepping back to view the full effect.

I turned to the mirror to admire it along with her. I'd never had occasion to discover my sister's secret talent for hair arranging before. But with my waves pinned to my head, I actually looked elegant—as well as older than a mere sixteen. I turned my head this way and that, admiring the white flowers.

"Where did you get them? Nothing in the garden has been flowering for weeks."

Airlie grinned at me, slipping a striking purple blossom into her own curls. "You just think that because you've been sticking to the inside passages since the snow started. But it isn't that deep, you know."

I raised an eyebrow. "It's definitely deep enough to kill flowers."

"Ah, but you're forgetting this is the Mages' Guild. There are some very powerful people around with plants affinities."

"Oh, of course." I shook my head, feeling foolish.

The royal gardeners might have enough power to keep the royal gardens healthy and the cook's herb garden in constant production, but the plants mages of the Guild could manage much more impressive feats. They'd probably coaxed the flowers to grow from seeds overnight.

"So who did you convince to provide these?" I ran a gentle finger over one of the petals. "They're beautiful."

Reluctance colored Airlie's face, and she began to bustle around, collecting the various items we'd left strewn across the room.

"Zeke dropped them off to me this morning, actually. It was thoughtful of him." She glanced sideways at me. "He probably spent all morning coaxing flowers into life given how many of the apprentices must want to wear them."

Her attempt at sounding casual fell flat, but I didn't question her words. Her awkwardness only made his gift of flowers more telling, and I had no desire to hear what significance she thought it might have. I was already struggling to master a foolish flush of disappointment.

"Thank you," I said instead. "I couldn't have managed this on my own, and the dress looks even more beautiful with my hair up."

She beamed at me. "It's been a fun day." She hesitated. "I miss hanging out, just us."

Impulsively I rushed across the room to give her a hug. "I miss us, too. And your dress is just as beautiful as mine."

She looked radiant in a deep blue gown that fell in elegant lines from her hips. I didn't doubt she would be in high demand at the ball.

"That's kind of you to say, but hardly true." She smiled to show she didn't mind. "It's a generous gift from Gia."

"I tried to say no, but she insisted, so..."

Airlie laughed wryly. "It's hard to say no to royalty."

I eyed her with concern. She would know better than me about the demands of royalty. How much was the constant effort to protect the Guild wearing on her? Was that why she had been looking so tired lately and skipping meals? I should have asked.

Before I could rectify my error, however, a peal of bells

sounded, ringing through the Guild building. Airlie laughed, her smile of anticipation so genuine that I resolved to ask her later. Tonight was for merriment, not serious conversations about heavy burdens.

We hurried out into the garden where the elements mages had cleared a snow-free path all the way to the palace. I gasped in delight when I saw a whole host of fireflies dancing and weaving through the air, lighting the scene and transforming it into something from an enchanted story book. A healer with a focus on animals must have bred them especially for the occasion.

A throng already stretched along the path, and we slipped among them. Laughter and calls of greeting surrounded us as we followed the crowd all the way to the great double doors of the palace.

Here two rows of footmen greeted us, their blue and gold livery shining in the light of many lanterns. Streaming up the steps and into the wide entryway, I experienced the palace for the first time as a guest.

With Gia, I had always darted in through a side entrance, or come around through the gardens. Now, for the first time, I felt the weight of the building. The history and power that upheld Tartora and its royal family pressed down on me. Part of me marveled at the beauty of the polished stone and deep, vibrant tapestries, a sense of security seeping from the solid structure. But a deeper part of me felt a slithering of unease. None of the current inhabitants had been alive for the atrocity visited on Calista, but this building had stood then. The forces who had slain my forebears had ridden out from these halls.

If everyone knew the truth, would the current generations turn on me as they had done on my ancestors? Did Airlie feel the same weight of hidden secrets and long dead mysteries that refused to stay buried?

A sideways glance showed me nothing but shining eyes and

slightly parted lips as she drank in the scene around us. And then we reached the ballroom door and the king and queen.

Having learned to curtsy since my arrival, I managed to drop into a creditable dip. Queen Celestine greeted us with conventional words she must have already recited a hundred times, but King Marius gave a more personalized welcome.

"We're glad to have you among us, Airlie, Royal Mage Apprentice," he said as if pronouncing an official title. Perhaps it was, for all I knew. "We look forward to the coming ceremony."

With a jolt I remembered what was to come at the end of the ball. How had I spent the whole day with my sister without it coming up in conversation?

Seeing the stiff way she held herself as she replied to the king, it occurred to me that she might have been as desperate to ignore the realities of our situation for one enjoyable day as I had been.

Others pressed behind us, forcing us on, and we moved along to Gia and Nikolas. I expected Gia to exclaim and gush, perhaps throwing her arms around my neck, but I had forgotten that with the court present, she was Princess Morgiana.

The regal incline of her head was angled perfectly, and her voice was soft and sure as she complimented me on my appearance. Only the warm glow in her eyes suggested the interest of actual friendship.

"I must thank you for your efforts, Cadence," she added. "The flowers in the ballroom look beautiful."

I smiled, curtsying carefully. "The gardeners did the work. I merely passed along your directions and requests. Happy Birthday, Your Highness."

Nikolas, who had always effected a rapid escape when Gia and I began talking about the ball, had no qualm cutting into the conversation.

"You look lovely." He didn't specify which of us he meant, but his eyes lingered on Airlie.

I had to admit they would make a striking couple, her hair several shades darker than his, but their eyes an equally intense blue. I couldn't help shuddering at the idea, though.

Two years of apprenticeship already loomed before us like a lifetime. I didn't want to imagine an actual lifetime spent in fear of the truth being revealed.

"Has Evermund returned?" Airlie asked, her words only just above a whisper.

Both twins frowned in unison.

"Not yet," Nikolas replied, equally quietly.

"But he'll be here before the ceremony." Gia sounded like she was trying to convince herself as much as us. "It's not until after the ball."

Airlie and I exchanged a look, but a footman gestured for us to move on, so we both curtsied again and stepped past the twins to the ballroom beyond. My steps faltered as I gazed around, a soft sigh escaping.

"Oh, Cadie, it's beautiful," Airlie murmured.

"I really can't take any credit," I repeated. "Gia had the vision, and the gardeners carried it out. I was just a go-between."

"Still...it looks incredible."

Only the endless lights—glittering off crystal chandeliers and candleholders and glossy metal lanterns—gave away the event was indoors. Otherwise the ballroom looked like a garden, trailing vines hanging down the walls and flowers blooming everywhere.

The throng of guests in brightly colored clothes moved among the greenery, swaying to the music of the small orchestra or strolling up and down the long room. Clusters of stationary guests around the supper table and along the walls watched the proceedings with bright eyes and broad smiles.

"It's just what I always imagined a ball would be like," Airlie breathed, her hands tightly clasped.

"Really? I thought I was the only one who dreamed about dancing at a ball. I never admitted it because I thought you would consider the idea foolish."

"We're all allowed a little foolishness." She shook her head as if to shake off the past. "Shall we start at the supper table or on the dance floor?"

"Definitely the supper table." I led the way toward it. "The pastry chef has prepared a feast."

I didn't mention my certainty that we wouldn't be there long before someone swept Airlie away to dance.

Surrounded by the fantastical setting, the guests were hard to recognize in their elegant garb. I eventually spotted a number of familiar apprentices, however, including Karielle. She swirled past on the dance floor, clasped loosely in the arms of Bryce.

Her attention was elsewhere, though, and when I followed the line of her gaze, I found Zeke. He stood out as effortlessly in the ballroom as he did in the dining hall, his golden skin glowing in the profusion of lights, and his black hair rumpled and enticing.

He stood in conversation with a glamorous woman who I recognized after a moment from the dining hall. I had seen her talking to him more than once in the past and had eventually discovered she was another of Augusta's apprentices, although she had graduated the year before.

She laughed—a chiming, bubbling sound—and rested her long fingers on his arm. I quickly looked away.

"If everything is as delicious as it looks, I'll be too full to dance," Airlie said, eyeing the table.

"Then come and dance first," an unfamiliar male voice said from behind us.

Airlie turned and smiled as if she recognized him, although he was too old to be an apprentice.

"If you insist." She put her hand in his outstretched one and let him whisk her away.

I watched for a moment, but they were quickly swallowed by the dancers. I tried to console myself with the accuracy of my prediction, and when that didn't work, I decided a pink cake might do the job more effectively.

Selecting one from the tray, I edged around the table, taking up an inconspicuous position at one end. The cake was consumed in moments, but I didn't reach for another, my stomach churning uncomfortably. What if no one asked me to dance the whole night? Every dream I'd ever had about a ball had included dancing, but I hadn't considered the fact that it was entirely likely no one would ask me to dance. After all, the only two males I ever spent time with had their pick of partners.

"Surely someone who's willing to brave the forbidden section of the library isn't scared of a mere dance floor."

My lips curled up at the familiar voice behind me, soft and low, just for my ears.

I turned slowly, seized by boldness.

"I'll willingly dance with you."

Zeke smiled approvingly. "I knew it couldn't be fear keeping you over here."

"Not at all." I chuckled. "I'm afraid it's nothing more interesting than a lack of acquaintance." I tried to keep my voice light. "People don't exactly fall over themselves to get to know the Guild's one remaining non-apprentice."

"Their loss." His eyes captured mine, something sparking in their depths that sent a shiver down my back.

When he held out his hand, I laid mine in it, my heart skipping a beat. He looked too handsome to be real in his formal finery, his warm eyes aglow.

"Perhaps I should warn you that I can't actually dance," I said as an afterthought, my eyes still trapped in his.

"All you have to do, Cadie, is follow my lead." His words were a low rumble, setting off answering vibrations in my chest.

He stepped backward, toward the dancers, and I followed along, ready to go wherever he might take us.

CHAPTER
NINETEEN

My heart rate sped up as his arm slipped around my waist, pulling me close. None of my imaginings had encompassed the solidity of his tall frame, or the gentle strength with which he held me.

Surrounded by a press of dancers, we felt totally alone. I didn't even feel anxious about my lack of skill, my feet easily following the rhythm of his steps. With his sure hand on my back, subtly directing me as we twisted and turned, we moved as one.

"See." He smiled down at me. "You're a natural."

I shook my head. "You're just a good teacher. Too good for this to be your first time dancing with an inept partner. I'll try to earn a position somewhere above the bottom of your list by not stepping on your toes."

He chuckled. "No one who knows you, Cadie, would put you at the bottom of any lists."

I pretended to consider the matter. "You might be right. I know my sister always had me at the top of her list of people so annoying she wanted to dump them head-first in the river."

He laughed softly, the sound traveling through his embrace as much as the air between us.

"Didn't the two of you live alone?" he asked. "So that must mean you were bottom of the list as well."

I grinned up at him. "Thus proving you wrong—something that probably needs to happen more often before your head grows out of all proportion."

His eyes crinkled in the corners, a laugh in his voice. "You would get on well with my mother." He paused, and the serious look that crept into his eyes sent another shiver through me. "I hope I can take you to visit my tribe one day. I think you'd like them. I know they'd like you."

I swallowed, my mouth suddenly dry. His tribe meant his family. They were basically the same thing for the nomads, even if not every member of a tribe was actually related by blood.

"I'd be honored," I whispered.

He pulled me closer. We were pressed tight now, almost too close to move freely, but I didn't protest.

"Cadie, I—"

"There you are!" A bright voice shattered the moment, and I turned to see Airlie, a broad smile plastered on her face.

I blinked, trying to bring the rest of the world back into focus. Somehow we had made it all the way up the dance floor and back to the supper table.

Zeke let me go, stepping back in one smooth, subtle movement, his usual smile on his face. My disorientation grew. It was almost as if whatever stolen moment we'd just experienced had never happened.

"Airlie." Zeke bowed with a flourish. "The woman of the hour. I hardly dare ask if you'd honor me with a dance."

Airlie rolled her eyes while I stared between them, not even pretending not to watch.

"She's not in a dancing mood." Nikolas stepped up beside me.

Had he been lurking there the whole time? I didn't even realize he was finished with his official welcoming duties. He certainly sounded sour as he watched Airlie and Zeke. Had she refused him, then?

The prince's eyes slowly turned to me, blinking as if he was only seeing me properly for the first time.

"What about you, Cadence? Dance?" He held out his hand, a beguiling note in his voice.

Seized by an intense desire to be far away from both Zeke and Airlie, I placed my hand in his. Before I had time to reconsider, he pulled me close and spun us both into the flow of dancers.

I didn't feel the effortless sense of oneness I had with Zeke, but Nikolas was a strong enough dancer to keep me from tripping over myself. After a few turns in concentrated silence, he gave a rough chuckle.

"Don't I even rate a look?"

Startled, my eyes flew up to find his laughing down at me.

"Sorry." I grimaced. "I'm not very good at this yet. I'm just trying to make sure I don't embarrass either of us."

"Maybe some embarrassment would be good for me. I'm sure Gia thinks so—and I could have sworn you do, too."

I opened my mouth but couldn't think of anything to say. What had happened to the bored and sneering Nikolas I was used to?

"You needn't be afraid to tell me what you really think," he assured me, the curve of his mouth and his eyes still laughing, although his voice was serious. "I might be here in an official capacity tonight, but in the small bubble of this dance, it's just us, and you can treat me like Apprentice Nik. I promise not to be offended."

I had never heard him style himself in Gia's manner before, and I couldn't help smiling. For once it was easy to think of them as twins, their similarity stretching deeper than appearance.

"There, that's better." He sounded satisfied, although his

face held a wicked look. "I'm quite willing to earn my smiles at a dance, you know. And I'll start by telling you that you look enchanting. That shade of green suits you. You remind me of a wood nymph, wandered from a painting—here to bewitch and bewilder mortal men."

His tone was perfect—half admiring, half joking—but I caught the barest flick of his eyes away from me, the smallest hint of anger slipping through along with it. I said nothing, letting the turn of the dance bring the object of his interest into view.

Airlie.

My sister still stood where we had left her, although the distance between her and Zeke had closed. Whatever they were discussing, both wore intense looks. As we spun again, she declared something with a look of finality. He responded with a silent bow before turning on his heel and disappearing into the crowd.

I stumbled, missing the next step. A sound of suppressed frustration from Nikolas made me stiffen and miss the following step as well.

"If I've promised not to take offense, you must as well," he told me in the same smooth voice. "Especially when I only speak the truth. You really do look enchanting."

I turned my face away, no longer able to see the similarity to Gia. Nikolas's charm was only skin deep.

He spun us several more times, until we reached the edge of the dance floor. I immediately pulled myself free and dropped into a curtsy.

"Thank you for the dance, Your Highness."

When I looked up, I expected to see anger in his eyes at what amounted to a dismissal on my part, even if it was couched in polite terms. But all I saw was boredom and irritation.

My mouth tightened, humiliation washing over me. Not

only had he been playing with me—toying with the less attractive version of the girl he'd really wanted—but I didn't even matter enough for my rejection to touch his pride.

With one half dance, he had curdled the magic of the night. My eyes began to fill, and I hurried down the edge of the room, moving on instinct back toward my sister.

"Cadie?" Her familiar voice washed over me, and her arms steadied me.

Drawing me with her, she moved us both back into the corner of the room where a potted plant offered me some shelter.

"What's wrong?" She sounded alarmed. "Did something happen?"

I swiped at my eyes, angry with myself now.

"Nothing important."

"Was it Zeke?" Her voice turned angry.

I looked up. "Of course not. He was with you, remember?"

I hated the hint of bitterness in my tone. How could I blame her when she had rejected them both? It wasn't her fault she had been the true object of both their interest.

"You shouldn't spend so much time with him," she said.

I stared at her. "What are you talking about? I said it wasn't Zeke."

She didn't seem to hear, apparently determined to see the topic through.

"It can be hard to keep your head when someone that good looking gives you so much concentrated attention."

I bit my lip, discomfort filling me. She couldn't be talking from experience since she certainly didn't seem to have that problem. I wanted to reject her words, but hadn't I warned myself against expecting anything of Zeke—only to immediately get swept away by our dance? For the span of those few minutes, I could have sworn we both felt the connection, and yet he had turned to Airlie without pause.

"What are you saying?" I asked, my defensiveness rising, despite the truth of her words. "Are you trying to suggest Zeke's being duplicitous?"

She sighed, the frustrated emotion of a parent when confronting a foolish yet recalcitrant child. My anger flared, my discomfort only fueling it.

"I'm sure he doesn't mean any harm, but that doesn't mean harm can't be done. I'm just worried about you, Cadie. I care about you. Zeke's charming, but he's charming to everyone. The girls who've grown up in court understand that, but you'd barely even spoken to a boy before we came to Tarona."

"No, because all the boys we met only had eyes for you!"

Of course Airlie didn't think it possible any attractive male could ever be interested in me. Why would they with her around?

She sighed dramatically. "You're just proving my point. You're still too much of a child to be safe around someone like Zeke. Don't act like I'm the enemy here. I'm only trying to protect you. I don't want to see you heartbroken by some nomad boy who's going to walk out of here in less than a year and not look back."

"You're imagining something that isn't there," I snapped. "Zeke is my friend—that's it. I'm allowed to have friends, aren't I? Or should I just sit around doing nothing, waiting for you to throw me some crumbs of attention?"

She stepped back, her face creasing. "What's that supposed to mean? I'm working myself to exhaustion protecting you and everyone else here. I'm sorry if I don't have time to baby you as well."

"You think you don't baby me?" I could barely control the volume of my voice. "You don't do anything else! But I don't need it. We both stopped being children the day Father died and left us alone."

"What do you know about being left alone?" My anger had

finally leached across into her, blazing in her eyes. "You have no idea how hard it's been for me, trying to carry on without Father, trying to find a way to activate my power."

"No, I don't know anything about that," I said, my voice icy calm. "Because you never told me. If you'd just told me everything, you wouldn't have had to carry anything alone. And I wouldn't be such a child now, burdening you with my ignorance." My voice dripped with sarcasm.

"You were so young." She sounded half-indignant, half-pleading. "I *wanted* you to have the chance to be a child. That's why I told Father—"

"*You're* the reason Father never told me anything?" I could almost feel myself growing taller, my fury making me swell. "So it's your fault I'm so ill-equipped for life! It sounds to me like I would be better off without you altogether. Maybe then I can finally grow up and learn all those harsh realities of life you're suddenly so desperate for me to understand."

"Cadence!" Her voice cracked like a whip, too loud for the setting, but neither of us broke eye contact.

"Fine!" she exclaimed after a moment. "I'll leave. It's not as if I *want* to dance and smile and play nice with people who are only interested in what I can do for them." She turned on her heel and dashed around the plant, plunging into the crowd.

I watched her go with glazed eyes, barely seeing the swirling dancers as my chest heaved with angry breaths.

"Cadence? Are you all right?" The soft voice took a moment to penetrate my consciousness.

I turned to see Karielle watching me with concern.

"You looked..." She waved her hands vaguely as if unable to put my expression into words.

I pulled myself back into the moment, shaking free the echo of my cutting words, and Airlie's angry replies.

"I'm...I'm all right." Or I would be. Airlie and I would be all right once we both calmed down. We always were.

For a moment she looked embarrassed. "I heard your sister telling Zeke off about you earlier. I couldn't help overhearing."

Heat rushed to my cheeks. That was what Airlie had been berating him about? How he shouldn't charm foolish little me? And Karielle had heard them?

I wanted to flee into the crowd like Airlie had done, but the last shreds of my pride held me immobile.

"She's not completely wrong about Zeke." Karielle spoke quietly, her eyes trained on the dancers.

A good look at her expression stopped my glare before it could begin. There were no hints of condescension on her face, just a self-deprecating sort of chagrin. Was it me she was thinking of, or herself?

"Zeke is far too charming. It's too easy to forget who he is."

"What do you mean?"

She looked over at me, a single crease across her brow. "He might be a nomad, but royalty is the same everywhere. No doubt his family already have a marriage alliance planned for him."

Her eyes strayed to where Nikolas and Gia stood to one side of the dance floor, deep in conversation. Or Gia was, at least. It looked like she was scolding her brother about something.

"Royalty?" I looked back at Karielle. "What do you mean?"

I strained my mind to remember my lessons. The nomad king's sons were fully grown, their children my age. But he had only granddaughters. Zeke couldn't possibly be one of them.

Karielle gave me a look of such honest surprise I couldn't doubt its genuine nature. She had thought me as aware of Zeke's situation as she was.

"He's no more just Zeke than Princess Morgiana is Gia. He's Zekiel, son of Annora, head of Tribe Nicabar."

"Nicabar?" The memories of my lessons on the nomads came rushing back to me. "They've been gaining power for years now. They're considered the most likely choice for the next rulers."

Karielle nodded. "King Fenix has been ailing for some time. The latest reports suggest he has only months to live."

"And then, most likely, the reign of Queen Annora will begin," I murmured, shock making my voice unsteady.

The only fixed structures built by the nomad tribes stood within their capital, the Hidden City. Located somewhere in the vast northern mountains above Calista, only tribespeople were permitted to know its exact location. There, all the tribes kept storehouses to protect their less portable treasures. And there, one tribe at a time made their dwelling—giving up their nomadic life for a single generation.

When a monarch died, the tribes gathered to vote on the new ruling tribe, whose leader became the next monarch. Once elected, in exchange for dominion over the entire nomad kingdom and precedence in all trade deals, the chosen tribe temporarily gave up their traditional ways and pledged to stand guard over the treasures of all the tribes.

The lack of heredity meant that right now, Zeke was a mere tribesman, free to move about as he willed—even to take an apprenticeship in another kingdom. But once the vote was cast, his life would change forever. For as long as his mother lived, he would be a prince.

It could be no coincidence his family had broken with tradition and sent him to complete his apprenticeship in Tartora. Karielle had looked to Gia when she mentioned a marriage alliance. Was the Tartoran crown princess the wife Annora had in mind for her son? Once the nomad crown sat on her head, he would have the rank to aspire to the match.

So much that had been a mystery now made sense. No wonder Zeke was given precedence and access beyond what his rank and position seemed to suggest.

Indignation stirred inside me. How could Zeke not have told

me his tribe and family? He had been the one to tell me he was a nomad, so he must have known I was unaware of the rest of his background. And yet he had left me ignorant so I could make a fool of myself.

My hot words to Airlie came circling back to bite at my conscience. She must not know the truth either, or she would have brought it up in our argument. But she had sensed it. If I was honest, I had, as well.

Two princes wandered the halls of the Mages' Guild, and both were equally out of reach.

"Thank you for telling me." I felt a new warmth for Karielle. Few people seemed to have much interest in giving me information.

"I'm sorry about Airlie," she said. "I have two younger sisters, so I know something about how it can be. No one knows how to so quickly infuriate us as our siblings—even when we love them."

I heaved a sigh and then forced a smile. "It's nice to know it's not just me."

She laughed softly. "No. Some things are universal."

Nikolas rounded the plant, looking at us both with faint displeasure.

"There you are." He was talking to Karielle. "Would you like to dance?" He gave the distinct impression he was doing an unpleasant duty—perhaps he had been instructed to dance with all the female Triumvirate apprentices.

Karielle threw me a single, loaded glance, as if to say, *see what we have to put up with from princes?*

But her curtsy was the perfect depth, and she put her hand in Nikolas's willingly. Once again I was struck with the uncomfortable feeling that Airlie had been right. Karielle understood the rules of interacting with royalty in a way I couldn't hope to do.

They disappeared, and once again, I found myself standing

near the supper table all alone. But this time the churning inside was far worse. The music washed over me, and an unknown length of time passed.

Apparently nothing was what I thought it was, and Airlie was right about my ignorance. It wasn't a pleasant realization.

"Am I allowed to ask you to dance again?" Zeke asked, breaking through my torpor.

I flinched, and he reached out a steadying hand, his face concerned. When I pulled away from his touch, his worry lines deepened.

"Perhaps instead of dancing, you'd like to get some fresh air?" He gestured behind us to where several full-length windows gave access onto a stone terrace overlooking the garden. A number of couples strolled along its length, enjoying the break from the crowded ballroom.

I nodded, knowing I couldn't handle being held in Zeke's arms for another dance. When he tried to cup my elbow with a guiding hand, I increased my pace, breaking the contact. When I burst out into the cool night air, I sucked in deep, steadying gulps.

Zeke stepped out behind me. "Is something wrong? You don't look like yourself."

I frowned at him, examining each angle of his face while he stood silent and confused under the scrutiny. He had sought me out again, noticing that I stood alone. Earlier in the evening I would have considered it a sign that the connection I felt between us was shared, but now that dream had been punctured.

And yet, I could think of no underlying agenda that might motivate his friendliness toward me. Was it just a general kindness on seeing a friend alone at a party? He was certainly no Nikolas.

But neither could I entirely dismiss the prince's behavior from my mind. Zeke lacked Nikolas's arrogance and unconcern for others—a product, perhaps, of not being raised a prince—but did that make what he was doing any different underneath? Whether he meant to or not, he was toying with me, just as Airlie had said.

The reminder of my fight with her made me sicker than the revelations about Zeke. She might be officious and overbearing at times, but what sort of sister would she be if she didn't try to warn me of obvious dangers?

I needed to find her and apologize.

"I'm sorry." I had meant to confront Zeke about not telling me the whole truth, but somehow it now seemed less urgent than finding Airlie. "I don't have time for this."

"Is something wrong? Let me help you."

I hesitated. He probably could help. "I just need to find—"

A stir inside the ballroom cut off my sentence. Both of us turned toward the closest door, moving closer to the building. Around us, others on the terrace did the same.

The first person through the door spoke briefly with someone on the other side, shock transforming his face as he took in her words. He turned back to us, horror in his eyes.

We all surged forward, meeting him at the door as a solid mass. Despite his horror, his expression suggested he relished the chance to have his turn as bearer of the news.

"Word has just arrived. The Royal Mage isn't back yet because he and his force are under siege!"

"What?"

"Impossible!"

"Under siege by who?"

The overlapping voices called questions at him.

"It's the raiders. Their retreat over the border was a feint. They circled around to lay a trap for the Royal Mage. He and his people are holed up in a farmhouse just out of the city. The mages among them are holding the raiders at bay, but who knows for how long?"

His pleasure at telling the news faded, swallowed by the awful nature of the tidings.

Zeke pushed the rest of the small crowd aside. "What is being done? Quick now!"

Everyone around us fell back, allowing a path for the two of us through into the ballroom. Now that I knew the truth of Zeke's background, I wondered why I hadn't seen it before. His bearing and air of command were so similar to the twins'.

"King Marius is to ride out within the hour, taking as large a force as can be mustered in that time." Someone from further in the room answered Zeke's question.

Zeke muttered an exclamation under his breath, diving into the milling crowd. The musicians had ceased their playing, and all dancing had stopped, leaving the dance floor covered in stationary guests discussing the news in an overlay of shocked voices.

Racing after Zeke, I clutched at his arm.

"What is it? Where are you going?"

"Gia," he said grimly. "What do you think she's going to do?"

It only took me a moment to imagine the scene. She would insist she and Nikolas be activated immediately so they could ride out with their father. Evermund was their cousin, and Gia was intensely loyal. I'd heard her myself arguing that a ruler shouldn't stay safe while the ones she loved were in danger.

Their parents would refuse, of course. But I had heard a childhood's worth of tales of Gia's inability to accept her parents' prohibitions. Her father was going after his nephew, and she wouldn't want to wait behind safely and tamely at the palace while he rode into danger.

"Quick!" I pushed him forward. "We need to find her."

CHAPTER

TWENTY

The size of the crowd impeded our progress, causing Zeke to growl under his breath as he fought a way through. Whatever awkwardness lay between the two of us, it was forgotten in the urgency of the moment.

By the time we struggled to the front of the room, there was no sign of King Marius. He must have already left the ball, probably to confer with the Triumvirate and the captain of his guard, who were also missing.

Zeke stood in the doorway, scanning the crowd that still filled the room. Unlike the king, no one else seemed inclined to leave.

"There." He pointed at someone, but I couldn't see who before his arm dropped.

I hurried in the direction he'd indicated, however, hoping it was Gia he'd seen. He raced behind, reaching my side just as I stumbled into a pocket of clear space and spotted Nikolas.

From the way Zeke strode over to him, Nikolas must have been our target. I joined them, my eyes darting around as I tried to find Gia.

"Where is she?" I asked.

Nikolas glanced between us, a frown on his face. It was obvious he was distracted. "Where is who?"

"Your sister." Zeke sounded impatient and frustrated.

Nikolas's face tightened. "I would recommend avoiding her for a while. She's in a foul mood after Father said our activation would have to be delayed—and that under no circumstances would we be included among the rescue force."

"Why aren't you with her?" Zeke leaned almost threateningly toward Nikolas, and I noticed for the first time that he was slightly taller than the prince.

Nikolas's frown deepened as he finally gave us his full attention, responding to Zeke's threatening posture more than his words given the lack of understanding on his face.

"She'll be back soon enough. She wanted to work on Mother alone—not that it will do her any good. Mother won't attempt to override Father on something like this."

"And would Gia know that?"

Zeke maintained his stance, silently demanding Nikolas consider the situation more fully.

"She should, but..." His words trailed off as horror filled his face.

Clearly he had been too distracted by news of the attack to consider his sister's behavior. But as soon as he gave the question his full attention, he reached the same conclusion we had.

"Come on. This way." He ran out of the ballroom, moving so quickly I could barely keep up.

Corridors flashed past, and I made no attempt to keep track of where we were going. When we finally paused at a solid wooden door, Nikolas only stopped long enough to grasp the handle and push the door open. It banged against the wall with the force of his entry.

The three of us tumbled into the room, me colliding with Zeke's solid back as he came to an abrupt halt.

"Gia!" Nikolas sounded furious.

I edged between them, finally getting a proper look inside. Gia stood frozen beside her bed, in the act of slinging a half full pack onto her back. As her defiant gaze moved from her brother, to Zeke, to me, a measure of guilt crept in.

"It's not too late for you to join me. All of you. The General is on our doorstep, and Father wants us to just shelter at home! Evermund is our cousin, and he's in danger right now!"

"Don't be a fool, Gia!" Nikolas crossed his arms and stood firmly in the doorway. "Father is right. Staying safe is exactly what the kingdom needs from its heir right now."

"That's no problem, then." She stalked toward him. "You stay here safe. If anything happens to me, you can be heir."

For the briefest moment, I thought he was wavering, but he merely dropped his arms and rolled his eyes, transitioning from angry brother to exasperated one.

"A pretty picture of me you have in your head if you think that's an argument that will sway me."

"But what about Evermund?" Her voice turned plaintive, the aggression draining out of her, just as it had out of him.

"Evermund is precisely why none of us are going to go," Zeke said, his face sympathetic but his voice firm. "Even if the three of you were to be activated right now, you would be next to useless out there with no training."

"I've got my sword." She patted the belt around her waist which supported a scabbard of brown leather.

"As does every one of the king's guards, along with activated and trained power," Zeke said, matter-of-factly. "You might as well be fighting with one arm. One arm can be helpful to defend yourself in a tight corner, but it will make you a liability in the field. Your father has experienced guards and mages to accompany him. You would only get in their way—potentially dangerously so, since they would feel obligated to protect you."

242

The last of her fight dissipated, and she threw the pack onto the floor.

"How infuriating," she said with surprising calm. "I hate it when Father is right. Why must it be the lot of a princess to sit in the palace and do nothing?"

"At least you're the heir," Nikolas said. "You'll get a reward for all the unpleasantness one day."

Gia wrinkled her nose, giving the distinct impression a crown wasn't the kind of reward she wanted. She didn't argue, though. Instead her shoulders slumped, and her discontented gaze latched on to me.

"Cadie!" She leaped over and grabbed my arm. "You understand!"

"Ah...Do I?"

She chuckled. "Don't think I haven't noticed how you are around Airlie. You don't like your family always telling you what to do any more than I do."

I grimaced. I obviously hadn't done as good a job of hiding my feelings about my sister as I'd thought.

"Family can be infuriating," I acknowledged, my unresolved fight with Airlie still hanging over my head. "And talking of family..."

"Don't worry, Airlie won't be going with Father," Gia said in perfect understanding. "Father said we're to stay at the Guild instead of the palace because it's the safest place for us given that here we have Airlie and a whole host of mages watching over us. So he's obviously not planning to take her with him."

An unacknowledged tension in my chest eased.

"I'm sorry your father is going to be in danger," I said, earning an impromptu hug from Gia.

"If we have to stay in the Guild, I'm staying with you, Cadie." She gave me a pleading look. "Please?"

"Are you sure?" I shot a glance at the two boys. "I'm not certain if..."

"If Father thinks there might be some danger, then the last place I should stay is my own room." Gia tilted her chin in a defiant way, daring Nikolas or Zeke to argue.

Neither of them did. In fact, Nikolas agreed for once.

"That makes sense. And you can stay in my room with me, Zeke. So I'm not alone."

"How delightful," Zeke said dryly. "And where will I sleep?"

Nikolas shrugged. "There's plenty of room on the floor. You can bring a blanket and pillow with you."

"It just gets better and better."

Gia hesitated, throwing me an uncertain look. "If you'd rather be alone…"

"I'm perfectly willing to have company." I smiled. "As long as it's not going to earn me a lecture from the king on his return."

If it kept Gia from haring off after the departed soldiers, I was more than willing to have a temporary room mate.

"Oh no, Father will be much too distracted with more important things," she said with a final lingering trace of bitterness.

She had already changed out of her ballgown, which lay crumpled on the floor, but I was still in my party finery. So she sent me ahead to change and prepare my room for her arrival. But after standing staring at it for several moments, I couldn't think of anything to do. I didn't have enough possessions for the room to be messy, and there was no way to produce a second bed.

I sighed. No doubt I would end up on the floor like Zeke. At least my room was equipped with extra blankets and even a couple of extra pillows.

A knock on the door made me hurry to unlock it and let Gia in. But at first glance, I couldn't even see her, my view blocked by the enormous pile of blankets and cushions filling her arms.

"I'm not kicking you out of your bed," she said with a firmness that suggested arguing would be fruitless. "I'll make myself a nest on the floor. It's a more comfortable night than I would have had if you hadn't stopped me leaving."

I bit my lip. Was she still upset at our interference? A trace of something less than serene remained in her voice.

But concern for her father and cousin could account for the lingering shadow. Which meant it was my duty to be as amenable and distracting as possible. There was nothing to be achieved by her lying awake all night, consumed with anxiety.

It took a little coaxing, but Gia was eventually willing to sit herself in the middle of my bed and be distracted by talk of the ball. Her conversation was dotted with abrupt references to the absent rescue party, but the rest of the time she discussed guests, dresses, dances, and other such birthday topics. She even bemoaned the magnificent cake prepared by the pastry chef and not yet brought out when the evening took such an unexpected turn.

"I'm sure they'll save you some," I reassured her, and she conceded that was likely the case before launching sideways into a speech bemoaning the delay of her activation.

Her words made something in the pit of my stomach unfurl and begin to writhe. Shouldn't Airlie have checked up on me by now? She must be excessively angry about our fight to stay away given the circumstances.

The same urgency that had gripped me out of nowhere on the terrace with Zeke reappeared. Where was Airlie? I shouldn't be sitting here—I should be looking for her.

But I repressed the feeling, stuffing it away. I had a responsibility to Gia. I couldn't abandon her to go racing around the Guild just to assuage my guilt and discomfort over my harsh words to my sister.

The emotions lingered, however, until it was me tossing and turning while Gia somehow slipped into a peaceful slumber in the middle of my floor. But eventually exhaustion overtook everything else, and I slept.

———

There was no knock to bring us gradually awake. My door splintered, the lock not so much breaking as dropping away entirely as the wood around it sprang improbably back to life, writhing with new, fast-growing green shoots.

For a crucial second, I couldn't think what was happening or where I was. And then I remembered who slept on my floor.

"Gia!" I leaped out of bed, falling mostly, as I flung myself down onto Gia's nest.

She gave a muffled scream as my bulk landed on top of her, shielding her from whatever was coming for us.

"Get up. Hurry!" Despite the terse tone, the familiar voice calmed my stuttering heart.

I disentangled myself from Gia's myriad blankets as she crawled out and leaped to her feet.

"What's happening?" she demanded.

"We're under attack." Nikolas stood beside Zeke, alarm on his face.

"The Guild is under attack?" I stared at them both.

Gia turned and dived back among her blankets, emerging seconds later with her scabbard gripped in her hand.

"I'm ready to fight."

I gaped at Zeke. "Do we need to fight? Is it that bad?" I winced as my voice squeaked.

"The opposite. You will *not* be fighting." Hayes appeared from behind the other two, his expression harried and eyes grim.

"What does that mean?" Gia demanded, planting her feet

firmly and giving them all a challenging stare. "I'm not hiding away while—"

"That is exactly what you will be doing," Hayes rapped out in a sharper voice than I had heard from him, even during the attack on the road. "And since my own life hangs in the balance of protecting yours, I won't hesitate to knock you over the head and drag you into hiding if I have to."

"You wouldn't!" Gia's eyes grew round. "I'm the crown princess!"

"Exactly!" Zeke gave her a determined look. "And that's why you're going to stop delaying us with this childish squabbling."

For a moment I thought she would take offense, but although she stiffened, she abandoned her protests. I trailed behind her as she joined the small cluster at the door, my mind racing as I tried to think through every possibility.

Gia was stepping through the doorway when I turned and dashed back toward my bed. The others continued on, only Zeke pausing in the doorway.

"Come on, Cadence." He sounded scared for the first time, as if he thought I might be planning to remain behind in some sort of protest.

Grabbing my pack from the trunk, my hand brushed against my mother's old book. I hesitated for less than a second before stuffing it inside, along with the first few fistfuls of material that came to hand. I ran back to Zeke, still stuffing trailing blankets into the pack.

"Just in case," I panted, racing headfirst out the door.

No one had said where exactly we would be hiding, and I could imagine a whole host of unappealing options.

We both ran, catching up with the others halfway down the corridor. I glanced back at the ruin of my door.

"Was that you?" I asked Zeke, a little awed.

He nodded. "There isn't time for niceties."

A fleeting sense of regret washed over me. I had felt safe in that room, but it was hard to imagine doing so again now that I had seen first-hand how little a lock meant to a mage.

We turned down another corridor and then another. Eventually we reached one I didn't recognize. The only decorations were large—simple wall hangings in the blue and gold of the servants' livery. At a guess, it appeared to be some sort of thoroughfare between the servants' rooms and the rest of the Guild building.

Hayes stopped, glancing up and down the deserted, darkened hall. No one could be seen in either direction.

Lifting the hanging next to him, he pressed a stone in the wall behind. A grating noise sounded, and a whole section of stone swung away.

"Hurry!" He held the hanging aside, waving us all through ahead of him.

Nikolas plunged into the darkness without hesitation, Gia following less eagerly on his heels.

"An elements mage would be nice right now," I heard her mutter.

"What about the fireflies?" I asked Hayes, regarding the darkness uneasily. "Is that something healers can do?"

"An excellent idea." Zeke gave Hayes a look, and the mage nodded.

"I know a way to attract them."

I bit my lip and stepped through the wall, propelled by Zeke's hand on my back. I had only made it a few steps when my faith was rewarded, sparks of light darting past my head.

Hurrying footsteps behind me were followed by the thump of the wall closing. Darkness settled over us, lit only by the glow of the insects. Without the light from the corridor, they shone brighter, and my eyes soon adjusted.

We walked through a narrow corridor of gray stone, uneven dirt beneath our feet. With every step we angled downward, until surely we must be underground.

248

"Are we beneath the gardens?" I murmured, and somewhere behind me, Hayes grunted an affirmative.

It was hard to measure time in the tense darkness, but it couldn't have been long before the stone of the passage walls ended, to be replaced by packed dirt. Moments later we stepped into a room of reasonable size. I turned slowly. Nothing but packed dirt was visible above, below, and on every side.

I swallowed nervously as I looked up at the ceiling and wondered what it would take to bring it crashing down on our heads.

"Don't worry," Zeke said quietly. "I'm a plants mage, remember. I won't let it bury us."

My breathing lightened. I had momentarily forgotten that his affinity included the earth itself.

"There's a reason he's with us," Hayes said, his skin washed out and unnatural looking in the strange light.

I tried not to be concerned that Hayes's best option had been an apprentice. Wasn't there a building of more qualified mages above us? How many of the strongest had gone with the king? Were the rest already caught up in fighting off the raiders, with only Hayes able to be spared as a last line of defense?

Or perhaps it was merely that Zeke had been there when Hayes arrived to collect Nikolas, and he had made a compelling argument for being brought along.

"And what about me?" I asked, trying to sound stronger than I felt. "Why am I here?"

"Because I would never have agreed to leave you behind," Gia said. "And there was no time for an argument."

"No one was planning to leave you behind," Zeke said firmly before glancing at me, his face softening. "You three are the only ones in this whole building who aren't activated. You're helpless compared to everyone else. But don't worry. You'll be safe down here."

He threw a glance at Hayes, but I didn't try to read it. Whatever doubts the two of them had, I didn't want to know about them. I had enough anxieties of my own.

"So everyone else is up there fighting?" I looked toward the ceiling again. "My sister?"

A heavy, uncomfortable silence settled over the hidden room. I looked sharply at Hayes.

"I'm sure not everyone is fighting," he said. "It's chaotic up there, but it was a targeted attack. They're looking for the prince and princess."

"The raiders?" I swallowed, my next words staying in my head. The raiders weren't only after Gia and Nikolas. They wanted me and Airlie as well.

"It seems the message that arrived at the ball was a fake." Zeke sounded grim.

"A fake?" Gia stepped forward. "What do you mean?"

"Evermund arrived half an hour ago," Zeke said. "He and his troops had to change routes to avoid a small rockslide. It delayed them enough to miss the start of the ball, but they pushed themselves hard, hoping to arrive before the activation ceremony."

"The raiders must not have been expecting him to make such good time," Hayes added. "It was supposed to be a surprise attack."

"So the General sent the message about the ambush to lure Father and his force away?" Gia asked. "To reduce the defense here? I suppose they learned from the failure of their first attempt." She sounded remarkably calm.

"But Airlie felt them coming? She warned you?" But even as I said the words, I could read the answer in his tense manner.

"Actually…" Hayes sounded reluctant. "Your sister is missing."

"Missing?" I sank onto the ground, my legs no longer able to hold me. That urgency I had felt. Had some subconscious part of me known she was gone?

"Thankfully we discovered her absence, and I ordered extra guards to patrol the Guild grounds. One of them stumbled on the first small group of assassins."

"The first group?" Gia sounded uneasy now.

"We believe they decided to give stealth another attempt," Zeke said. "But at the same time, they sent multiple teams to give themselves a better chance of success. We just have to wait down here until all of them have been found and eliminated."

"But Airlie?"

Had he forgotten my sister was missing? What did I care about the safety of our hidden hole when Airlie was up there all alone?

"We did a thorough search of the Guild looking for her," Hayes said. "And there was no sign of the assassins at that point. I'm confident she was gone before they arrived."

"What's that supposed to mean?" I could hear the rising panic in my voice and tried to rein it in. "Is that supposed to be reassuring?"

"Of course it is." Zeke's calm tones washed over me. "We have no reason to think she's dead, Cadence."

"No, just gone! I don't understand it. Are you saying she was abducted?"

Hayes shifted uneasily. "I'm saying we don't know."

I stared at him for a long moment before comprehension broke. He thought she'd run away. He looked uncomfortable because he thought she'd deserted her job of defending the Guild and run off, leaving Gia and Nikolas exposed to attack.

But why would she...My thoughts ground to a halt.

We'd fought. I'd told her to leave, and she had said she would. She couldn't possibly have taken me seriously enough to flee the Guild...Could she?

"If Airlie's not up there, we can't stay down here!" Gia strode over to Hayes, locking eyes with him despite the height difference. "All three affinity heads went with Father. Even the seconds all went except you."

"That's why I'm here," he agreed. "I will keep you safe with my last breath. I can heal—"

"No!" She shook her head. "With the rest of them away, the Guild is your responsibility as stand in for the Head of Healing. You're the only leadership left in the Guild. You can't be cowering down here with us. We need to go up there and direct the search for the assassins." Her volume escalated. "We can't stay down here, under all that dirt, closed in, trapped. We need to—"

"Keep their targets away from them," Zeke cut in, heading off her panic. "Everyone else will be safer without you around. It's you they want."

And Airlie. I wanted to scream the words, but they lodged in my throat. They believed she had left before the assassins' arrival, but how could we be sure? And even if she had, that meant she was out there alone in a night filled with roving bands of raiders. I trembled.

"Maybe you should get out those blankets?" Zeke suggested in a soft voice. "It's cold down here."

I stared at him uncomprehendingly, and he nudged my pack toward me with a significant glance in Gia's direction. I started, nodding and fumbling at the clasp with nerveless fingers.

"Here." I thrust a blanket at Gia, and she accepted it without demur.

"I think a drink would be a good idea to calm everyone's nerves." Hayes's voice sounded strained, but it was hardly surprising in the circumstances.

He drew out a portable silver flagon from a small pack of his own, handing around cups to everyone. Whatever tea it contained had a calming aroma, and I wrapped my shaking hands around the cup.

Before I could begin drinking, however, Zeke called me

softly. Responding instinctively to his familiar voice, I stepped aside to join him.

"I thought it might be a good idea to catalog whatever else you have in that pack," he said. "Just in case."

As he spoke, he moved, shielding me from view of the others with his body. Removing my cup from my hands, he held it along with his own untouched one. I looked from the cups to his face to find a warning expression trained on me.

"This is nice," Gia said, while I continued to stare in confusion at Zeke.

"What...Why is...?" Nikolas's words slurred together followed by a muffled thump.

I pushed Zeke aside to see the prince's body slumped on the ground. Hayes, who supported an equally unconscious Gia in his arms, gave us a rueful look.

"I couldn't catch them both."

CHAPTER

TWENTY-ONE

"What have you done?" I rushed over to help Hayes lower Gia gently to the ground.

Zeke flung the untouched contents of both our cups against the far wall. "I recognized the smell."

"I figured you would. Quick thinking with Cadence."

"I still don't understand. What happened? Are they—"

"Just sleeping," Zeke said quickly. "Do you remember the sleeping herbs my mother developed? Hayes was very interested in them when I first arrived at the Guild, and I ended up teaching him how to make them."

"A marvelously useful invention, and yet another argument for the value of cross-influencing." Hayes stood, brushing his hands together briskly.

"You put them to sleep? But why?" I wondered if I should be nervous, but it was hard to be scared of the man who had saved my life on the road.

"How long do you think they would have lasted?" he asked, packing the flagon and cups away. "Princess Morgiana was already talking of charging off. Do you think they could have endured hours of tense suspense without cracking me over the head and making a run for it? All with the noblest of intentions, of course."

"There are three of us and two of them," I said, resentful on their behalf.

He raised an eyebrow at me. "Are there? So you're telling me you couldn't be convinced—two hours from now—that you should side with the princess, obey a royal order, and go out to look for your sister?"

"I wouldn't put Gia at risk." I met his eyes steadily.

I wanted to find Airlie but not at the expense of anyone else. She wouldn't want that.

After a moment, he dipped his head. "Very well. But I couldn't be sure of that."

"I'm not to be trusted either, I suppose." Zeke gave him a knowing look.

Hayes shrugged. "You're almost as much royalty as the two of them. Your injury, death, or abduction while under the care of Tartora's Mages' Guild could cause serious problems for the kingdom. Consider it a gesture of trust that I didn't force the potion down your throat as well."

"Do you think you could?" Zeke sounded genuinely curious.

I held up a hand. "This is not the time for the two of you to start testing each other's strength. We need to work together, remember."

I paced up and down, trying to gather my scattered, terrified thoughts.

"The twins might not be able to put themselves in danger," I said accusingly, "but if the raiders do find us, they can't defend themselves either."

"Then it's a good thing I have the two of you to help me." Hayes spoke calmly, but I could see the tension beneath his facade. No doubt he was second guessing every decision he'd made since the Triumvirate rode out and left him filling in as Head of Healing.

"I don't know how much good I can be." I frowned. "And what about you? The fireflies are a boon. And you'll be essential if it does get as far as injury. But will your powers be of use otherwise? There are no animals down here to call to our aid."

Hayes shook his head. "It doesn't work like that. I might be able to attract fireflies, but I can't control all animals. I can only heal them, and sometimes influence them, if I can get them to trust me."

He strode over to take up a guard position by the tunnel entrance. "I may not be able to call for an army of animals, but if anyone gets close enough to lay a hand on any of you, I won't hesitate." He looked sick at the bold pronouncement, however.

"Most healers hate to use their ability to harm," Zeke told me quietly.

Hayes gave us a steady look. "If it comes to it, I'll do what needs to be done. And if someone actually breaks through and it comes to hand-to-hand fighting, I can use my ability to wake the twins."

I bit my lip. "And if they come after us with their abilities instead of charging through the tunnel with swords?" I didn't point out it was the more likely eventuality. Neither of them would need the reminder. "Last time we had Airlie..."

"That's where I come in." Zeke's voice was low and deadly, and his presence at my side was the only thing allowing me to maintain my calm. But I couldn't help remembering that it had taken both him and Sutton to fight off only two attackers last time.

"Wait! What about Evermund?" I asked. "You said he came back sometime after Airlie disappeared but before the attackers arrived. Is he up there now fighting them?"

Hope filled me. But one glance at Hayes's face dashed it.

"At that point, we thought the true ambush was intended for the king, not the Guild. So Evermund left his exhausted troops behind and took fresh forces with him to ride after the king."

"But the king already took everyone he could muster…"

No one answered, and I swallowed hard. If Evermund had taken everyone left, it must be lean pickings indeed up there.

"And so you grabbed the twins and came to hide here," I whispered.

Hayes wouldn't meet my eyes. "There wasn't much time to think, but it seemed like the best option."

"And so we guard them." I tried to put steel into my voice, earning an approving look from Zeke.

He moved closer to me, and memories of the ball suddenly flooded my mind. How long ago it seemed. With everything that had happened in the hours since, I had put my tension with Zeke out of my mind. But here in the darkness and the quiet, with only Hayes to keep us company, it came rushing back.

I moved away from both Hayes and Zeke, needing space to breathe. Dragging over Gia's blanket, I laid it gently atop her sleeping form. After a moment's hesitation, I did the same to Nikolas. All the while my thoughts sped far faster than my body, my gaze slipping sideways to watch Zeke.

Did I really have a reason to be angry with him? He might have come to my room for Gia, but he had also stayed back for me when he thought I was falling behind. Over and again, he had noticed me when I felt overlooked and abandoned. Did it really matter if he kept some of himself back? I hadn't told him the full truth about my history either.

And was it his fault if I had created something in my mind that wasn't there? We could be friends even if he preferred Airlie. And we could be friends even if his mother had hopes for a marriage alliance with Gia. He had never suggested anything to me beyond friendship, the one thing it was in his power to give. The desire to blame him slipped further and further away. I didn't need to confront Zeke, I needed to pull away from him.

If I avoided ever being alone with Zeke, I could protect myself from imagining something that wasn't there. Gia wouldn't abandon me once she was an official apprentice—I believed her when she said that—so I would just have to keep her around as a buffer in the future.

A thump from overhead shook the ceiling, sending dirt sprinkling down over us. I jumped, the reality of our situation rushing back. My focus on Zeke had only succeeded at keeping the fear and tension at bay for so long.

A sound like distant thunder accompanied another shaking of the ground around us. This time whole clumps of dirt shook loose.

Hayes said something I couldn't catch, and Zeke hurried toward me. He crouched between the two sleeping royals, and I realized Hayes must have sent him to protect them.

Pressing both hands against the ground, he closed his eyes. I held silent, despite the rising tension winding my insides tighter and tighter.

Another boom shook the walls around us as well as the ceiling. Dirt billowed into the room from the tunnel, but Zeke didn't move. It was impossible to tell from his stillness whether he was using his ability to keep the earth around us intact.

The tension inside me wound tight enough to snap.

"What is it? Are they trying to get to us?"

Zeke's eyes sprang open, his gaze catching mine.

"They know we're down here. One of them can smell the air, like your sister."

"What?" I swallowed. "How do you know?"

"I can hear them through the root system." He nodded toward his hands which still pressed against the dirt. "They're up there, in the garden among the plants, talking."

I stared at him. I had no idea such a feat was possible. But I needed to focus on the raiders. It must be my imagination after his revelation, but I could feel them up there, four of them.

"How is it possible that one of them can do that? I thought Airlie was stronger than anyone in the last—" I cut myself off. There wasn't time for such questions. "Never mind. What are they doing to find us? Have they found the tunnel?"

"I've closed it off."

"Wait, what? What does that mean?"

"I collapsed the tunnel."

"Collapsed it?" I looked around wildly. "You mean we're trapped?"

"They would already be here if I hadn't."

I swallowed. "What next, then?"

The shuddering repeated, dirt now coating all our hair.

"Are they going to bury us?" I forced the words out around the lump in my throat.

"Not if I can help it." His voice sounded strained, his face no longer impassive as it had been before.

"Hayes!" I called in a panic. "Hayes!"

The mage sprinted toward us, abandoning the tunnel entry that was no longer a point of weakness.

He dropped to a knee beside us, our eyes meeting over Zeke's bowed head.

"Did he finish collapsing the tunnel?" he asked.

So that had been Hayes's instruction. I nodded.

"But he's only an apprentice," I whispered. "And there are four of them."

Or I imagined there were. I brushed the thought aside. What difference did it make?

"Can't you do something to help him?" I pleaded with my eyes, dismayed at the fear I saw reflected back at me. "Give him more strength, or..."

"You know it doesn't work like that. I would if I could, but I can't. They're so much stronger than we expected. I don't understand how—"

"Drag them into the tunnel." Zeke cut me off, his head back up and his eyes on Hayes. "If it comes to shielding them, it will be easier in the more confined space."

Hayes didn't hesitate, scooping Gia's tiny frame into his arms and staggering away. I couldn't carry Nikolas, but I grabbed the packs and sprinted after him, depositing them just inside the entrance to the narrow tunnel before rushing back to Zeke.

"Shield them? Can you do that?" I asked.

He grimaced. "Some plants mages could. It would be better if I was plants cross elements. If everything else collapses, we'll need to keep a bubble of air around us to survive. I don't know…"

Hayes grasped Nikolas under his arms and began to drag him back toward Gia's prone form.

"If only I could help you." I wrung my hands together, fighting to breathe in the increasingly thick atmosphere. "What if you activated me right now? I…I think I've been ready for a while now. If I was under your influence, could I lend you my strength—as little as it might be?" I was babbling, spouting ideas no matter how little sense they made.

"If you activated me, it would mean I had some connections to plants, wouldn't it? No matter my own affinity? Maybe I could help. Maybe I even have an elements seed, like Airlie. It does run in families."

"I'm still an apprentice." His voice sounded strained. "I'm not permitted to activate anyone."

Another shudder sent us both rocking as the ground beneath us rippled. I gave him an incredulous look. That couldn't be the real reason for his refusal. Did he think me too weak to do any good but wanted to spare my feelings? It was hardly the time for such niceties.

"I know I'm weak. But surely every little bit would help? What if I can provide the extra bit of strength that means the difference between life and death?"

Some detached part of me marveled at the irony of the situation. After all my protestations that I would never risk activating my ability, now I was desperate to convince Zeke to do just that. But trapped beneath the ground, faced with death, all my excuses were stripped away, and the truth stood bare.

It hadn't been fear of the potential ruin I might cause that held me back. It had been resentment and jealousy. I hadn't wanted everyone to compare my weak ability with Airlie's strong one. I hadn't wanted to yet again be nothing but a weak shadow of my older sister.

But my defiance had been childish. I wouldn't find my own path, separate to my sister, by diminishing myself. My ability, however weak, was part of me, and neither my jealousy nor my father's cryptic pronouncements should be allowed to strip that away. If I'd admitted that earlier, I might be more help now.

"You're not weak." Zeke looked me in the eye, his muscles trembling with whatever unseen effort he was expending to keep the earth above us from collapsing. "And you're right that you're ready to be activated. I have no idea how strong you're going to be, but I've never even heard of someone ready so long before their birthday. There's every chance your strength will exceed your sister's."

I shook my head. Was the strain making him lose touch with reality?

"Master Colton tested me himself, remember? He found me weak."

"No, he couldn't identify your affinity."

"That's the same thing."

"In some cases. But not in yours. Colton just didn't recognize your affinity."

"That doesn't make any—No." I shook my head. "Never mind that. We don't have time. Will you activate me or not?"

Still Zeke hesitated while the last seconds of our lives counted down.

"You have to promise me no one finds out," he said after what seemed an age. "For both our sakes." He glanced across at Hayes, who was crouched over the unconscious royals, gesturing for us to join him. "You can't let Hayes realize you're helping me. Which means, whatever happens—good or bad—I'll have to take the credit. Can you live with that?"

I didn't hesitate. "This isn't about heroes or villains. It's about keeping us all alive." But even as I said it, I knew if we survived but this went badly, I would never be able to let him take all the blame. Which just meant I had to make sure it didn't go badly.

"Very well. I've never actually done this before, so give me a moment."

He closed his eyes, and the air between us stirred. A tendril of power reached out, passing through me as if I had no physical form. A cracking sensation deep inside sent a riotous burst of life racing through my body to my brain. Connections formed instantly, opening up a whole new web of sensation.

Neither of us had moved or spoken, but I knew instantly and with absolute certainty that four mages stood in the garden above us—two plants mages, one elements mage, and a healing mage. I could even sense the duller glow of Gia's elements seed and Nikolas's plants one.

And the web of power! It sparked between Hayes and the twins, where he kept a monitoring hand on each of them. It spread out from Zeke, a hundred tiny roots that dug through the earth, holding it in place above us. It pushed down from above where our enemies sought to burrow down to us. It even pulsed in the walls of the room, the leftover power from some long-ago plants mage who had scooped this hideaway from the earth.

I could see now how one apprentice had managed to hold off the raiders for so long. They weren't trying to bury us outright, but rather dig themselves a path to reach us.

I couldn't hear them—that was a skill I didn't possess and might never have, one that belonged to a plants mage. Whatever this was, I didn't think it was a plants ability. The roots and tendrils and vines I could sense all around me were made of pure power, not of green growth.

Zeke's eyes met mine again. "Now you can see why they want you alive," he whispered, and I shivered.

I didn't know what was going on with me, but this wasn't weakness, and I refused to let the raiders seize me before I had a chance to explore my ability for myself.

"How do I help?" I asked.

"I…I've never trained a power mage. I don't know." He stopped, drawing a deep breath as the mages on the surface sent a fresh surge of power burrowing down through the earth above us.

A large clod dropped, nearly hitting him in the head, and anger surged through me. Three times now the General had sent his people for me, and I'd had enough. If I had power after all, then I intended to use it.

I closed my eyes, imagining myself as a giant oak—stronger than storms, stronger than centuries. I didn't bother to crouch beside Zeke—I didn't need the connection with the earth. The power I needed was all around me, floating in the air. I sucked it in, and then I pushed it out.

I pushed with everything I had in me, sending a tidal wave of pure power through the soil above us, driving back everything in my way. It pushed out the brigands' power that had been digging down toward us, before rolling over them and carrying on through the Guild.

The air around us cleared, and for the first time in a long time I drew in a deep, unfettered breath. Opening my eyes, I smiled at Zeke.

"They're gone. They're running and will soon be beyond where I can sense them."

He watched me with wide eyes, his features frozen.

"What just happened?" he whispered. "I felt your power in every root in the network. And then it was just…gone. All of it. I can't hear anything anymore."

I winced. "Sorry. I don't know how to do anything with finesse yet. All I could think to do was push all the power away. Including yours."

He shook his head. "Don't apologize. That was…incredible. I've heard tales, but I've never seen…"

He fell silent as my head jerked up, my attention caught by something in the distance.

"There are more people coming. Mages. Lots of them. But I can't tell…" I lifted my arms and then let them drop helplessly. I could tell their exact numbers and affinities, but I couldn't tell whose side they were on.

"Let me listen again. I'll just need a minute to send my power back through the roots." He swayed slightly as he pushed his palms down flat once more.

I watched him, my brow creased. "You're exhausted. Don't push yourself too hard."

His eyes sprang open, a grin breaking out on his face.

"They're our people! King Marius and Evermund together. They're rounding up the remaining raiders, and—"

I put a hand on his shoulder. "Break free. Let it go. You've already expended too much. You're going to collapse." I grinned at him, giddy with relief. "And then we'll have more unconscious people than conscious people down here, and where will we be?"

Slowly I stood, tugging him up with me, breaking his

connection to the ground and the system of roots it contained. Instead of leaning on the dirt, he leaned on me, and when we both made it upright, he maintained the connection.

His hands curled gently around my upper arms as he looked down into my face with something uncomfortably like awe.

But the moment stretched out, growing and changing. Something warmer and stronger than awe sparked deep in his eyes.

"You were amazing, Cadie," he whispered. "I never dreamed..."

Despite the cold of our underground cave, his warmth spread through me, reaching from his hands all the way down to my toes. No one had ever looked at me the way Zeke did now.

"Zeke!" Hayes strode across our hiding hole, his clothes and visible skin coated in dirt. "What's happening?"

Zeke fell back, and the punctured moment reminded me sharply of the ball. He gave me a warning look, but I didn't need his reminder not to blurt anything out in front of Hayes.

"Reinforcements have arrived." The exhaustion was showing in Zeke's voice at last, as the reality of our survival sank in. "I could hear them through the roots. They knew you planned to come down here as a last resort and were talking of digging us up."

"I made him disconnect," I said, in case Hayes might be tempted to ask for an update. "He's exhausted, and I'm worried about him pushing too far."

"I can help with that." Hayes held out a hand, an inquiring look on his face.

Zeke accepted it with relief, some of the weariness leaving his face as they made contact.

I frowned. "I thought you couldn't help him."

"I can't increase the strength of his ability. I can't touch his power at all. But I can ease his physical tiredness."

I nodded as if I understood, but I didn't really. I was the

opposite. All I could sense of the people above us was their power.

It hit me suddenly, and my knees gave way. Sinking down to the floor, I put my head in my hands.

I wasn't weaker than Airlie—quite the opposite. But what would happen if I told all the people up there? If they had thought her ability unique, what would they think of mine?

I glanced up to find Zeke watching me, an intense look on his face. Was I imagining the warning he was still trying to convey? Probably not. He had told me we couldn't tell anyone I was activated.

But it was more than that. What did he know that I didn't?

I put my head back into my hands. I had succeeded in helping my friends, and I now possessed the means to step out of Airlie's shadow forever. And yet, here I was, hesitating. And it wasn't just because of Zeke, either.

For the first time, I truly understood how it felt to be in Airlie's position—the weight of impossible power. And I hesitated. Maybe life away from the glare of expectation wasn't so bad after all.

TWENTY-TWO

"It seems like Zeke isn't the only one exhausted by our ordeal." Hayes reached a gentle hand for my shoulder, his eyebrows raised inquiringly.

I nodded, too tired for words, and he completed the contact. Fatigue lifted, my head clearing and my muscles loosening.

"Thank you," Hayes said quietly.

I looked up at him, startled. Did he know?

But his eyes moved sideways to Zeke. "Not all strength is connected to our ability. Thank you for staying with him and giving him the strength to keep us safe."

"Oh...you're...welcome."

A rumbling began above us, causing both Hayes and me to look toward Zeke.

"That will be the rescue effort," he said confidently. "Don't worry. They've got plenty of plants and elements mages to ensure we come out safe."

I glanced over at the still, silent twins.

"Now might be a good time to wake them," Hayes said, and we both nodded.

I trailed after him, watching as he knelt down and touched

a hand to each of their shoulders. A moment passed, and then Gia blinked, followed a second later by Nikolas.

As soon as his eyes opened, he surged upright, glaring at Hayes.

"What happened? What did you do? Did you drug us?"

"It was a harmless concoction," Hayes said. "To help you relax."

"Relax?" Nikolas glowered down at the crumpled blanket where he'd been lying. "You—"

"Let it go, Nik." Gia put a hand on his arm, giving him a look I couldn't read. "You know Father will have authorized him to do whatever was necessary to keep us safe." She looked past Hayes to me. "I suppose we are safe now?"

I nodded, and Hayes chimed in, obviously relieved to have made it through the waking so easily.

"We had to collapse the tunnel to keep them out, but then they tried to collapse the entire room on us. Zeke held them off, though."

"He was incredible," I added, speaking only truth.

The rest of Hayes's assumptions I let stand. His version of what had happened was a great deal simpler than the truth.

Gia rushed over to Zeke and flung her arms around his waist, burying her face in his chest.

"Thank you!" When she pulled back, she sounded like she was crying.

He patted her back, exchanging an awkward look with Nikolas over her head. Her brother just shrugged, so Zeke continued his patting.

"I never want to be in an enclosed, dark space again." Gia stepped away from Zeke and crossed back over to hug me instead.

I embraced her back, glad she hadn't been conscious for most of it. If she was already inclined toward a fear of small spaces, it was better for everyone she had been asleep.

The longest, deepest rumble yet opened a split in the side of the room, letting stronger light flood in. Two people stepped through the hole.

"Master Drake! Master Augusta!" Hayes had never sounded so relieved.

Drake's eyes swept over us, and he turned to bellow up the tunnel behind him.

"They are all here, and all well."

Distant sounds of cheering drifted down.

Drake bowed. "Your Highnesses." He gestured for Gia and Nikolas to exit into the tunnel.

They both went without hesitation, and I stumbled along behind them, still overwhelmed despite Hayes's assistance with the fatigue. Zeke stayed a step behind me, leaving Hayes to bring up the rear with the two masters. I could hear him murmuring to them at a fast pace, relaying everything that had happened.

I only half listened, having even less desire to correct his tale on this second telling. Only when Drake spoke was my attention fully caught.

"We had already realized something was wrong and started back when Evermund caught up with us. When he saw we weren't in trouble, we all realized the true ambush must be back here. We sent our fastest horses on ahead with our strongest fighters—and reached here just in time it seems."

"We would have been dead without Zeke," Hayes murmured. "He knew what they were trying to do. He could hear them through the network of roots."

"Could he now?" Something in Augusta's voice made me turn to glance back. She was watching her apprentice's back with a speculative gleam in her eye. "What an interesting ability." She raised her voice slightly. "I look forward to hearing all about it once you've had some rest, Zeke."

"Of course, Master Augusta," he called back, a rueful set to his mouth.

I raised an eyebrow at him, and he grimaced. "Mother isn't going to be happy I revealed that particular trick."

Ahead of us the light of dawn stole in through the mouth of the tunnel. A few more steps, and we strode out into the cold early morning air.

I took a deep breath, closing my eyes as I reveled in how pure it felt. It wasn't just the freedom from the clogged and dirty air below ground, however.

Before my activation, it had been as if I saw through a thin layer of blindfold, seeing only hazy lumps of dark and light, although it had grown stronger as my seed matured. But now I saw with perfect clarity. The heaviness I had sensed in the air at the Guild was power. Back at home, in the wilderness, the air had been clear, but here power floated everywhere.

Or it did normally, anyway. The wave of power I had sent up through the ground had pushed all power before it—both aggressive and friendly. The air of the Guild had never been so clear.

Another difference struck me. I could now sense everyone around me, thanks to their ability—an invisible tapestry that marked every presence. But it wasn't an entirely new sensation. I had always been aware when people were near, an ability I had taken for granted. It had just been hazy and indistinct compared to this new feeling.

And while I had always thought I reacted to being pressed in by crowds, I had felt no terror at being underground and enclosed as Gia had. Only now did I realize it was the unfamiliar sensation of so many abilities around me, not the physical confines, that had caused my previous reaction.

How little I had understood myself.

King Marius hurried over, wrapping one arm around each of his children.

"You have done my kingdom a great service today, Zekiel of Tribe Nicabar. I will not forget it."

Zeke bowed deeply. "I am pleased to have been able to assist."

Master Colton hurried up and placed one hand on each twin. After a moment, he pulled away.

"They are both healthy, Your Majesty. Although sleep would be recommended." He looked toward me and Zeke, and then Hayes just beyond us. "For all of you."

"What of the raiders?" Zeke asked.

"Fled, all of them." The captain from our training shook his head in disgust. "They must have heard our approach."

Zeke glanced at me, but I kept my face carefully impassive. The timing had worked well, and I was more than happy to allow the assumption to stand, letting the reinforcements take the credit for our victory.

"They were powerful." Hayes looked between each of the members of the Triumvirate with concern.

"That explains how they got cleanly away, then." The captain nodded, looking pleased his guards hadn't been to blame. "And from a preliminary sweep, plenty of mages are complaining of damage they did on their way out."

I bit my lip. How much of that damage had actually been from my inexpert effort to repel our attackers?

"And the General?" I asked, remembering who was responsible for all this.

"He'll be off licking his wounds beyond the border." Evermund strode over from the direction of his suite. His words were confident, but a line creased his brow.

He directed his next words at me. "Where is Airlie?"

"I don't know." With my newfound ability, I could have stated with confidence that she wasn't anywhere on the Guild grounds. But I refrained from doing so.

The crease in Evermund's brow deepened. "She's still missing?"

"Yes." The king sounded displeased. "That will have to be investigated."

I shuddered. How terribly the timing had worked out. What trouble would now be waiting for Airlie on her return?

It was still a better scenario than any other, however. I had to believe she would return.

"There is time for such things later," Colton said. "Sleep is what is needed now. For as many of us as can afford to be spared from guard duty and healing."

Gia looked over her shoulder at me as her father ushered her away, and I managed to produce a wan smile. It seemed to satisfy her.

Zeke, however, looked more determined as he strode toward me. But Augusta cut him off.

"You heard Master Colton's orders. Bed, oh apprentice of mine. And in the morning, we will have a long talk."

Her keen eyes brooked no opposition, so he was forced to turn away, leaving me alone.

But I wasn't alone. Evermund still stood before me, the crease still there between his eyes.

"Where is my apprentice, Cadence?"

"I truly don't know. I wish I did." I bit my lip. "I'm worried about her."

His expression softened. "Of course. Come. You can sleep in her room tonight, so you can be the first to greet her when she returns."

I smiled my gratitude and stumbled after him across the trampled garden. Stepping into her room, however, I was hit with a wave of pain. I had driven her away, and now I had no idea if she was even safe.

I buried my face in her pillow and cried myself to sleep.

The sun was high overhead when I awoke. For a long time, I just lay in bed, remembering everything that had happened the night before and marveling at my new ability.

But the constant reminders of Airlie all around me drove me out of bed eventually. I could sense Evermund's presence—or at least the presence of an elements mage—next door in his sitting room, and I couldn't put off our conversation forever.

Unlike those closest to me, I couldn't yet identify the feel of Evermund's ability. I would need to rectify that given the way Airlie and I were still bound to him.

"Ah, you're awake." He nodded a greeting as I stepped into the sitting room, sounding far too alert for having ridden through most of the night.

"Has she returned?"

My eager question died on my lips at his expression.

"Sit down." He pointed to a seat in front of a tray laden with food.

I sat eagerly, my stomach gurgling in response to the smells floating up from the plate. Evermund spoke while I ate, his tone brisk and businesslike, despite the worry in his eyes.

"Airlie disappeared last night during the ball. No one actually saw her leave the palace grounds. That's important."

I nodded, confused.

"Unfortunately, someone heard her final words to you."

He bent a questioning look at me while I racked my brains to remember just what had been said. She had exclaimed, too loudly, and then she had said she would leave. That she didn't want to be there with people who only wanted to use her.

"Oh no," I whispered, my fork stilling in my hands.

"Yes, precisely." Evermund ran his hand through his hair. "I still have some influence, so officially she has been declared a missing person. There will be an investigation into her disappearance and attempts will be made to discover if she might have been abducted by the raiders before their presence was discovered. But already there are other voices—"

"People think she left," I stated flatly. "That she abandoned the Guild and the protective responsibility she'd accepted for Gia and Nikolas." I stood. "That's not what she was talking about. It's all my fault. We had an argument, and I made her angry. She was just lashing out at me, talking about the ball. She didn't mean..."

"Sit." He waved me back down. "I'm relieved to hear you say so. But do you think there's any possibility she might have left of her own volition? Perhaps intending merely a short break? Is there anything about Airlie I don't know?"

I froze at his last question, and he gave me an odd look for a moment before the corners of his eyes crinkled.

"Anything that might be relevant to her disappearance, I mean. Naturally sisters have secrets they have no interest in sharing with outsiders."

I slowly dropped back into my chair, annoyed at myself for having such a visible reaction. It had been a natural enough question for him to ask, and I had better be more prepared in the future. He might not be the only one to ask questions about Airlie during the investigation, and if any of the questions were asked with a healing mage in the vicinity...

I swallowed, unable to force myself to take another mouthful. It had been bad enough carrying our shared secret before, let alone now that Airlie was missing and I had even more dangerous secrets of my own. For the first time I could understand why Airlie had considered my ignorance a protection.

Thinking about her reasons for silence—however much I disagreed with them—reminded me of his original question. It was one I could answer with confidence.

"No. If my sister has one defining trait, it's her responsibility. There's no way she just left. Not when she knew we were all relying on her ability to keep us safe. If Airlie is gone, it's not because she chose to go."

Terror swept over me at my own certainty. Where was Airlie now? Was she even still alive? Was she trapped somewhere, terrified and alone...

"Breathe." Evermund's calm voice broke through my haze.

I looked up to find him directly in front of me, his steady gaze holding mine.

"Remember that the General wants her alive. Your sister is an incredibly valuable tool, and she's also not weak and powerless. They'll keep her alive, and she'll bide her time until she can find a way to escape."

"Or until we find her," I said with determination.

A smile spread across his face. "Precisely." He hesitated, and it faded. "But be aware it may only be us making any serious attempt to look for her. Those unfortunate words at the ball..."

"It doesn't matter." I stared down at my fork, my fingers white where I gripped it. "It doesn't matter if everyone else gives up. I will never stop looking for her."

"And neither will I."

I looked up at him, bewildered by his support.

"She's my apprentice," he said simply. "She was my responsibility, and I left her to Sutton. And while I haven't known her for long, I agree with your assessment. I don't believe she just walked out." He hesitated again. "She was my responsibility, which means you are, too."

"Me?"

He raised an eyebrow. "Need I remind you that you're not of age? You're not even old enough for your own apprenticeship."

I bit down on my tongue. Clearly he couldn't sense the change in me, just as Colton hadn't been able to sense my affinity.

"You will live here, in Airlie's room, until she returns," he said.

"Are you sure? I won't get in your way?"

I couldn't help but ask, although his offer was a relief. It meant I wouldn't have to live in constant uncertainty, wondering if the Guild might kick me out when sentiment turned against my absent sister.

"Of course I'm sure. It's what she would expect of me."

I couldn't help grinning at that. There was no doubt his words were true. And no doubt that if he didn't house me, she would have something to say about that on her return.

"Thank you," I said. "And this way we can work together to find her that much faster."

He smiled, but his eyes had grown distant, his mind already racing on to the next thing.

"Will you be all right here on your own for now?" he asked. "I'm needed with the Triumvirate."

"Of course. I'll be fine. Go." I waved him off, and he left without a backward glance, lost in abstraction.

As soon as I was alone, I set my fork down, my appetite gone. No matter how I tried to clear my mind, my thoughts circled back to either the events of the night or my missing sister.

New interpretations for situations kept springing into my mind, new ways to view so many aspects of my life.

I had taken Zeke's interest in me as a sign of his true friendship because he had nothing to gain by it. But he had known about my strange power. He had known that Colton's failure at my testing had another interpretation. Had all of his interest since then been motivated by my ability?

His knowledge threw everything about our relationship into question. Was this how Airlie felt? Always wondering if people were truly interested in her for her or were merely interested in her power?

"Cadence!"

Zeke's familiar voice in the doorway to the garden made me flinch. Standing up, I slowly crossed the room, meeting him halfway.

For a moment I was intensely conscious we were alone, the memory of his hands on my arms in the darkness of our refuge filling my mind. He stepped toward me, reaching out as if he was remembering the same thing.

But I stepped back abruptly, and his arms dropped to his side.

"Are you all right?" he asked quickly.

I nodded. "I'm fine. But I want all the answers this time."

CHAPTER
TWENTY-THREE

He spread his arms wide. "Ask away."

I took a deep breath. "What sort of affinity do I have? You said something about a power mage? Is that what I am? How do you know about it when no one here does?" I stopped the flow of questions with an effort of will.

He sighed. "Of course others here know about it. Some, anyway. The old records aren't destroyed—just restricted to a section of the library forbidden to both apprentices and the general public."

"Is that what's in there? Books on a fourth power affinity?"

"That and the full histories of Calista. Because the two are bound together, of course."

"Of course." I sat down on the nearby sofa, trying to process it all. "That's how the Calistans were storing power, like you told me about? Because they were power mages?"

He frowned. "I don't know how they did that. I haven't been able to find any information on it, despite my late night searches. Storing power isn't part of the ability of a power mage, as far as my people are aware. But much has been lost in a hundred years."

I looked across at him. "So you have power mages among the nomads?"

He shook his head. "The Calistans had all the power mages. It was a rare ability, and they managed to acquire all the families with a strong power bloodline generations ago. Which was part of the problem, of course. If there had been power mages in other kingdoms..."

"So, you know, then." A flush crept up my cheeks. Apparently none of my secrets had been secrets from Zeke. The imbalance of it galled me.

"That you must be Calistan? Yes. Although it was only after you found me in the forbidden section that I actually confirmed for certain you had a power seed."

"You tested me?" But even as I asked the question, I remembered how the air between us had turned thick, and how his brief flash of excitement had been followed by disappointment when I clearly knew nothing of power mages.

"So the invasion, the massacre, it was all aimed at power mages."

He nodded. "It was never intended as a general massacre— but rather a highly targeted one."

"That doesn't make it acceptable!"

"Of course not." He sounded shocked. "It just explains how they convinced themselves their actions were justifiable."

"But my grandfather must have escaped. He would have been just a baby..." I shook my head. "My father once told me a story about his father. He said his house burned down, and my grandfather was the only one of his family to escape, carried to safety by his nurse. He never told me we were Calistans, so I didn't realize the true story he was telling. But it makes sense now." I shivered.

Zeke watched me, the wonder on his face making me uncomfortable.

"I took an apprenticeship here in the hope of studying any

old records of power mages," he said. "I never dreamed I would meet one—activate her even!" His expression turned dark. "But if you think there was interest in Airlie, you can't imagine what sort of interest there will be in you, Cadence, if the truth is known."

"Will they want me dead?" I asked in a small voice, thinking of the invading army, and the nurse creeping away with a sleeping baby in her arms.

He grimaced. "After nearly a hundred years, I would hope not. But it's possible. Those who know of the power affinity have been taught it's dangerous."

"Is it?"

He shrugged. "All power is dangerous. My fist is dangerous."

He strode over and dropped to a knee before me, putting our heads at the same level. "I don't want to leave you in the dark, though. You have incredible natural strength, Cadie—how early you were ready for activation shows that. But you will also have much greater access to power than the power mages of old because it has been so long since there were any of them in the kingdoms. You are powerful—and will only become more so as you master your ability—and there will always be people who are afraid of that."

"I don't understand. Why does it matter how long it's been since the last power mage?"

"Power mages have an affinity with power itself. It makes their ability flexible in a way that other affinities are not. But it also has limits. When the rest of us use our power, we leave traces behind—fingerprints, if you will. Power mages have an affinity with those traces of power. It allows them to manipulate everything from people, to plants, to the air itself."

"But it requires other mages to have gone before them," I said, realizing where he was going with the thought.

He nodded. "And for a century other mages have been leaving traces behind, but there have been no other power mages to use them up. I can only imagine power has been building everywhere. And you alone have access to it."

I chewed on my lip. No wonder I had woken to find the air already thrummed with power again, the effects of my blast overturned as the power I had thrust away settled back down. I could only imagine how concentrated it must be at the Guild.

"So what do I do?" I asked, as much to myself as to Zeke.

"You let me train you."

I looked up. "What?"

"I activated you, that makes you my apprentice."

"But you're still an apprentice yourself."

"Is there someone else you would rather have as influencer? Given my study, I'm probably one of the leading experts on power mages—the second-best option to an actual power mage as trainer."

"I see it as vines, did you know?" I asked inconsequentially, distracted by the reminder that I was under the influence of a plants mage. "Vines and tendrils and roots and branches."

"The power, you mean?" When I nodded, he stood, striding up and down. "Fascinating. The influence of my plants ability must have affected how you understand the power and how you shape it. I suppose it makes sense, but I would never have guessed..."

"If I train with you, can we keep it a secret?" I asked, before he could be distracted by the theoretics.

He paused his pacing. "Evermund insisted you stay here in Airlie's place." He waited as if it had been a question, so I nodded. "Then I think it's easy enough. You'll need to do something with your days. I can offer to help teach you in anticipation of your apprenticeship."

"And when I get to seventeen and they want someone to activate me?"

He grimaced. "We have time before then. We might even be

able to put them off until after I graduate. Then my tribe could invite you to visit our kingdom."

He nodded, as if the matter was solved.

I regarded him silently, keeping my own counsel. If he was willing to train me in secret, it wasn't an offer I could turn down. If I was honest with myself, it wasn't an offer I wanted to turn down.

Even now, when I was annoyed with him, I felt the pull of attraction. And spending time with Zeke was always enjoyable.

But visiting the nomad lands was another thing altogether. For one, I wasn't leaving Evermund until we'd found Airlie. And for another, while the Tartorans might decide to kill me, Tribe Nicobar might decide I was the perfect tool to ensure Zeke's mother's ascension. I had no interest in either future.

I had only begun to discover my path, and it was mine to determine.

"Very well," I said at last. "I'll train with you."

He gave me his most blinding smile, making me glad I was already sitting.

"You won't regret this, Cadie. You'll see. We'll make a brilliant team."

I smiled back, unable to help my instinctive response. But underneath a layer of caution remained. Zeke spoke as if the information about power mages was freely available among the tribes, but could that really be so? Given the level of trade between the nomads and the Tartorans, surely some word would have made its way across the border if that was the case.

Zeke had more answers for me than anyone had ever had before. More answers than Airlie even. And he was promising to help me puzzle out more. But that didn't mean he wasn't hiding something. And just because I liked him didn't mean I wasn't going to find out what it was.

"There's something else," Zeke said, making me start. "Can

you sense the people around you? That's supposed to be one of the most basic abilities of a power mage."

I nodded. "I could do that even before I was activated."

"Really?" He regarded me with a curious light in his eyes before giving a brief shake of his head. "We can talk about that later. For now, I'm going to need your help."

"My help?"

"With Airlie gone, the Triumvirate has decided that I can guard the Guild."

"You? How? I thought smelling intruders on the air was an elements ability?"

"It is. But the plants masters are in the middle of setting up a perimeter of greenery all the way around the Guild. The network is going to be connected back to those parts of the building I frequent, and I'm supposed to listen for any assassins who might try to sneak past it."

I raised an eyebrow.

"I know." He rubbed the back of his neck. "It's not a great plan. I only agreed because I was hoping you would do the actual monitoring. It should be easy for you—even easier than it was for Airlie. And if you ever do sense someone who's out of place, tell me, and I'll pass the information on. It's quite convenient, actually, since it provides us a smokescreen for your ability."

I stared at him for a moment. Airlie had gone—whether she ran and then was taken or was plucked from her room was irrelevant. She had gone. And apparently I had to step into her shoes. It was a responsibility I didn't want.

But there was really only one answer I could give.

"Of course. If I sense intruders, I'll come straight to you."

He was right that an explanation for our knowledge would prove convenient.

"Cadence!" Someone else barreled in without knocking. "And Zeke! You're here, too!"

Gia looked just as pleased to see Zeke as she had been to see me. "I heard you were going to stay here, Cadie. I think it's perfect." She looked at my face and hurried on. "Just until Airlie gets back, of course. Because I'm sure she'll be back any day now."

"I hope so." My voice must have sounded dejected because Gia brightened even more, as if determined to cheer me up.

"I came to tell you the news. Have you already heard?"

"What news would that be?" Zeke watched her with an exaggerated wariness. "I think I've had enough surprises for a year at least."

She narrowed her eyes at him. "I'm not so sure it'll be a surprise for you. Although I'm sure you'll never share how you managed to exchange messages with your family so quickly."

Zeke's expression smoothed out, a slight smirk lifting his lips, as if he did indeed know what she was referring to.

"Well?" I didn't like being the only ignorant one. "What is it?"

"Father just received an official missive from King Fenix. The nomads are sending a delegation at the end of the spring! Can you believe it? The historians are currently scouring the records for the last time such a thing happened. Beyond a single ambassador, the nomads don't normally deign to leave their own lands. But three tribes will be sending representatives."

"Will they stay here?" Zeke asked.

Gia shook her head. "That's the best bit. Father and Mother realize how significant this is, and they want to extend the greatest welcome possible. And since they know how much nomads dislike being penned into cities, they're going to plan a tour of the kingdom. We'll travel through Tartora, and the nomads will travel with us."

Zeke whistled softly. "That's a neat arrangement, and very considerate. The tribes will take it as a sign of honor."

"Exactly as intended. And of course we'll all accompany the tour."

No wonder she looked so excited. This was adventure outside the palace, just as Gia wanted. And Zeke looked pleased as well, presumably because of the compliment to his people.

A smile gradually spread over my own face as well. I hoped Evermund and I would have located Airlie before spring. But if we hadn't, then a tour of the kingdom might be the perfect opportunity to look for signs of her. After all the years we'd spent together, I was confident I would recognize the feel of her ability—if I could only get close enough to her.

"Am I really to be included?" I asked.

"Of course!" Gia threw herself onto the sofa beside me. "The Royal Mage will have to come, so you'll come with him as his pseudo-apprentice. And my best friend, of course. Even if he doesn't get you a spot, I will."

"And will you get one for me, too?" Zeke used a wheedling voice that made Gia giggle.

"As if I don't know that you'll be more popular than ever. Everyone will want your insight into how they can impress your tribe."

"Tribe Nicobar is to be one of the three?" I asked.

"Naturally. They claim they want to check up on Zeke after the attack. The timing certainly suggests the two are connected, and I'm convinced Zeke must have been involved. I just don't know how."

I looked up at him, but his enigmatic smile gave nothing away. If his tribe was coming in response to the attack, it wasn't to check on him but on me.

But I didn't mind the idea. It would give me a chance to check them out myself without committing myself to their care.

"Why isn't it spring already?" Gia sighed. "I don't like waiting."

"We are all aware," I said dryly. "But personally I'm in no hurry to wish my life away."

I met Zeke's eyes, and an understanding passed between us. If the Tartoran court and the nomad tribes were going on tour in the spring, then I had only a few short months to learn how to use my power.

When I met the future queen of the nomads, I would do so not as a scared girl without family or control, but as the first power mage in a century. I just hoped it would be with my equally impressive sister at my side.

Note from the Author

I hope you enjoyed the start of Cadence and Airlie's adventures. Their story continues in book two, Vines of Promise and Deceit.

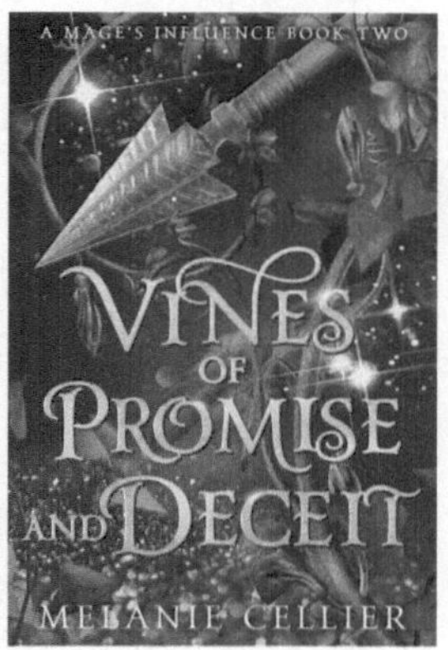

Or for more fantasy, romance, adventure, and intrigue, try my completed Spoken Mage series where a world of written magic is upended by the first spoken mage, starting with Voice of Power.

To be informed of future releases, as well as A Mage's Influence bonus shorts, please sign up to my mailing list at www. melaniecellier.com.

And if you enjoyed Seeds of Glory and Ruin, please spread the word and help other readers find it! You could start by leaving a review on Amazon or Goodreads or Facebook or any other social media site. Your review would be very much appreciated and would make a big difference!

HIDDEN CITY
NOMAD LANDS
KINGDOM OF CALISTA
CALINARA
CELADON RIVER
VIRIDIAN RIVER
LAKE ATERRA
CADENCE'S HOUSE
HUNTING LODGE
KINGDOM OF TARTORA
TARONA
CELADON RIVER
VIRIDIAN RIVER
NOMAD LANDS
N
S
E
W

ACKNOWLEDGMENTS

After writing twenty-five books in my first two worlds, it was both daunting and freeing to start an entirely new world. I'm looking forward to getting to know all of its inhabitants better.

I'm so grateful to my fantastic readers who support and encourage me. You're the ones who keep me coming back to my keyboard when it all feels impossibly hard. Thank you for giving me the gift of your valuable time.

And I also owe an enormous thank you to my team who go above and beyond every book—

My betas: Rachel, Priya, Katie, Deborah, and Ber

My editors: Mary, Deborah, and my dad

My cover designer: Karri who deserves an award for her patience in helping me work out what I wanted in this new style

My map artist: Rebecca

My family: You put up with my odd hours, stress, and strange schedules, and I love you all more than words could say.

And to God, who is always there no matter what life throws at me. Thank You for all your many gifts.

ABOUT THE AUTHOR

Melanie Cellier grew up on a staple diet of books, books and more books. And although she got older, she never stopped loving children's and young adult novels.

She always wanted to write one herself, but it took three careers and three different continents before she actually managed it.

She now feels incredibly fortunate to spend her time writing from her home in Adelaide, Australia where she keeps an eye out for koalas in her backyard. Her staple diet hasn't changed much, although she's added choc mint Rooibos tea and Chicken Crimpies to the list.

She writes young adult fantasy including books in her *Spoken Mage* world, her *Mage's Influence* world, and her various *Four Kingdoms* and *Kingdoms of Legacy* series that are made up of linked stand-alone stories that retell classic fairy tales.

www.ingramcontent.com/pod-product-compliance
Lightning Source LLC
Chambersburg PA
CBHW060757190726
48285CB00002B/470